Digital Nervous Breakdown

Hemant R. Joshi

VISHWAKARMA
PUBLICATIONS VP ®

Digital Nervous Breakdown

1st Edition - Published by Vishwakarma Publications in December 2016

ISBN - 978-93-85665-50-9

This is a Work of fiction, Names, characters, places and incidents are either the product of the author's imagination or are used fictitiously and any resemblance to any actual person, living or dead, events or locales in entirely coincidental.

Published by:
Vishwakarma Publications
283, Budhawar Peth, Near City Post, Pune- 411 002.
Phone No: (020) 20261157
Email: info@vpindia.co.in
Website: www.vpindia.co.in

Cover Design
Sumit Yempalle

Typeset and Layout
Gold Fish Graphics, Pune.

Acknowledgements

Sumit Yempalle, you have been a source of inspiration always. Thank you for inspiring me to write this, and for the book cover. Nikhil Shankar, thanks for bringing to my notice hundreds, or thousands of errors in the book. My family, my first supporters and critics, I am sincerely thankful for all the inputs. All my friends from birth till date, thanks for surrounding me with stories.

INDEX

Prologue

"Wait a second. Why is the Wi-Fi connection not working? Let's restart it," he wondered to himself. It had been twenty minutes now since his internet connection stopped working, and he was trying all methods that he knew to somehow get it up and running.

After restarting 5 times, he was frustrated now and called his service provider, just to hear- "Service is busy." This aggravated his vexation, which led to the highest level of anger and a feeling of betrayal. But he was helpless without the most essential requirement of his life- a stable internet connection.

He went out for a stroll, but his mind kept wondering about the internet, eventually leading to a sense of loneliness. He returned after a while, hoping that the internet would have started working again, but it hadn't. He tried calling the service provider again, but that led to disappointment once more. To take his mind off things, he started watching a TV series, but his mind was too tensed for him to even have an artificial laugh. The episode ended in some time, but he remained the same. Realising nothing was working, he decided against watching another episode. His mind did not allow him to.

He called his friends who had the same service providers, to clarify whether it was only his connection or others were facing problems too. He heard rumours of there being a power outage at the internet service provider substation, which had led to this predicament. The bright side of all this was that it was providing time to introspect, but he did not have the appetite for anything other than work currently. He was clearly troubled due to the faulty connection.

This night was turning into a living nightmare for him. A situation which any normal person today could empathise with. But he had a reason for overreacting. At the same time, he had no control over the situation. Frustrated, vexed, angry, and helpless, he decided to call it a night, as he had to be at office the next day.

ASHTRAY

Jai's cubicle had been the second, or perhaps his first home for the past four years. And why not? It was among the most splendid office spaces, and had what Jai loved the most-free food, including the necessary four meals a day. Jai would usually sit on his desk overlooking the glass facade of the building. On the other side of this facade was the breath-taking view of the city's skyline, with lights twinkling all around, telling him that he was not alone-swarms of people similar to him were working in the buildings that formed the skyline. The locale of his office was one where anyone would want to be. It was the IT hub of the city, and as a result, the infrastructure here was top notch. On his office desk, which was right opposite his boss' office, sat his computer and a few files. A typical office desk it was, by looking at which anyone would start feeling sleepy. But, Jai had grown habitual of it. He could not afford to sleep. His project head was a shrewd manager, who thought everybody out there was at his disposal. But no one had the audacity to speak up to him, as his past records showed an impeccable commitment towards his work. The boss had almost resurrected the company from bankruptcy during the economic depression. Jai could not even afford to check messages on his phone frequently, over or under the table. But, the pay cheque, the good food and the view, apart from the excellent projects he got took all these worries away from him.

Jai spent most of his time here; and had really nothing at home to be there for. His home was almost an hour's journey from here, and Jai tried to avoid leaving the office at peak hours to avoid the traffic and the rush. To add to the distance, his roommates were not his best friends; he just went along as they had to manage the rent. He preferred going home just for the sake of a good night's sleep. On normal days, he would leave office at around 8 pm, to reach home just in time for dinner.

Today again, he did not want to go home, but it was as if work was calling him there. It was the exact opposite of his usual days. One could see from his face that he was anxious and eager to go home. He finished e-mailing the daily report to his boss and decided to leave for home. As he started to prepare, a call from an overseas client arrived. It took him a long, dreadful fifteen minutes to get off the phone, which he then transferred to his boss. His boss in turn, ordered Jai to finish the client's request today itself, as the client was highly valued. It took him another half an hour to do the job, after which he mailed a report to the client and to his boss.

Frustrated now because of the delay, he packed his bag, shut down his system and went straight to the coffee machine. He grabbed a cup of coffee from the machine, after waiting for about 5 minutes in the queue. A light hearted banter among his peers was not of his interest today, unlike any other day. He had a very important job to do today. Sipping the coffee on his way, he went to the elevator.

In the elevator, he met Ramesh Shetty, an old friend. Ramesh light-heartedly punched him in the back, "Dude, how come you are leaving for home today? Mom coming? Hahaha," he laughed. After thinking for a few moments, Jai found himself jeopardised just to reply- "Why do you care? Just leave me alone". Ramesh noticed that odd behaviour and tried to check if everything was alright. "Nope, everything is fine, Ramesh" was the placid reply when he asked. Although Jai did not let anything out, there was something that made Ramesh wonder. The elevator bell dinged, as they reached the parking floor. Exiting towards the parking lots, Jai fumbled a bit, and as was visible from his grim countenance, he was disturbed.

He seated himself on his bike and left for home. On his way, the signals troubled him, increasing his anxiety even further. He even tried honking away the lights one time, only to realise that he was making a fool of himself. The crowded streets and the polluted air added to his frustration. It turned out to be a long, long ride, for it was the peak hour rush. After driving for almost twenty-five minutes, he abandoned the highway for the service roads, which led him into smaller lanes and even smaller *gullies*. But, this route saved him some precious time. After another half an hour, he reached his building.

He hastily parked his bike, got to the elevator and went up to the 4th floor. He got the keys to his house from his neighbour and opened the door. He pushed the door inwards making a loud noise, banging the door on the side wall. His roommates were sitting in the hall, watching the cricket match between India and Sri Lanka.

Ignoring all the people in the hall, he went straight to his bedroom. He switched on the lights and the air conditioner, and looked around for his laptop. He found his laptop lying on his bed in the same position that he had left it, and fired it up for the upcoming challenge.

He started his daily routine now, which included only coding. This routine had been set for about two months now. This was his passion for life. Working all his life he had developed some of the best coding skills, which were popular among all his colleagues and friends. In college, he had a good chance of getting a high paying job, but since the job was not fundamentally related to developing software, he decided to work elsewhere. In his current office, he had won many coding challenges, and everyone in his office always approached him for his codes.

His ways were not too complicated, but he followed a sophisticated and understandable procedure for his codes. But the code that he was currently working on was completely different. It was a piece of software that his roommates could not decipher, and they no longer wanted to know. Jai did not like to be disturbed while he was coding, and his roommates respected him enough to not disturb him.

As the laptop switched on, it was time for him to get to work. First up, he opened a web browser, and logged into the wifi connection to check if it was working. All the phone calls he had made to the service provider the earlier night had come to fruition. Yes, he had access to the internet. A few seconds later, an e-mail notification popped up on his desktop, and this was the e-mail that he had been waiting for all day long. In the salutation was written Mr Rajinder Shukla (senior consultant, NIC). Jai had sent an email to NIC this morning, and was eagerly waiting for the reply.

NIC- the National Informatics Centre has been the backbone of all the IT operations of the Government of India for the time since its foundation. This centre has been the go-to place for all the governmental informatics jobs. NIC oversees the operation of many governmental web sites, databases and their maintenance. Government's secret databases and intelligence agencies' databases are also maintained by the NIC.

The e-mail Jai had sent to the NIC had been responded to, and surprisingly quickly too! He read the e-mail, which dismissed the claims he had made in the trail mail. He had been thrashed for sending spam mail to them, although Jai's e-mail included details that could be very important. Clearly disappointed at his effort, he again started constructing a mail, this time much more detailed, to be sent to the NIC. He looked onto every detail that he should have included in the earlier mail, and ensured that all his claims were supported with examples. He took about an hour to compose this mail, and proof read it three times. He then sent it, this time specifically to Mr Rajinder Shukla. Mr Shukla's e-mail address was in the trail mail, in the contact details.

He then went back to what he originally had planned to do. He struck off a few entries in the to-do list, as he had already completed them the earlier day. Now, he had to start designing a code whose diagram was lying beside him. He continued to code and design for the next fifteen minutes. The world around him ceased to exist when he started to code. The atmosphere of his room was tranquil, the air conditioner was usually set at 22 degrees Celsius. This ensured that the laptop was never heated too much. The only noises that could be heard were the faint honking of cars on a nearby street, but they were not loud enough to bother Jai.

His roommate, Harish called him three times before he was actually heard. In the fourth attempt by Harish, Jai heard Harish calling him for dinner, whose loud voice seemed capable of penetrating any sound-proof glass. Jai responded with an equal pitch, making it certain that the previous calls of Harish were unheard. He closed the laptop lid gently, switched off the air conditioner and went to the dining table. Harish had already served the dinner. Sarthak Joshi, his second roommate was also already there, waiting for Jai. Much more relaxed now, having received the dose of coding for his project, Jai asked Harish why only Bhindi (ladyfinger)is served these days. "Aunty gets only Bhindi, maybe it is the cheapest'". By aunty, Harish meant the cook at their place. She made delicious food and all of them had a feast almost every day. On hearing this, Jai's lips widened, and he smiled for the first time in hours.

All the eyes turned to the television as the commentator's voice became louder. "Whoa! Good fielding," uttered Sarthak, on viewing the replay. After this, no one talked, all of them watched the match between India and Sri Lanka on the television. But the silence was broken when Dhoni got out and the match turned in Sri Lanka's favour. "What man! This is not done…" said Sarthak, leading him and Harish into a long discussion. Jai realised that this was not the time for getting involved in petty conversations; he had something very important to do. So he silently finished his dinner, and got off the dining table. He now remembered he had to make a few phone calls, before getting back to work.

The first call was to his mother. *"Maa-Kar lunga,"* (Mom, I will do it) he kept saying. He was 29 now, and his mom claimed that no girl would marry him if he did not marry in a few months' time. He was annoyed after a few minutes, but still kept talking to her, knowing that talking to him made her happy. He tried changing the topic under discussion-his marriage, into something else. But this took him nowhere. His mom found ways to ask him the same questions. After a gruelling call lasting five minutes, he finally breathed peacefully. On other days, he would have not minded the call going on for so long, but nowadays he had found something else to keep him busy. His peace didn't last long, as he found himself answering another call. This time it was Rita, who was his girlfriend since early college days. Again he tried to end it at the earliest, but it was not possible this time around. After a long, long call he was finally on his own, reaching his computer to get to work again.

'Not today,' he thought and switched off his phone, satisfied that no call will be as important as the work that he was about to do.

As a hobby, Jai worked on small level hacks and created viruses, which he sometimes used for teasing his friends. About three months ago, he had started working on a virus which he had thought up in one night. He had something big in mind then. It was late in the night when he had just returned from office. It was a Friday, so he did not have to sleep early. He therefore was surfing through some random articles and blogs over the internet. For a reason not even known to him, he started clicking hyper links of an airline's web site, checking where the web site ended, and how it linked to other web sites. He kept visiting these links for almost an hour, discovering the linkages to other web sites when it struck him. He was viewing the seating arrangement of an airline when a vague idea occurred to his mind. He developed the concept further through the night, and there it was. He had the concept for a virus that could prove destructive enough for the world.

The project had reached its ending stages now, and Jai had started testing it against his self-made web sites. Project ASHTRAY, as he proudly called it, was capable of disturbing the largest information systems in the world. It consisted of a deadly virus, spread through an uncurbed Distributed Denial of Service (DDoS) attack which was way more potent as compared to today's DDoS attacks.

The DDoS is a special kind of attack where a user is not allowed access to the system, as the attack holds the system's resources. It might be used to tamper with the data present in the databases. Modern day computers are capable of curbing small DDoS attacks, but the one Jai had developed could challenge even the most advanced computers.

Regarding the potential threats, he knew that the attack could disturb the nation's latest biometrics database-the 'union identification database'. The government planned to use this database to unify various identity proofs, and to give each person in this largest democracy a unique identification number. These IDs were then going to be used to link everything from bank accounts to governmental services among other governmental systems to form one unified system. It was indeed a large project, and the government had been putting in a lot of funds to make sure that it was implemented correctly.

While Ashtray was poised to destroy such systems, Jai did not intend to do any harm to them. Instead, he was making a thesis to be submitted to the Government of India, specifically to the NIC, regarding the subversive nature of the attack, averring that if someone else developed something similar, doomsday for the system was just around the corner.

But, he was mistaken. He thought the attacks might be capable enough to disturb the country's best information systems. The unknown reality was that the attacks could disturb the largest of the databases in the world that ran into petabytes of data.

What would happen if the world's largest email service providers were hacked, and customers' secret data was tampered with? Which hacker would not want to throw such an attack on global web companies? Software giants control the world these days, and minute anomalies can lead to large repercussions, such as financial losses, loss of confidentiality or massive electronic theft. Although there is always a risk at the top companies regarding various attacks, the threats are averted almost always, thanks to the excellent intelligentsia they have. These companies have special teams that monitor the threats and work towards their avoidance. Whenever a threat is suspected, the companies make it a point that it is removed even before it can touch the surface. These companies are throwing tremendous money into research leading to security. Often, people like Jai, who can crack attacks, help these companies.

But since Jai was unknown of the potential, he thought of the governmental databases as the summit. For the same reason, he was trying to contact NIC, and his two earlier mails had not been fruitful in setting up a meeting. His first mail was not replied to, and the second was the one to which he got the reply from Shukla. With the mail he had just sent, he had high hopes of getting a reply. He opened his checklist again.

His tasks for the day were clearly defined. But Jai would usually complete a few tasks scheduled for the next day as well. This would help him finish his job earlier, he thought. But in the process, he was overworked. He had visible dark bulges under his eyes now.

Picking the next item from the checklist, he started attacking his own self-made small web sites and databases. All that he had done till now was bearing results to his project, as almost all that came in the way of Ashtray was turned to ash. But still, since these websites could not match the humongous databases that could be affected, he was unaware of the real danger. Neither was he aware of the time that would be taken for the virus to infect a huge governmental database. It might even take hours, which could be enough to mitigate the effects of the virus or it could take microseconds, enough to destroy all the data. He continued working till 1 a.m. and went to sleep today, much earlier than his normal schedule of sleeping at almost 3 a.m. Before sleeping, he just hoped that Shukla would reply to his mail on time. With a sense of pride for having created a huge virus on his own, and at the same time fearing its implications, he let his eyes close, to wake up only when his alarm beeped in the morning.

The next day, again the same cycle repeated. This cycle had been going on for the past two months, ever since the development of Ashtray had intensified. His routine after returning from office was set-attending a few phone calls, switching off the phone and working on ashtray was all he did. He ignored his parents, his girlfriend, his friends and well, almost everybody once he began working. Whenever there was a call from his mother, he never talked to her openly about what he was doing, and same was the case with others.

One day, his mom, naturally worried about her son, called his roommates. Harish described how he and Sarthak felt about his behaviour those days. He told her that Jai had been obsessed with something big, which left him very less time to do anything else.

Sarthak, on the other hand, talked about Jai's coding to his mom, and about Rita as well. He explained to her the full situation that Jai had with Rita.

As if there was a smaller burden on Jai's head, his mom called him right after talking to Sarthak, obviously infuriated about him having a girlfriend in the first place. She gave him a long harangue about it. It soon turned into a tiring, ugly argument. Jai wanted to get out of it immediately, as he did not want to complicate things at hand. After a phone call that lasted about 10 minutes, Jai banged down the phone, shattering its screen, as the plastic lid on the back side came off. He soon realised what he had done, and searched for the parts of the phone that were thrown off because of his reaction. He was able to find the battery and the back cover. He put the battery and the cover in place. But, his phone failed to start again. He tried doing it two more times, to get the same result. It did not matter to him anymore, and he got back to his work. After about an hour, he realised his mistake, and called his mother using Harish's phone. He was surprised to find his mother relaxed on the phone this time, but this gave him a sense of confidence to work further. The call did not last long this time.

He stuck to this routine for the next few days, when an unexpected thing happened. On this day, Jai had asked for a leave from office. He wanted to switch the level of testing to a higher level. His initial testing phase was over and all the web sites that he had developed for testing were not able to give good results. That is, the virus had clearly affected them. Now, Jai initiated an attack to a system which had a much bigger database, both in terms of size and security. He was busy with this, when he got a call from the NIC. In a frail voice, someone from the other end said- 'Hello, is that Mr Jai Goyal'-Yes, he said. Jai's day was made fruitful when he heard the next line.

"Sir, I am speaking from the National Informatics Centre. The centre has decided to give you a chance to discuss with us your virus attack." This call set him up for a meeting with Mr Akshay Unnikrishnan, the Senior Security Engineer at NIC, as told to him. At this moment, he ignored the haphazard tone of the caller. He just knew that the date was set for 31st March, 3 days from then.

02

CHAPTER

THE CALL FROM NOWHERE

Rajinder Shukla was the chief of the Information Sciences division of the NIC. This division was responsible for tuning and maintaining the databases operated by NIC, which currently held the data required by various governmental websites and information services. NIC was the backbone of all governmental web sites with its services being used by even the secret agencies. Rajinder babu, as he was fondly called by some in his office, had been a man who began office at 9.00 a.m. sharp and ended at 6.00 pm, on normal days. In between these two, there was hardly any rest that he needed, apart from the lunch time between 1.00 pm-1.45 pm.

A man in his mid-forties, with an overgrown beard and a moustache that covered most of his lips, Shukla was the go-to man at NIC, delivering solutions to the toughest problems, ranging from replacement of a chip to the replacement of a web server. Every day he got requests for retrieving sensitive information by security agencies, reporting hack-attacks, and requests for information to be given to Intelligence agencies. His solutions to these requests and problems were much sought after, and the secret agencies could trust him with their secret data. Being at an important post at NIC, he could not disclose any work-related details outside his office. Due to this, he found himself in awkward situations at times. But this was a small price he had to pay, compared to the highly revered job he had.

As he had been in this position for the past 5 years, he was well accustomed to the threats to this office and to its countrywide operations. Almost every day, he got reports from his associates about the threats and attacks that were detected. The pattern of the reports to be given that Shukla advertised amongst his peers was one which had the solutions first, followed by the problem. This way, he said, the reader was able to think in terms of betterment of the available solutions first, saving some precious time. The format of the report was strictly followed, at least while the reports were being given to Shukla. Almost all the reports said that the attacks were carefully evaded by the team, courtesy the brilliant team that Rajinder Babu had garnered over the years. The attacks evaded varied from trivial pop-up viruses to the deadly database-altering viruses.

30th March was seemingly just another day in the life of this civil servant. He was comfortably seated in his cabin in the office, which was on the fifth floor of the building, facing the main street. He could see a series of buildings that housed many governmental departments and employed many powerful people. He was going through some reports regarding the possibility of a new data intelligence wing within NIC. The government wanted to deal effectively with the menace of cyber-crime and had appointed Shukla on a three-membered advisory committee. Shukla had to ensure coordination among various investigation agencies, and had to set up a new intelligence wing. He had been on the committee not by his choice, but the work had been forced upon him. As a result, he wanted to finish it in a hurry and deal with better situations at NIC.

While he was busy going through some statistics, he received a call from a neighbour in Gwalior, saying that his father was ill, and needed to be hospitalized. He cqalled his mother, but her phone was not reachable. This news was enough for his heartbeat to race. Full of fear, he arose from his chair, and headed straight to the railway station. He had no luggage with him, not even his precious laptop. On his way, he booked a ticket on the first train he could get which was scheduled to leave not before two hours from then. He waited in the station waiting room thinking about his father and the cause of his hospitalisation-gastroenteritis. "Why does he have to eat so much oily food? It does him no good," he wondered. His mind was filled with such thoughts, when he realised that he did not even get a phone charger. So he bought one from a store on the station. Instead of going back to the waiting room from here, he decided to take a walk on the platform to divert his mind from the worries. But that hardly happened, although he kept walking.

As he was wandering, he met his friend Unnikrishnan, whom he had known for some time now, since they had been spending time at the tea stall near his office. It was a normal practice for Shukla and his colleagues to go to the tea stall near the office complex in the evening. Here, these people had an opportunity to interact with some of the mightiest people in the governmental jobs. The stall served as the perfect place to informally discuss upcoming projects. However, everyone knew that some things were too risky to be discussed, and they were avoided. The tea that was served was to fit the description by a connoisseur. This was a tea stall where Shukla could go any time of the day, be it summer, winter or the rains.

"Why looking so tensed?" asked Unnikrishnan. "I might have a problem at home," said Shukla, trying to bring the conversation to an end. "But Shukla, what is the matter? Your parents are alright?"

"I am afraid not. I got a call from mother that dad needs to be admitted to the hospital. Gastroenteritis…"

"Okay. Is it very serious?"

"I am not sure yet. I will know only when I get there."

"Okay sir, I will not bother you with my queries right now, you should leave; the train to Gwalior is arriving in sometime. Please let me know about his health once you know."

"Oh yes, thanks Unni. Bye," said Shukla, as he left to reach the spot where the indicator showed D3, the bogie in which he had to get in.

Shukla hurriedly got into the train and anxiously waited for the train to leave the station. It was one of those days when he wished that he had a charter plane, so that he could just reach home in not more than half an hour.

As Shukla lay on his berth, watching the fan rotating over his head, he was reminded of his beloved, heroic father. The father that a child looked up to, a father who was a friend, a father who was his hero. He was reminded of the time when he got a job at NIC, his father was the happiest person on the planet- "Son, you have made us proud," his father had exclaimed. He was reminded of the unparalleled love and care he received as a young child living in a small city, and how his father had taught him to dream.

His father had always given him insights to dream big and his present day reputation as the go-to man for finding solutions was because of his father. He and his father had the best weekends together when he was a child, as they would certainly find something that needed repair in the house. Then they would do it without any help from professionals, modifying and improvising things. Shukla was reminded of one such day when his father had bought him a computer, when Shukla was 25 years old. The reason for buying the computer was to allow him to play with the computer. Too early in the computer age, Shukla had started to explore computers, and dreamed of changing their expensive nature back then.

His phone vibrated amidst this nostalgia. "Hello, Rajinder Babu?" said the person on the other end.

"Haan speaking, Mohan," said Shukla as he recognized the familiar voice. Mohan Verma was Rajinder Shukla's associate, who had been with him for more than two years now. Mohan was one of those trained by Shukla, and under his mentorship, Mohan had learnt the most diplomatic ways to deal with situations. He had been recruited five years ago, and after training under Shukla for a year, had moved to lower level projects. After a promotion, he now had the highly busy role of being Shukla's associate. "Sir, this person called Jai Goyal called, and said he had an appointment with Mr Unnikrishnan. I said that there is no Unnikrishnan here, but he arguably said he was sure that he got a call from the NIC that an appointment had been fixed with Mr Unnikrishnan. Sir, what do I do?" he continued. "Sir, I also don't know anything of any Mr Unnikrishnan in our office. So it seems to be a spam call, but he had sent a mail regarding some demo of a virus, to which you had apparently replied."

"Yes, I saw his mail a couple of days ago. Seems like just another threat, but he insists that he can explain the full depth of the matter by presenting. Fix an appointment, or rather you hear from him and take a call. I shall not be coming for a couple of days. I have to go home now; papa needs to be hospitalised. Okay?"

"Okay sir, let me see what I can do. If anything serious turns up, I shall inform you. You take care. Bye," said Mohan, and hung up the phone. It seemed a bit weird at first, Shukla was unable to think why Unnikrishnan was involved at this point. His mind was completely thinking about his father. Unnikrishnan and Jai had been side-lined at the moment. The train journey lasted six long hours. He took an auto-rickshaw to his home from the station.

As Shukla reached his home, he found his mother watering her carefully curated rose plants in the garden. With a certain sense of guilt and a fear, he thought that something had gone terribly wrong. He predicted that the worst just happened, and his mother was still not able to digest it- she was rather in a state of delusion. As he approached the gate, his mother came running towards him. She opened the gate, looking at Shukla bearing the coldest face she had seen. "What happened son?" she asked.

Shukla was now muddled, but he was also very curious to meet his father. She calmed him down, and took him inside. Shukla saw his dad, comfortably seated in his chair watching the India-New Zealand cricket match. His face turned cherubic, and he chuckled, his eyes turning watery. He barely managed to stop tears from running down. Shukla went to the bathroom and came back a few minutes later, to find both his mother and father comfortably seated in the dining room.

The three of them ate dinner together that day. After eating, his mother asked "Why did you have to come without informing? Are you here on work purpose?"

"Mom, you were the one who asked someone to call, right?" he retorted. Looking at her confused face, he realized that it was not his mom, but somebody else, who had done this. Now he could think of Unnikrishnan's involvement. But, why would Unnikrishnan be involved? Unnikrishnan, as known to Shukla, was one of the nicest government employees Shukla knew. Unni, as Shukla would address him always, was a large-hearted, hilarious personality. Shukla had known him for a long enough time to know that he would not play such a prank on him.

Baffled about the phone call that his neighbour had made, he rushed to his phone, and called Mohan. He told Mohan to find the details of the phone call, and to trace back Unni; to call him for questioning at once. Shukla now thought that his meeting Unni at the railway station was not coincidental, and tried to link back everything, but to no success. "There is a connection, but where?" he thought.

Mohan started working almost immediately, checking for the phone records in the logs. He called the police too, and explained to them every bit of it. But, as it seemed irrelevant, the police did not heed the issue. It was only because of the respect that Shukla had that they even looked into the records of Unnikrishnan, which showed nothing suspicious. But that did not derail Mohan, who began the investigation himself. He knew that someone who had done this to his boss certainly had some big thing in his mind. Before reporting anything to the head of NIC operations, he tried to trace the call himself.

In an hour, he was able to decode that the call was made from somewhere in the city itself. After an investigation by his internal security team, he found out that it was nothing but a prank call, as certified by his investigation team. He notified Shukla of the same. But why the prank call in such a way? And why at this moment? Mohan too was convinced that there was something here that led to Unnikrishnan. Mohan did not close the investigation as a prank call, and went out hunting for Unnikrishnan himself, without informing anyone yet.

Shukla thought that nothing in his office could be as precious as the time he spent with his parents, and decided that he would stay for a couple of days, now that he had come here. So he delegated all his work to his subordinates and notified Mohan about the same. The Intelligence wing work that he had already begun was to be halted for a few days. The next meeting of the committee was not before 7 days anyway, so he had the time. He started thinking of ways to spend the next two days peacefully, without the bustle of work, and the sleepless nights. He was rather happy to watch the India-New Zealand match on TV with his father.

The next morning, the 31st of March, brought to him the calm of the town side. It was a lovely morning, the sun had just risen, and the birds had begun chirping. He woke up at 6 am, and decided to go out with his father for the walk that his father was famous for, covering a circle of 5 km in just an hour. This walk brought him the fresh air which he had not breathed in many years, it seemed. Despite the financial-year-ending workload elsewhere, Shukla was able to finally manage a holiday with his parents, after a long time.

This walk, the 'Panch' walk, as his dad called it, had been the best time one could spend with Mr Shankar D Shukla, Rajinder's father. The old man had never missed the walk a single day, which everyone in the neighbourhood could bet on their lives. Also, Mr Shukla was famous for his views about several topics and people liked talking to him in general, when he was walking. As they both started to walk, Rajinder started asking dad about his plans, health, food and related stuff. They both cherished such conversations, which eventually led into politics, heating up as they reached home. The discussion obviously now turned to the elections and who would win them this time-the time when the country wanted a change. The discussions continued till they reached home. His mother waited for them, with tea ready on the table. His father went to get the newspaper first, and started sipping tea as he read the front page. "What does it say?" asked Shukla.

"Election news, mostly," replied his dad. This started a conversation among all of them regarding the elections. The three of them talked for a while, after which his father went back to the newspaper. His mother now went to the garden to water the plants. Shukla started watching the television. But he was also thinking about the person who had made the prank call. Although prank calls were common to his job profile, they never related to his parents anytime. This was the first time, and Shukla was sure that he would get to the bottom of the matter, and get those rascals. And then it clicked. Why did Unnikrishnan ask him if his parents were alright even before knowing the condition?

"Yes, it does relate," he said to himself. "But how? Perhaps, Jai Goyal and Unnikrishnan are colluding, and deliberately wanted to make me stay away from the office. Well, but they know that the NIC is not run by one person. But, the functioning of the advisory committee? No, the committee is not even made public yet," he muttered to himself. His eyes were fixated on the TV, but his mind was thinking deeply. He tried to think properly of what could be the proper linkage of all these events. Was something big coming? While thinking of all this, his finger was on the volume up button, and he was pressing hard, increasing the volume to its maximum. When he did realise this, he switched off the TV, and decided to lie down.

After some time, around 11.00 a.m., Shukla got a call from Mohan.

"Sir, that man, Jai Goyal, has not yet arrived for the meeting, shall I cancel his appointment?" asked Mohan. Mohan sounded rather annoyed with Jai when he said it.

"It is your call Mohan, I am out of it," asserted Shukla.

"But sir, it is just that there is something wrong about this, Jai's phone call, Unnikrishnan and everything else."

"Did you get to question Unni?"

"No sir, he has been on leave since yesterday and will not be in office for two days. I tried to get to his cell phone, but it was not reachable."

"Typical. My suspicions are coming true. Anyways, wait for communication from Jai for a day or two, and then maybe finish the issue as a prank. I will handle it from there."

"Okay, sir," said Mohan, and hung up. Mohan decided to cancel all his appointments on that day, and sort out the issue. He tried

Jai's phone to inform him to come the next day, but the phone was unreachable. He went back to what he was doing earlier, looking into the background of Unnikrishnan. Although Unni seemed involved in this matter, his records and background said nothing suspicious about him. Mohan now decided to inform the matter to the NIC head, and he went to his office, only to find that he was not there.

After some time, Mohan got an anonymous call:

"Hello, is that Mr Mohan Verma, the associate of Mr Shukla?"

"Yes that would be me," said Mohan. "What can I help you with?" he asked.

"Sir, I have been asked to notify to you that the meeting with Mr Goyal will not take place because Jai has been involved in an enquiry, and that he is not available."

"But, may I know the reason?" asked Mohan. "Sir, this is a matter of a higher order, please do not interfere with the proceedings," said the man on the other end, and hung up the phone.

Higher order, what is that? The secret agencies? The security intelligence agencies? But they would need the help of NIC, inevitably. The higher order would be safe only if Jai could explain the security threats that he had created to Shukla. The person calling was not even remotely from NIC, as Mohan could surely say.

He tried calling back the caller, but to no fruition. Whenever he tried, the phone was unreachable. He called Shukla and informed him about what had just happened.

THE MAIL THAT HAD ARRIVED

As soon as the news reached Shukla, he went through the mail that Jai had sent him earlier. Reading it over again, he just came to realise that he might have made a huge error, by not heeding to this person. He went over the mail thrice just to see the depth of the matter. He realised that the life of this kid, Jai, could be in serious danger. Jai's project was exactly what any notorious group would want. Jai could have been taken by a gangster. A group of terrorists could have come to know of his activities and could have turned him. His project's source code could be modified to get unimaginable and dangerous effects. It brought a scare to his face, now that he saw the effects of the virus that Jai had created.

He told his mom that he would be leaving for Delhi the next morning. His mom stayed mum, and gave him a go-ahead, as she knew how important her son's job was. She went to the kitchen, starting to make laddoos and a bunch of aloo parathas for him. Made with utmost care, these parathas were something that Shukla missed in his daily routine. They were partly responsible for his being at that position.

His mother knew that every time Shukla visited home, he would have to leave soon, owing to the important position that he held. His dad felt rather proud to watch his son go to work.

Shukla packed his stuff to leave the next morning. He got a cab to drive him to Delhi early in the morning, leaving as early as 5.00 am. It would take about 5-6 hours, he estimated.

Upon reaching Delhi, Shukla went straight to Mohan's house, as it was a Saturday.

"What happened with that person who called?" he asked. "Sir, no report about where he called from or who he was. Absolutely no trace sir," said Mohan.

"What about his tone, his voice, anything? Trace him back somehow!"

"His voice was hardly distinguishable from a normal voice. A voice that is a bit too croaky, as if he was about 50 years old, but nothing more. Apart from this, I could infer that he seemed to be a trained diplomat, and he did not falter even once while speaking. It did seem that it was some agency. I fear it was some agency, not sure if it is good or bad."

"Interesting. Is it a foreign intelligence agency? I guess it should be. Anyways, whoever it is, the code, if it reaches them, is going to have huge effects. Okay, let's go to office, we might have to deal with a situation."

"Yes sir, I will be ready in about 10 minutes. In the meantime, make yourself at home," replied Mohan. Shukla took a round of Mohan's house, as it was the first time that he had been to Mohan's house. He walked into the kitchen and picked up bread, some butter and jam from the refrigerator to eat. Although he had eaten the parathas in the cab, he felt very hungry. "Nice house man," he complimented as Mohan came to the hall. Mohan was flattered, and started describing the features of this flat that he had purchased in the last month. He described how he got the best deal, with a scenic view on the outside, a pool and a gym always waiting on the ground floor, among the others. Mohan made tea for Shukla and finished sipping the coffee that he had made for himself earlier. Shukla meanwhile finished his jam sandwich.

As they reached the office, Mohan was made to answer another call, this time from a known number. The caller said -"Can I speak to Mr Shukla?"

"Sir, who shall that be? And what is this call for?"

"Tell him it is Unnikrishnan calling." Mohan's eyes suddenly widened and he had goose bumps. As much as he wanted to curse Unnikrishnan right there, he resisted and sincerely did what was expected of him.

After transferring the call to Shukla, Mohan instantly went to his computer. He started perusing that mail which Shukla had received from Jai. He was trying to link this e-mail to Unnikrishnan. But he could not get any trail which led to Unni.

"Yeah Unni, how are you?" Shukla spoke with a totally unperturbed look on his face and a calm voice. He wanted to abuse Unni, but first wanted to confirm what he and Mohan thought.

"I am fine. Sir, how is everything at home? Good, I suppose," Unnikrishnan asked.

"Do you know anything about a person called Jai Goyal?" Shukla asked, unable to resist, and in no mood for chatting.

"No sir, I don't know anybody having that name? Anything I should know?" On hearing this reply, which seemed a blunt one, Shukla seemed to be convinced about his fears.

"No I don't think so. And yeah, everybody is fine back at home," said Shukla, as he was now almost convinced that Unnikrishnan was involved in the whole incident. As Shukla was about to speak something, Unnikrishnan started.

"Good to know that sir. I called to tell you about something weird that happened yesterday. At the tea stall, I was having tea at around 12.00 noon, as I was feeling a bit dizzy. As I was waiting for my tea, I saw two people, an old man, about 55, and a young guy, about 30 sitting beside my table. At first, I did not bother myself to look into the matter. But, as the boy seemed too tensed, I was naturally inclined to know what was happening. I managed to overhear a few lines. It seemed they were talking about some hacking stuff, and the younger guy, though reluctant at first, was explaining something for a long time to the older guy." Unnikrishnan paused for a moment to check that the phone connection was still live.

"They both felt much tensed. At first, I thought they might be workers at your office. But, the older man did not appear to be a guy who worked at NIC, as I know most of the senior staff. So I delved a bit deeper. I sat there for about 35 minutes trying to listen to their conversation. The young person even wrote something on the tissue papers. While writing, he was explaining something to the other person, which I could guess to be a flow chart. Irresistible now, I even tried to approach them. But when I tried, the old man pulled off the younger one by his collar, and almost dragged him into a car. I decided not to interfere there, but was a spectator of the whole sight. Sir, I think it might be a matter of concern." Shukla silently listened to the whole story.

He was shocked to hear this. He could clearly see where this could be heading. Some terrorist group might actually have got hold of Jai Goyal. Or he himself might have had nefarious plans. Shukla also cleared the air of suspicion hanging over Unnikrishnan, and was about to tell him what he thought. But he still did not know why Unnikrishnan's name was used in the first place.

"Sir, are you there?" asked Unnikrishnan.

"Oh yes, thanks a lot Unni. Can you come down to the office sometime today? I want to discuss something with you."

"Okay, I am in office right now, but will be free in the evening, around 4.30 pm. I can come then, if it is okay."

"Of course, please come."

Unnikrishnan arrived as promised. Shukla explained to Unnikrishnan the whole scenario and sensed that he was frightened about being involved in something big and terrifying. Shukla tried to placate him, but he realised that Unnikrishnan was not someone who would be ready to deal with dangers and fears. The discussion was not at all fruitful, Unnikrishnan was so frightened that he was not even able to describe the two men. He was panting the whole time. After a lot of convincing, Unnikrishnan looked normal, the fear did not show on his face. But on the inside, he was very scared.

Shukla's fears were also steadily picking up. What was this? What was going to happen? Where was Jai at that moment? All these thoughts started pipelining into Shukla's brain. All this seemed too troublesome for Shukla to take alone. Although he had a good experience with managing databases and virtual attacks, this was the first time when people disappeared in front of him. This was something much bigger than the normal cases, he knew now.

He decided to go to the higher authorities, specifically to Mr David Fernandes, who had been his boss and the head of the NIC for the past 4 years. David had a reputation of being the best in the office for virtual security matters, and had helped in drafting India's cyber security policies, dealing with all the sections of the government diplomatically. He had an exceptional acuity for such matters. He had been an adviser to the National Investigation Agency on matters of intelligence too, and he had great friends there. He was also an advisor to the Prime Minister on matters of Informatics and cyber forensics. Rumours at NIC were also saying that he was once a member of an intelligence agency, although he himself remained discreet on the topic.

So, he seemed the appropriate choice for Shukla.. Shukla forwarded the mail to David, which read as follows:

David,

In the past few days, there have been a certain set of disturbing events that have happened. The first of them is this mail which I got, which led to a series of events that I would like to explain face-to-face.

Rajinder Shukla,

Senior consultant.

Sir,

I am Jai Goyal, a computer scientist working at a leading IT firm. As a hobby, I engage in some ethical hacking activities, and have been an enthusiast in this field for the past 7-8 years. When I had the chance to start building stuff of my own, I started. Today, I can hack some of the better systems in the world.

What concerns me when I say this is my latest project, 'Ashtray' which could reduce the governmental databases to ash, modifying and tampering data leading to a series of breaches. It consists of a deadly virus, capable of making an uncurbed Distributed Denial of Service (DDoS) attack which is way more potent as compared to today's DDoS attacks. The attack is so effective as the method through which it spreads is different from the normal ones. After the DDoS attack which proceeds in a particular manner, the database fields are modified abruptly, and the memory may be flushed multiple times. The attack is uncurbed because I have devised an algorithm that makes it flourish in a chain reaction manner. It spreads on an exponential scale. It also has some smart features, including those to adapt to the systems and create its own atmosphere there. And above all, today's antiviruses, firewalls and other security measures are not enough to curb this attack. This is because of the repeated attacking on a system unless it is affected. I tried using various antivirus programs that are used today, and could find none that gives protection against Ashtray. It may seem speculative if I do not present any example at this point.

To use ashtray, I started with some small websites, which were attacked simultaneously, without any intervention by any firewall/proxy. I was able to easily access sensitive data, and could have easily tampered with it, without leaving a trace. Then I tried the website of NIC, and although I was able to bypass all the security measures used, I did not alter any content. I also went through the website of the Ministry of Information and Broadcasting, and because these websites had similar regulations, it was easy for me to trespass into them. But these were the small ones, now I tried the UID database. I passed through their website again. A thing of mention is that I had only bypassed the databases at this point, I could have easily denied access to the users. Although I had not initialised the full program till this point, I could easily reach the inner sections.

The bigger problem lies with not being able to detect the sender of the attack. The masking of the system is done in such a way that the IP address of the sender is shown from the same network. The situation worsens when the chain reaction leads to multiple attacks in a short span of time, which would again trigger a DDoS attack. This could lead to complete inaccessibility of the computers.

To demonstrate the same, I want an appointment with you, but am unable to get it through your desk. But, I want to thank you for replying to my first mail.

Regards,

Jai Goyal.

That day in the afternoon, David called Shukla, asking him to meet him at the earliest possible time. Shukla had a report to make regarding the intelligence wing to be submitted to the ministry. Before starting, he called David and fixed an appointment for having a meeting with his team. The appointment was set for 5.30 that evening.

After an initial glance at the mail, David spontaneously started seeking methods for mitigating the scare. David had an experience of 23 years now with the government, him being the member of the Indian Administrative Services' batch of 1991. He had served various offices till now, and had seen many challenges. He was sure that this would be one of the many, and his team would be able to solve it.

Before the meeting of the two, David made some calls to his expert team, gathering valuable inputs from its members. The whole team was ordered to report at 5.30 in conference room #3.

David had carefully picked this team up over the past few years, and the members were trained to solve problems of highest importance within hours. Even Shukla viewed them with high regard. Such was the training of these team members that they had to attack some systems themselves at times, to update their skills. One such incident was when the team had to create a whole dummy NIC main centre, and crack down the whole centre. After this was done, they had to find solutions to avoid the hack, and implement them after building the whole system after it was crashed completely. The team had performed this job in ten days and had celebrated for the next five days.

Among the team members were the best cryptanalysts and the best mathematicians. Algorithms were designed in a flow, and there seemed no other place which would have such smartness. All these skills were used to make algorithms of very high statures, and they were implemented very quickly. Although it was a team of only nine people, these nine people were always involved with some agency outside of the NIC. Even the foreign governments had employed them on projects and missions. One could easily wonder, why would anyone with such high skills work for the government? But, these people had an obligation to their boss, David. While recruiting them, he had told them that they could work as freelancers, but were not allowed to be permanently employed after their stint at NIC. This was required to save the sensitive information from private players and the not-so-friendly groups.

Shukla on the other hand, somehow tried to complete the report. He tried focussing for the next hour, twisting and turning on his seat. Having typed only three lines till now, he realised that he was not able to do it. He instead typed a letter to the ministry informing that he would vacate the position, and the government should search for someone else. He was already too occupied currently, and this work could be done by someone else as well, he thought. He then gave the resignation-preparing job to one of his interns, describing completely what to write in the mail. Shukla then watched some videos related to hacking on his computer screen.

He then decided to seek help from outside. He first thought of asking permission from David, but decided not to, fearing that David would not approve of it. He took out his phonebook from his shirt pocket. The first two calls that he made were unreachable. On his third call, someone at the other end finally responded.

"Hello, may I speak to Dr Aravind Sharma?"

"Yes, who is this?" asked the person at the other end.

"Tell him that his friend, Rajinder Shukla has called, and it is something important that he wants to discuss."

"Okay, hold on for some time," said the person, putting the phone on hold. Aravind Sharma had been a classmate of Shukla in his engineering days, and they were in contact as Shukla would seek the opinions of Sharma on various occasions. Aravind was a faculty member at the Indian Institute of Technology, Kharagpur and had dedicated his life to the study of system security and other types of security. His doctoral thesis had won him international accolades. He was frequently called by people throughout the world, and lived a life delivering lectures at various colleges and universities. His research papers were not so famous, but his teaching methods were so popular amongst the students, that they could tell anything that he had taught in his class. Shukla was certainly privileged to have an acquaintance of Aravind's stature.

"Hello, Shuklaji! How are you?" spoke an ecstatic Aravind.

"Aravind, I need some information on certain techniques that are used in construction of DDoS attacks today, and to see how antiviruses help prevent them."

"Oh sure, I will be happy to help. Shall we do it online, because I would not be travelling to Delhi in the coming days?"

"Of course, it is alright. The matter needs urgency, so…"

Shukla and Aravind discussed the problem. Aravind had the real foresight of the problem. He could clearly see the implications of Ashtray. Shukla had to be satisfied with whatever he could gain from the little information that he gave to Aravind, considering the secrecy involved. But to his surprise, Aravind's vast knowledge made him realise what Shukla wanted to say exactly. He also recommended that he could tell people at IIT about it, to which Shukla said a big no. It was too sensitive a case, and any disclosure could mean trouble. They talked for almost an hour.

Shukla got all the information that he needed for the moment, and then made a checklist of all the things that Aravind had told him. Although the checklist had 9 main items, Shukla was well aware that they were just the beginning of a long list that could keep growing at a rapid rate.

04

CHAPTER

ENGINEER IT BACKWARDS

April 1,2

As the hands of the clock neared half past four, the anxiety and fear on Shukla's face kept accruing. He had been looking at the system attacks reported to him that morning by one of his associates. The attacks had been a huge pain for Shukla, for the location of their origin was just so trivial! They were traceable, but the address was too ironic to be true. These attacks had been coming from a location whose IP was traceable. But the strange thing was, the IP addresses were of the same network of NIC. It seemed strange, because the systems at this office were amongst the most secure systems in the country; their IPs were very hard to obtain for an outsider. Shukla tried 5 times using different techniques to find the origin, but to the same result. The IP address being of the same network, he searched for similar attacks on other computers to see if it was only this network, or all the internal networks were responding in the same way. But, it came to no fruition. After two hours of pondering over the issue, Shukla was still on the problem. But yes, he was now convinced that it was Ashtray. The attack could be from the time Jai had attacked the NIC main centre for trespassing, as he had claimed in the mail.

"But the attack was under control, as told by Jai. So what was the problem? Did Jai know the real implications of his virus, and did he really control it? If he did not, I better find him and send him to jail! Why do people have to create such things, just tell us the threats!" All these thoughts made way into his mind.

But he soon realised it was time to prepare for the meeting with the boss. He ordered three members of his team to be there at the meeting with the boss. After this, he himself used the information Aravind gave him to verify this attack was Ashtray indeed . He jotted down all that he could think of, every fine detail in that mail that could be a hazard. He highlighted the specifics of the mail, the chain reaction, which he did not comprehend completely till then, and prepared notes on all the points that he came across as threats. He then picked up the notes he made during his discussion with Aravind, and searched the internet for reports of similar attacks.

"Sir, it is 5.30, shall we go?" asked Mohan, shaking up Shukla who was deeply buried into his computer.

"Yes, yes," said Shukla, and got up from his place. Mohan called the other associates in the office, and they all went to Conference Room #3. Boss was already waiting there, and had his own team ready for action. He had been in discussion with his team for a long time now. In all, there were 4 people in Shukla's team, and 6 in the other team.

The teams gathered, as Shukla projected the mail on the projector screen. After all, he did not get the time to create a presentation of it. For the next 10 minutes, he was the only one speaking in the room, not because there were no doubts, but because the people were just dumbfounded by the danger lying ahead. The teams discussed the attack thoroughly, and Shukla even explained the technical details that could be implemented with this framework. He explained his conversation with a friend who explained him the prospects of such attacks. But, he did not disclose the name of Aravind. People in both the teams participated in the discussions, discussing solutions among themselves. Meanwhile, Shukla and David got into a conversation among themselves while the teams were busy, Shukla starting to report the attack that happened earlier in the day.

"Sir, my team earlier in the day reported an attack which

at the first instance seemed to be just a commonplace attack. So, routine protocol for its disintegration had been initiated. But the disintegration did not happen very easily. The problem was, the IP address pointed to the same network. Sir, I have an inclination to believe that it is…"

"Wait a minute, what did you say? Is this related to Ashtray?" David was terrified.

"Sir, you heard it correctly. And I guess even you can see what has happened," replied Shukla. "There is certainly a connection between this attack and Jai's testing phase," he added. Then Shukla addressed the whole team there. His team explained the nuances of the attack that they had mitigated. The other team members were not new to such discussions, and initially just thought that it would be a routine attack and could be easily prevented. It took some convincing on the part of Shukla's team for the other team to believe in the power of the attack.

After an hour of discussions, David had orders ready for his team, and so did Shukla. Both the teams were asked to cooperate and work together in preventing this crisis. The teams were not used to coordinating their work with others at NIC, as David's team mostly worked in other offices, while Shukla's team was the one which operated within NIC. The teams were ordered at once to get the implementation details, use whatever means necessary to track the criminal, and at all times be secretive of the mission- "Raakh" (ash).

David was to head the investigation team, and Shukla was ordered to make a team of his to find the man anyhow. But Shukla had no clue how much effort it would take him to get to Jai, so randomly he selected the team size to be 2 people. The team comprised of Mohan and Vineet Singhal, another of Shukla's trusted aides. The investigation team that David headed comprised of all the members that were present at the meeting, apart from Shukla and his teammates. All the teams got to work at once.

The investigation team started chalking out all possibilities about the hack. The team made an inner circle whose job was to reverse engineer every attack that had been incoming since the mail had arrived. And it was a mighty task. Daily, this place got 30-40 attacks, small or big. Sometimes, due to constant cyber warfare, this number could go to as high as 100-120 attacks. And it was a humongous task just to keep a log of all the attacks, let alone reverse engineer them. To go through the code of each one of them would take another 8-10 days at least, and there was the issue that the team might not be able to focus on the future. It might happen that the real attack was yet to come. The threats might not be prevented in such a case. Complete discord was coming up if the teams were not able to synchronise their efforts.

After a few minutes of pondering over these concerns, David made three teams, one for reverse engineering, that is, to check the code of the virus, and try to get hints to break it, one for mitigating any future threats of a similar kind, and the third team.

The job of the third team was to put all the systems to a test. It had the job of using the virus that had attacked the system and applying it to any potential system that could come under attack. The main job here was to seek recovery options first, as the effects of this test itself could be fatal. This was a tough job, as the slightest of errors while controlling the attack could create havoc in other systems. In other words, this team's job was to hack the system. The team started working early the next day, beginning in full swing with a list of 13 potential systems, which the investigation team had found to be critical. These were identified on the parameters of vulnerability, sensitivity and demand.

Apart from these teams, no one knew what was happening. David wanted to know the problem in detail first, and then tell everyone about it. He was sure that these teams would finish the issue off. The atmosphere at the NIC building was still calm, and people were hopeful that the effects of this attack would not be long lasting. Everyone was certain that the teams would curb the virus in a short time. The members of the first team worked at their respective desks. The members of the second team were seated in David's office initially, but they soon moved out to occupy a round table in Conference Room #1. The third team was working in conference room #3 itself.

All the teams were to report directly to David, who himself got occupied with the second team. This team was to develop firewalls and up the security level at all their data centres. Although the job seemed a bit clichéd as compared to the other two teams, this team had to ensure that no threat had already gotten into some system and destruction had not already begun. To do this, they had to check with the first team as well for the attacks that were handled, and go through each log of these attacks, if available. The job was tedious.

The three teams were at work.

The first team reported at 11.00 am, which seemed too early, and thus gave signs of gloom. "Sir, the code of this virus keeps reordering every 15 seconds, we are unable to even save it in parts to engineer it backwards. It is encoded in such a way that the code will change-dynamic reordering of the code is used here," they reported. Engineering backwards was to get the code and the output, and to rejig the code to see what exactly was happening at all the locations in the code. But now, as the original program was designed to shuffle the sequence in a span of 15 seconds, the difficulty that this team faced was paramount. Jai's virus would keep changing the sequence of instructions if it was connected to the internet.

"Do whatever is required, if you are unable to find the code that is causing shuffling, read the code enough times to get what you want. There has to be a point where it will stop. Make as many copies as you want. However smart he might be, his code has to be breakable," said David.

"Sir, we are trying to develop a code to stop this, but we are unable to get anywhere with it till now. We are trying to develop a tool so that the sequencing of the code is kept constant, but, to implement this, the machine needs isolation," said the team leader.

"Keep working, isolate, switch the backup terminal on for some time," said David, and turned back to the work he was doing.

Meanwhile, Shukla and his investigation team got to their job, and were scanning the life history, bit by bit of Mr Jai Goyal, an 'honest citizen' who had disappeared. They had the power to get everything, right from his birth till yesterday. Every phone bill, electricity bill, all the other bills, his certificates, and everything. But on a careful analysis, he seemed immaculate. There was nothing that could seriously question his integrity. The only thing that one could be certain of was that Jai had the potential to be a very good hacker, visible from his certificates. Satisfied that the primary checks did not give any significant leads, the team turned to the second round of their investigation.

This round included gathering information about all the people he had relations with. These included almost every person whom he had talked to in the past 5 years. Shukla had to reach out to NIA to get these records. But to get to them, he would first need to explain all of this to them. He was under strict instructions to keep this case low profile unless some concrete facts were found. So he turned to David. David's past experience at NIA was of paramount importance as he had made many friends there.

After some convincing, David agreed that a team from the NIA would be needed inevitably. So he decided to make a call to a member of the NIA. At first, Shukla thought that NIA itself would feel threatened on hearing about the attack. But they trusted David, and were sure that NIC would deal with it effectively. But David was asking to have an investigation team for the matter. This would be a bit confusing for NIA. Although NIA would agree to David's demand, they would have to report the matter to the higher authorities.

Now it fell on David's shoulders to keep it low profile and at the same time include the NIA. It seemed a bit paradoxical. He would now have to request the NIA to keep it tight, and that the government should not be involved yet. The inclusion of the NIA also implied that the higher authorities of the government could politicize the situation. This could have serious repercussions, if not contained in time. But, he was confident that he could do it as he had been a 'good friend' of NIA. NIA's information system was also a part of the 13 systems identified by team three.

So David called Mr. Amit Joshi, his trusted man at the NIA, whom he had known since his NIA days, and had been a good friend. Earlier, David had avoided calling Amit as he knew that Amit was a busy person and to burden him unnecessarily was not good.

"Hello, Amit Bhai?"

"Yeah David, tell me," said Amit.

"I need to talk to you today. Matter of high concern. So, tell me when I should come, rather, can you come here?"

"Okay, but what is it about?" asked Amit.

"It is work related stuff, but very, very important. Meet me today at my office in the evening. Okay?" David spoke hurriedly

"Let me check my appointments, hold on," said Amit.

"We don't have time for appointments, please, this is highly important," David said, negating Amit.

"Actually, I am free, so I'll come by say, 5.30 in the evening?"

"Yes! Do that, this is urgent," replied David and got off the phone.

Amit had known David long enough to see that he was tensed, and he could clearly see that either the NIA was in some big trouble over cyber issues, or it was some personal tension that David had at NIC. He decided to check what was happening before he went to meet David. He told his associates to check for any reports of heavy cyber warfare going on, and if it were, to see if there were any related to the NIC. NIA was the investigation agency that had investigated many cyber-attacks, and had the best of the investigators in their teams. Amit was startled to know that in the past fifteen days, the reverse of what he had expected had actually happened. There was not a single cyber-attack seen on NIA's databases. While this seemed like a personal achievement for him, he was worried that it could mean something to David. It could also have happened that systems might have stopped reporting attacks. Of course, the first observation felt utopic, so he was convinced his reporting systems were not working properly anymore.

In the evening, David described the situation completely to Amit, who was just astonished, as the central information system of NIA was amongst the 13 identified systems.

"We need to keep this a secret," said David. Amit nodded. "And that is the reason why I am trusting you with it," added David.

"Well, yes David, tomorrow morning I will send over a few of my people here. What will be their exact jobs?" Amit felt obliged to act urgently.

"Sir it is fieldwork for which I need your people. I will call Shukla for an introduction and then he will explain it to you," said David, as he reached out to his phone to call Shukla.

Shukla was busy in the field, and had gone to Jai's office for the first leg of the second round of his investigation. He had been roaming for half the day, and the other half he spent in Jai's office, interviewing his colleagues. Although Shukla would need NIA to question other people that Jai knew, he thought that it was better not to waste time and started with Jai's office.

"Yes sir, I have known Jai very well. We have always seen him in the office, working zealously on his codes. His projects are generally top notch, and his boss is always pleased with his performance." said one person to whom Shukla enquired about Jai.

"Did you notice anything suspicious over the past days?"

"Yes sir, he did behave a bit weird for the past few days. Normally, he would not leave office until late at night, because he liked it here, nowadays, he is always in a hurry to leave office. Initially we thought it was because of his girlfriend, but that was not true. His roommates said that he would keep coding something every day on his laptop, and would hardly ever speak to anyone."

"Okay, I can see why he behaved weird. Can I meet his close

friends here, and his boss?" asked Shukla.

Shukla started asking questions to Jai's boss, and was hardly surprised to have an almost similar conversation with him too. After an hour of discussions with these people, he now had a lead. He had the contact details of Rita, but he believed that she was not the person who would have any more information than he had gained till now. He told Vineet to contact his roommates, and decided to go back to office. While going back, he got a call from David telling him that the NIA was with him and he needed to meet Amit Joshi for discussing the exact nature of work.

"Sir, I will be at the office in about 20 minutes, can you please hold Mr. Amit till then. I certainly have to discuss the matter with him."

"That would be great, I will check if he can wait," said David.

Amit decided to wait, and both David and Amit started discussing their time together at NIA. Although David had not been a permanent member at NIA, he had made a bond with many people there. After coming to the NIC, David hardly had the time to talk to anyone at NIA, and would certainly miss those days. David saw that the investigation team was continuing their work, as he explained to Amit what was exactly happening. He also showed him the reports of the first attack that the system had sustained, and then spoke specifically about the threat to NIA. Amit responded with a pale expression over his face, but David soon assured him that the NIC team would not let anything happen to any database.

Amit was curious about Shukla and constantly made queries about him to David. David's replies portrayed Shukla as a person who could always be banked upon to find solutions to their problems. Amit's curiosity to meet this person was high after this discussion.

Shukla arrived, as promised. The three of them got into long discussions, and Shukla described the problem which he had. He described the need to get Jai's contacts and also described his experience at Jai's office.

"Sir, we need expertise in questioning. In my experience today at Jai's office, I could see that I was certainly not able to press the matter, and was naively believing whatever the people were trying to say. Also, I believe your people might have their own 'techniques'."

"Not to worry, Shukla. People at NIA are trained for such things. And I assure you full cooperation from NIA. But I need an estimate of the number of investigators that would be needed."

"Very true. But sir, now that you know the full problem, you are the best judge."

"If you say so. I feel two investigators would be enough, as the job is mostly about questioning. Apart from these two, I will make an investigation team that would help you in finding leads. But it will take some time for me, as it needs to be done covertly. All my covert operators currently are into something or the other. You should begin the work with the two investigators first. I will send them tomorrow straight to your office."

"Sir, thanks a lot. I look forward to working with the NIA," said Shukla.

THE AGENTS COME AGAIN

April 3,4,5,6

Shukla remembered the day when he got the first e-mail which had a very abstract and a highly unconvincing description of Ashtray, as he was riding in his car. How he wished he had not ignored that e-mail! All the thoughts about Jai being with the wrong people were very prominent in his mind. He was also checking the news time and again to check that no mishaps were happening anywhere. He was so worried that one time, when he read about a train derailment, he started to link Jai's involvement in it. He was somehow also able to convince himself of the same. He had enough reasons to believe that Jai had been turned. The car moved at a steady pace, apart from a few bumps on the otherwise smooth road. It came to a halt in front of a gate, guarding a recently renovated, freshly painted bungalow. Shukla had reached Jaipur, to meet Jai's parents. He rang the bell.

"Who is it?" asked a frail, old man's voice from the inside. "Sir, this is Rajinder Shukla from NIC. I need to meet your son," replied Shukla. At once the old man stood up from the rocking chair, went out and opened the gate. He was surprised and anxious. "Did you find him?" asked Mr Goyal as he came almost running to the gate. Even he did not know where his son was. Jai's mother had been worried too much over her son going missing. She wept through the days and nights, nothing could bring a smile to her face. Mr Goyal, on the other hand, had made more than a hundred calls to try and find his son.

"Sir, I have come to inquire about him. I am unable to reach him, his phone is off, and he hasn't been at his house. I wanted to meet him as he was assisting us on matters of national security. I also went to his office, but could not find him. I had called your number as well, but the phone was off."

"No he hasn't turned up here. Even we are worried about him. Is he in trouble?" He paused for a moment, before beginning again- "I am going to the police station to lodge a missing complaint," he said, with a scared look on his face. Shukla could see the fright on the father's face, but was helpless, as he himself knew nothing about Jai.

"The NIA is working with us, so going to the police is redundant," said Shukla. All this was too troublesome for Jai's father, who tried to keep calm, but was clearly not at ease.

"The NIA is involved! That means real danger!" exclaimed Mr Goyal.

"What is all this about? Has my son been in trouble? No, I know he would never do anything wrong. He is just a young, working engineer," said Mr Goyal, his eyes becoming watery.

"Sir, I assure you that he has done no wrong, in fact he was about to assist in matters of national intelligence. You should be proud of him. He is about to be one of the best security experts in the country!" Shukla exclaimed, trying to assure him.

"Regarding this, I need to know more about him. Would you do us a favour? It is very important, in fact a matter of international security to find him."

Mr Goyal looked the man from top to bottom to verify his authenticity, and nodded.

They both talked for over 2 hours. Mr Goyal explained everything from Jai's birth to his admission in school, then to college, and how he was able to get a job of his choice. He spoke about his relation with him, Jai's childhood and his interest in computers. Jai's mother too joined in the discussion midway, describing Jai's career goals and his girlfriend, Rita. His mother also told Shukla about his habits for the past few days, most of which Shukla already knew. Then she left to pray for her son, and it was Shukla and Mr. Goyal who kept talking.

"Sir, I shall let you know if I find any leads," said Shukla, as he was about to leave. Mr Goyal nodded, hopeful that Shukla and his people would find his son soon.

For the next 3 days, Shukla was travelling, meeting Jai's friends, his colleagues, his college and school teachers, and many more people. The only considerable information he had gathered was that Jai was furtively working on something, as was confirmed by his roommates. But the roommates had no idea as to what had happened on that laptop.

Although Shukla had gathered little new information, he was thanking God for having found Jai's laptop. This could prove to be the best piece of evidence of what had happened, and above all, it was highly possible that Shukla would find the source code of Ashtray on it. Earlier, he had assigned the job of investigating data on Jai's laptop to Mohan. Mohan claimed that he had acquired good amount of information from the laptop.

All this travelling was being done to check if Jai was really into something malicious. But if he was, it was still unclear why he would involve NIC in the matter. He could have just done what he had to do. This argument slightly bent Shukla in Jai's favour, but Shukla still looked into the matter very carefully. To find Jai was the second motive of the mission, while stopping Ashtray was the first.

Shukla made a rather smart plan with the laptop. He decided to make a trap using the laptop, rather than take it away at once. If anyone would come to take it away, links could be easily found. He told only his investigation team about it. Even Jai's roommates were surprised to discover that he did not take the laptop when he had found it. To clear the haze in front of them, Shukla told them that the laptop had been encrypted, and if even tried to open, it would lead to self-destruction. So there was no point in taking the laptop.

But the investigators were able to get what they wanted from the laptop.

While Shukla kept traveling, Mohan was busy decoding every aspect of Jai's laptop. Although the investigators could not get his laptop, they did make a copy of Jai's hard disk and that was enough for them. The hard disk was embedded into a new system, and the system was configured exactly the same way as Jai's laptop. Apart from this hard disk, they were able to retrieve three more hard disks, mostly containing movies, games and pictures. But considering the smartness of Jai, the investigators had duplicated every hard disk that they could find. Mohan had to check every file on these hard disks, and discover links to contacts to whom Jai had contacted. He finished sweeping the whole hard disk, only to find a huge collection of movies and games. Ashtray's source code was not directly visible, but was certainly in there, Mohan was sure. He reported the contents to Shukla.

"Sir, nothing suspicious on the laptop, nothing in particular that could establish a link to Jai's disappearing."

"Okay, I'll be at the office tomorrow, let's try and connect all that we have till now," said Shukla. Vineet was traveling in other parts, so the three decided to meet the next day, and connect the dots. Shukla was very excited about finding the complete code of the infamous Ashtray, as was everyone else at the NIC.

The next morning as they met, all the facts gathered by each one of them was stated, the whiteboard was full with details and they had to arrange another one for Mohan's findings. David was called up later to discuss their findings, and the investigation team of Shukla had been left out, as Shukla wanted to keep Jai's laptop a secret for the time being.

Vineet came up with some constructive evidence. There was a possibility of a hack group called '4dm1r4ble' to be linked, but the probability was too small. Nevertheless, the team had to now find members of this hack group, which in itself was a daunting task, as the group had a reputation of not being in one particular location, and used aliases wherever they went. So they got to work. They had to link the fake passports to original ones, that is, link the aliases to real names.

This was to take a long time as they had to consider every possible combination of fake and real passports, before drawing any conclusions. By evening, they were able to locate 4 members, three of them in Brazil, and one in India. So the fourth member was scheduled to be grilled the next day. Along with these three, the two questioners from NIA were also included now in the discussion. The hacker was in Ahmedabad, and Shukla's team had to take the first flight in the morning.

After the long meeting that lasted almost till 3.00 pm, Shukla went to finish some other work. The ministry was not allowing him to be left off the advisory committee, and Shukla had to deal with it. His resignation was not accepted. He had to meet the other members of the advisory committee today. The gruelling meeting lasted almost an hour, draining Shukla's energy completely. Almost dark now, Shukla decided to call it a day. The people from NIA decided to stay in the office for some more time, as they had to report to Amit about the findings of the day. Mohan made the flight reservations for the next morning, and left.

After getting a good sleep, Shukla left his home at 4.30 am, as the flight was scheduled for 6.30 am, and the airport was an hour away from his place. The streets were empty, and the early morning breeze induced sleep in him. He was being driven to the airport, when suddenly his car was stopped. The car's sudden stopping woke Shukla up. For a moment, Shukla was scared. Frantically, Shukla rolled down his window, while his driver opened the door. It was a cop doing routine checks, and Shukla almost burst out laughing. "What a coward I am," he exclaimed! The car again took pace towards the airport, and reached there at 5.30 am, exactly on time. The others were yet to arrive, so he had to wait outside the airport. After a few moments, Mohan and the NIA people arrived, leaving only Vineet. The security check announcement was made now, and it was getting late. Shukla called Vineet, just to the disappointment of hearing- 'The number you have dialled is currently unavailable' in English and Hindi.

"Why do they even keep phones if they don't want to answer," grunted Shukla. All the others kept quiet. Mohan called Vineet's landline, to find that he had left for the airport at the scheduled time, confusing him. He told this to Shukla, who was now scared, and his inclination to believe that something fishy was happening kept growing. Shukla was now in a dilemma, whether to leave for Ahmedabad, or to find Vineet. But there was also an uncertainty; had Vineet actually disappeared, or were his communication channels not working, as does happen often in calamitous times.

After thinking for a few minutes, Shukla decided to let the interrogation be taken over by NIA. He and Mohan were to stay back to check what had happened. If Vineet arrived, Shukla and Mohan could take the next flight from the airport, which was an hour later. So they were certain about not losing precious time. But the wait at the airport was completely in vain. They waited till 7.30 am, post which Shukla decided to go to the office, to announce the problem and to get help from others.

And so Shukla called back his driver, who drove both of them straight to the NIC headquarters. Meanwhile, the NIA team had called upon a few more members, a contingent of 4 people now, with the inclusion of two more people from NIA. The team had the job fixed, to interrogate the person who was a part of the group, and to possibly arrest him, if Jai was found. This was a fairly procedural task, with all the four members of the NIA trained for such circumstances. In fact, they were happy that none of the members of the NIC were there, as they could have ruined the interrogations by not allowing them to interrogate freely.

The team reached the destination, the location at which they were to find the suspect. Thanks to their furtive searching techniques, they were even able to find the person there. But certainly, he was not Jai. After questioning this person for the next two hours, they were convinced that the trip to Ahmedabad was in vain. The hacker they found had already left the group, but still he was able to convince them that the hacking group had changed their stance. Their ways of questioning had all failed to get results this time. '4dm1r4ble' had been dismantled a few months ago, and its members were actually now assisting various national governments. The investigators decided to leave him there itself, and left to come back. On their journey back, they were doubting the methods that they had used to zero in on this group. But they were dejected, as they were hopeful of finding some information leading to Jai.

Earlier, as he reached the office, Shukla headed straight to David's office, who was not there at that moment. David was assisting the teams on the hacks, who had been working days and nights, with hardly a person who had left for home since their work started. Shukla found him in conference room #2, where David was having a meeting with the teams. Shukla barged in the room, and interrupted David with a loud "Sir!"

The whole team had their eyes on Shukla now, who looked wronged. Shukla looked at all of them once, and thought whether he should continue the discussion in private with David or tell them all at once. He decided to first tell the matter to David, and then announce it out loud.

"Sir, one more situation!" exclaimed Shukla. Shukla told him about Vineet's disappearance. Both of them now sat and discussed everything that had happened after 31st March. Shukla clearly explained the events that culminated in Vineet going missing, and wanted some concrete advice from the senior. But David had nothing that could help deal with the situation. He rather decided to tell the other people there, and see if anyone could come up with something. He felt like telling everyone at once, but resisted till Shukla finished talking. The other team members were still in the room, and wondered what had happened. After 15 minutes of discussion, David announced- "One of our own, Vineet Singhal, has gone missing since today morning." The atmosphere in the room turned chaotic with this announcement. Was Ashtray turning human bodies into Ash?

"Calm down people, our job just got doubled," Shukla said, looking down at the ground. He took a long pause after this, and then came back to normal. David had started discussing with the people there about this incident, and Shukla joined in.

After an hour of discussion, the team was given instructions to track down Vineet's belongings. Shukla and David agreed that Shukla would continue with his job, and David added 5 more members into Shukla's team, as they had to now even track Vineet. The disappearance of Vineet somehow propelled every member of David's team to give their maximum, and the work continued in full swing.

The NIA was now on a full red alert, with such hideous activities happening, but Joshi somehow had to manage to keep this tight lipped. Shukla understood the constraints on Amit Joshi, and decided not to bother him with more NIA investigators. The four NIA members that were sent to Ahmedabad were to be used full time now.

In the afternoon that day, Shukla received a call on his phone, but the number seemed fishy, so Shukla told Mohan to record the call. But the call was put off. After sometime again, another call was received, but this time it was his wife calling. He had forgotten to tell her that he was not in Ahmedabad, but in the city itself. He talked to her for some time, and was worried about his family more than ever now. Normally calls to his wife would last a few minutes, but today the call lasted longer, about ten minutes.

After this, he received a call from the team that had gone to Ahmedabad. Shukla was exasperated to hear their report, as he was watching everything going downwards. There was not the slightest link which could help him find Vineet and Jai. The investigators also questioned the methods used to reach to the hacking group, but in the end, Shukla convinced them that it was the only possible lead that could be used.

Earlier, NIA had looked up recent activities of many fraudulent organisations, and could not link Jai's involvement with anyone. 4dm1r4ble was chosen because its members had recently conducted a massive phishing campaign. The NIA thought that this could have been a precursor to Jai's virus, and had reported to Vineet about it. Vineet had then looked up the possible effects of phishing into Jai's ashtray, and although he thought that it was redundant, this was the only possible lead. So he had to report it.

Mohan had already started looking out for Vineet, contacting people whom Vineet knew. Mohan was a person who had good contacts with everyone at NIC, and Vineet was his one of his friends there. So naturally he was worried about him. He made sure that Vineet's parents were not worried, and he even went to their house to comfort them. He spent a considerable amount of time before getting back to the NIC headquarters. He was able to get the numbers of each of Vineet's friends, and after returning to office, started contacting each one of them. The list included his friends from school, college and work. After calling most of them, and getting a 'wrong-number' reply from many, Mohan was sure that none of Vineet's friends knew about his whereabouts. He was convinced that as was the case with Jai, no one would have noticed anything.

After finishing the call from Ahmedabad, Shukla went to David's team, and saw what the progress in securing the systems was. He was trying to freshen his mind by talking to people there. He discussed the progress with the team for about an hour, discussing minute details about everything. He advised the team to break the work down into stages, and even showed them the chart to work properly. Although the teams knew what they were doing, they had to listen to the trite suggestions that Shukla made as a courtesy to him.

After a while, Shukla did realise that he was saying things that the teams already knew, and was actually wasting their time. So he thought of going and having a cup of coffee instead. While he was at the machine, his office landline rang. He ran to the phone, almost spilling half of the coffee that the machine had carefully poured into his glass. Panting, he picked up the phone, forgetting to tell someone to record the phone.

"Sir, this is Vineet." Shukla's eyes opened wide. "Where are you?" asked Shukla.

"I need you to meet me after office hours today at the tea stall near the office. Keep it discreet, do not let anyone know about this, we will be in trouble if anyone knows. 6.30 sir, 6.30 in the evening." Shukla clearly recognised Vineet's voice.

RENDEZVOUS

April 6

"But, but tell me where you are curr…" The phone went dead. It was this phone call that had either given Shukla the greatest news of the day that Vineet was alive, or he had to be worried now more than ever, for Vineet was in danger. Shukla felt a bit peaceful at first to hear the voice of Vineet, but that did not last long. He was partly sure this time that Vineet was kidnapped. Shukla faced a crisis now, all these situations had started to affect him. His health seemed to drop and his head was hitting sixes on the inside. He wanted to get off this problem now. "Enough!" he screamed, his voice loud enough to reach five desks on either side of his cabin. Everyone around turned their eyes to him. "Nothing, sorry," he said, and sat back in his chair. He did not explain anything to them at that point.

"Sir, shall I get you some tea or coffee?" asked Mohan with a concern. "You better shut that door on your way back and let me be alone for some time," Shukla barked, showing him the direction of the cabin door. "Okay, sir," said Mohan politely, and left. Mohan was naturally worried and went straight to David to explain the situation to him. David exemplified his calm image by telling Mohan to leave the man alone, giving him some time. He surmised there could be some personal tension that Shukla was undergoing.

After a few minutes, Shukla called on Mohan, apologised for shouting, and decided to tell him what had exactly happened. He was about to tell him everything about the phone call. But a moment later, he changed his mind. He just thought, "What if I go there, and things actually change for the better?"

"Nothing..." he said to Mohan. "I just needed to say sorry for my behaviour earlier on."

"That's okay, Shukla ji," replied Mohan, feeling a lot better after the apology from Shukla. He felt bad when Shukla had shouted at him, which was natural.

Shukla delegated Jai's search related work that had to be done the next morning to Mohan, contemplating that he might not be there the next day. Then, Shukla explained every detail of the plan of action for the coming days, and told him exactly how he had to communicate with the other teams on the issue. He also instructed Mohan to keep the NIA involved, as their investigation strategies had had the highest impact till now, even though the progress was meagre. He told him everything he had in mind for the future. And he told him all this in a tone as if it was his last day at the office. Mohan was confused now.

"But sir, why are you explaining all this to me right now?" asked Mohan.

"I need every member in the team to know what has to happen!" Shukla continued, not heeding Mohan's question. "Okay sir," said an obedient Mohan, knowing for certain now that something was wrong. "Is there anything else sir?" Mohan kept asking three-four times, to which he always got a negative. He decided not to bother Shukla at that moment, and he would speak with him the next day. Hence he decided to leave Shukla alone for the time being.

"Shall I leave then?" he asked.

"Yes, Mohan."

Shukla now headed to the boss' office. They discussed the progress of their respective teams, and Shukla was amazed to find that David's team had started taking huge leaps towards security. They had done a lot of research to arrive at the current stage.

Shukla needed a few things before he went to the tea stall. He wanted a voice recorder and a camera. To get them, he would have to get permission from David first.

"Sir, I need a voice recorder and a camera, my phone camera is not good, and the investigation might be aided if I have them with me all the time."

"But Shukla, you can take them whenever you want. Just make an entry into the system, and take them. What is the big deal?"

"No sir, actually if I have it all the time, I would save making entries repetitively. My team always needs the equipment, and the NIA people do not disclose the details captured on their cameras. Please allow me to have them. I need a note signed from you for getting them for a longer time."

"If that is what you want, take them. I will make the arrangements, just go to the storage bay and ask for them."

"Thank you, sir, thanks a lot."

The use of cameras during Shukla's investigation was not very significant. While interviewing others, the NIA used a camcorder always, and the video and audio was always available. And David knew this. He momentarily grew suspicious of what Shukla was doing. But he did not want to cause any obstruction to Shukla, having faith in whatever he did. He called the storage bay to order them to give Shukla whatever he demanded.

At 5.30 in the evening, Shukla left for the stall, well before the time to see if he could spot any activity related to Mohan. He waited inside the stall, well hidden from the outside due to the darkness inside the stall. He knew the shopkeeper well, and had him briefed too about the situation. The shopkeeper had instructions to watch out for anything suspicious, note all the groups of people who were coming, and ultimately, to note the people who were to meet Shukla. He had been provided with a voice recorder to try and record the conversation between Shukla and the other party. Shukla waited there, checking every aspect of the stall. He visually inspected all the chairs and tables too.

It was 6.15 pm now, Shukla saw nothing in particular that could raise questions as to who the people that he was meeting could be, even though he was sure that Vineet would be there. An important person, whether good or bad, would have security checks before reaching there. If the person was of a small hacking gang, then one or two people could have accompanied him. Shukla had enough experience with the security procedures that are followed by high authorities, and looking at the situation, he could clearly see that it could be just Vineet he was meeting. "But, why in such a manner, if only him? He could have just come down to the office." he thought to himself. To be ready in time, Shukla decided to go freshen up and be back at the decided time. He went to a nearby restaurant, and washed his face in the washroom.

He was back exactly at 6.25 pm. Still, there was nobody. He could just wait anxiously now. He occupied the table which was the closest to the stall, so that his voice could be recorded. The wait was over soon.

At 6.30 pm, he could sight Vineet coming from a distance. He was flanked by three more people, who did not seem at all to be of the 'bouncer' kind. Their bellies bulged slightly outwards, and their shoulders were working hard to keep the arms hanging, it seemed. As he was walking, the three people walking with him said something to Vineet, and at the next crossroad, they were walking in three different directions, the fourth direction being towards the tea stall. Shukla tried to gain as much sight of the three people as he could, and his phone was just about to come out for taking photos. But it turned out that the people disappeared faster than his phone came out of the pocket. He tried to keep his eyes on them, but looking out in three directions was not possible as he did not have any volunteers there. So he ignored them, and concentrated on Vineet. He indicated the stall owner to switch on the camera and the voice recorder, and started to analyse Vineet's approach towards him.

As Vineet approached, Shukla tried to capture the look of fear, pain and agitation on his face. Shukla was analysing Vineet, looking at him from top to bottom multiple times. As he was doing this, Shukla gave him a wide smile, and a tear almost dropped from his eye. But he was equally muddled as well. The fear that he expected on Vineet's face was not there. Vineet seemed to be just normal, as if nothing had happened in the day. He seemed to be perfectly normal, if not more peaceful.

Vineet came up to the table, gently pulled a chair, and ordered a cutting chai for both of them. He then checked his phone, seeking a moment's excuse from Shukla and then looking back at him.

"Hello sir, how's it going?" He asked casually. Shukla was even more confused.

"Where have you been the whole day? What has been happening? Who were those people? What did they say to you? Did you meet Jai? How does he feel?" This was the beginning of the array of questions that Shukla wanted to ask. But he somehow resisted for the time being, and just replied a nonchalant "Fine, where have you been?"

"Sir, I thank God for showing me this day. Something very important has happened today. While coming to the airport in the morning, I was able to meet some erudite people, the same people who were walking with me earlier."

"Vineet, be clear about what you want to say. All of us have been worried about you, and I can't take any more surprises, or suspense. Please get to the point."

Their chai arrived, and Vineet took a pause to sip some out of the traditional kullhad (earthen mug)in which it was served. He then checked his phone, which seemed to be working like a beacon, ringing after every few seconds. It appeared to Shukla as if someone was constantly keeping a check on Vineet.

"And what is wrong with your phone," Shukla asked.

"Just a second sir," he said as he seemed to reply to a message. Then turning the phone silent, he kept it on the table, and began talking.

"Sir, the mission has taken an altogether different form up there."

"What? Up where? Whom are you talking about? Please talk clearly man."

"Sir, please let us talk on the way to my home. Let's take a cab. It will be better if we do not talk in a public place."

"Vineet, I am not getting into any car until and unless you tell me the situation. And if you need a private place, why not head to the office. I am sure they will allow us to have a discussion there. And in fact, everyone will be happy to see you back. Please explain."

"Sure sir, I will. Let's first go back to my place. You don't have to worry, everything is going to be alright, sir. Office not really possible sir, this is something that needs you, and if we drop the slightest of hints to NIC, we could blow it up completely."

"We? I am not working for some terrorist group, and if you are, I am going straight to the NIA to report you. I am sorry, if you cannot explain, I am not coming with you," said Shukla, as he started to get up from his chair, until Vineet began. Vineet was irked by this statement. Shukla thinking that he was involved with some terrorist organisation was not justified, he thought.

"Sir, how petty can you think. I have been trained by none other than you, and for you to think that I am working with some terrorist group is just not acceptable. I assure you that nothing of that sort is happening. Just that the mission is way more important that we think it is. Please believe me, let us talk while going back. And if you want to back out, you can, but just hear me once before that."

Shukla was in thought again. What if this guy was to be believed? But then, if he were right, why not explain to him right there. What

53

was the need to go home? He tried pressurising Vineet into explaining to him there itself, but he would not. After a few minutes, Shukla decided to give it a shot. He said "let's believe our man," to himself. His instinct now said there was nothing wrong, as did the peaceful look on Vineet's face. Both of them decided to leave. Shukla didn't realise that he had gulped in 5 cups of 'cutting chai' while all this was happening. He paid the tea stall owner, and signalled him to keep the voice recorder till he came back. "Apne pass hi rakho" (Keep it with you) he said aloud, to deceive Vineet into believing that he asked the stall owner to keep the change. They decided to take a cab. Shukla told his driver to go home, as he would mostly not work in the night, and would reach home on his own.

The cab they got into was a white Maruti Swift, the driver a stout, bearded man who looked as if he had not bathed for a year. He was chewing tobacco, which had always irritated Shukla throughout his life. On occasion he had even given lectures to people about the harms of tobacco. This time was not different, he wanted to do the same. But he was too tired, and decided against it. Shukla scrutinised all the particular details about the cab. He noted down the registration number of the cab on his phone and tried sending it to his office. But he could not send it, there was no network on his phone now. The driver started the engine and the journey began. Vineet's house was an hour away, so that meant enough time to take a nap if Vineet did not explain anything to him.

"Sir, should I start or shall we wait to get back home?" asked Vineet.

"No. Go on now!" Shukla said, knowing that his sleep was far less important than the matter at hand.

"Sir, what idea do you have about the working of this world? Do you know how these ecosystems function? Do you have any idea?"

"Mr. Singhal, I am in no mood for environmental education right now! I am frustrated. Please do not inflame my mind. If I do not see you explaining clearly what is happening, my eyes will close automatically. You get that?"

"Sir do not worry; this is about the predicament. Believe me. Just answer my question."

"Okay what?" said a sleepy-eyed Shukla.

"Sir, have you ever wondered how the biodiversity of this planet flourishes? The harmony between the numbers of smallest of amoeba to the largest of whales, how it is so organised, despite being chaotic?"

"Listen Vineet, to me all this is turning out to be baseless. Still, I guess the diversity must be very well organised. What are you trying to say exactly?"

"Sir, what is the count of trees, herbs, shrubs, animals, aquatic animals, in fact the whole flora and fauna on this earth?" He went on, ignoring Shukla's question.

"We have the Unique Identification database here for the humans. What is there for the animals, the plants and others? What is it that keeps everything working in a perfect balance?"

The word database woke up the half asleep part of Shukla's brain, which had been passively listening till now.

"Sir, the unique identification database is being prepared for many plans of the government, what for the plans of nature? The natural cycles such as water cycle? Birth dates of all the living beings? Will there not be an information system that manages all the life that exists on this planet, and all the possible life coming later on? What manages deaths, generations, Sun's heat, greenhouse effect, temperature and all the other things?"

Shukla was completely driven out of his slumber now. He felt refreshed, and was actually starting to think about the questions Vineet was asking. The concept of a huge database struck him now, and he actually started to think about the possibilities of the connection of ashtray with it. His ears suddenly forced him to listen to the talk by Vineet.

"Another thing, what is important for the survival of the fittest? A competition sir, a competition. To make this competition, there has to be two of a kind at least. The competition exists because there is a winner and a loser always. What if there are no winners, only losers? It will change the definitions of our existence. All these small things, all of them if taken into consideration could just baffle a person. Science provides us with logic, but how is this humongous system managed? Things don't happen automatically, as you yourself had taught us in the early days of our training. So what is the answer to the management of universe precisely? The MBAs of today might manage big corporations that control the world, but who manages the world itself? I know that you would guess the correct answer, and would negate yourself with equal haste."

But how? Such a huge informatics system seems unimaginable.

"Yes Vineet, I can see the answer-a very big information system, but yeah, it is unimaginable at first. I think it is not possible. Otherwise how would we have altered the natural processes of birth and death and actually have pushed our life spans to such huge extents. I think if there had to be disharmony, it already exists, for example just look at the number of tigers left in the world. The informatics would have hardly done anything to prevent it. And no, God did not order their deaths, it was the selfish motives of us, humans, which disrupted the harmony."

"Yes sir, there have been changes, no doubt. But sir, it was not only Darwin who stated the theory of evolution, but the higher order too agrees with it. They do condemn the morbid crimes of the humans, but to manage harmony, adjustments need to be made, to ensure that the world goes on. We now do acknowledge our tigers and vow to protect them sir, see the change that has happened over time. Time is respected everywhere."

"Okay, I can partly agree with you on that. But if that is the case, where does this informatics system exist? It certainly has to be something palpable, and should actually physically exist. And I am sure about this."

"Oh yes sir, I do agree that such a system does exist. In fact, I paid a visit today morning to that place. I have been chosen to serve there, and my first task is to invite you there. I think I have talked enough for now; you can go to sleep if you want now. We can talk later…" he finished.

"Yeah, you expect me to sleep, now that is certainly not happening. Please explain to me why we are the chosen ones, and not the others?"

"Sir, does that mean that you acknowledge the work and are willing to go there?"

"That depends on the work and the other terms and conditions."

"Yes sir, surely it does."

Vineet did not talk anymore, ambiguously stopping the conversation, but he had done something very important. He had managed to get Shukla's consent, even though Shukla did not say it out loud. Shukla did ask one more time, but Vineet told him that he would talk about it when they got home. It had been less than thirty minutes since they had gotten into the taxi, and the driver was now starting to speed through the mostly empty streets. Streets being empty was highly unlikely at that time of the day.

Vineet had just managed to charge up Shukla's brain, whose sleep had now drifted far from him. But he knew that every coin had two sides.

THE HAZE CLEARS

April 7

"Look Vineet, I am mesmerised with this little fictitious story of yours, but let's focus on work currently." Shukla ended the silence after a while, realising that all this was too good to be true, and he found it completely unrelated to his work.

"Sir, this is completely in harmony with our work."

"God's database actually exists, and the person whom we were searching for, has also been found."

"You found Jai, where? Well that's some good news finally." Shukla sighed, and this was in a way reassurance for the story that Vineet had just told him. He now began to believe in the story.

"Yeah, that man, Jai Goyal. Sir, he is one of the smartest people I have ever met. He has impeccable logical and coding skills."

"Certainly no doubt about that," said Shukla. "Now, explain everything that has happened since morning, please. And don't digress this time!" Shukla was impatient now. The car was speeding rapidly. Shukla did not even notice that the tires skid a few times, being completely captivated by Vineet.

"Sir, this morning, when I was in my car while traveling to the airport, far away, I managed to spot Goyal. Naturally, I drove towards him, and asked him to get into the car. But I did not realise there were other people with him too. There were 3 more people, the people whom you saw earlier. All of them got into the car, and told me to drive wherever I wanted to go. I was about to call you, when a strange thing happened. Of the three people, one person, who was on the pillion seat, removed a steering wheel from his backpack, and aligned it to the car, with God knows what! He controlled the car's steering wheel through his wheel, while I was just holding the actual steering, which rotated in harmony with his steering wheel. I simply do not know how it happened, there was no physical connection with any wiring in the car. Obviously, I was terrified."

Shukla's head turned to the driver of the taxi, his heart pounding loudly now.

"Don't worry sir, no danger with this car." He continued by reiterating the point he had just made- "My steering wheel was jammed completely for me, and the car moved towards the airport, but was being controlled by this man. In the meanwhile, Jai started talking. He explained to me whatever I told you about the databases. We were approaching the airport. Their actual plan was to pick you up. I was acting as the middleman. But suddenly, the man who was driving took a U turn, saying he had orders from above. I just thought that you were saved, which was very good. Later, I don't know how, but I slept on the journey. When I woke up, in front of me was this huge place, which seemed like any giant software company's office, just that the size of this one was too huge. At first, all the things that Jai told me started to play in my mind. And suddenly I screamed- Is this it? To which Jai replied- Yes."

"We went inside, myself being so enthralled by looking at the place that I was unable to speak. Jai started- "This place is the data centre of the world, it has the record of all the flora and fauna on planet earth. I was picked up to serve at this place. The best of the lot, those who have been great scientists in their lives on earth, are handpicked to work in this place, and serve mother earth,' he said." Vineet paused.

"He continued his explanation saying that the effects of Ashtray were just too big, and that it was the biggest regret of his life, unless it proved to be of some use. When we were walking to a giant screen over there, the screen started flashing his activities in the past three days."

It had so happened that since March 31, the day when Jai was picked, it had taken about 4 days for him to understand whatever was happening there. In the next 3 days, he started working. The screen showed a summary of his work till now. Jai told Singhal to ignore it currently.

When all this was being explained to Shukla, he remained a stone, and no part of his body tried to move. Vineet paused to look if he was even awake. "Go on," said Shukla.

"He explained to me the necessity of the database. For example, the food cycles inherently depend on this for their running. But most importantly, he said that ashtray was capable of having dire consequences at that place too. He did not mention a particular domain or area, but certainly said that it could lead to a disaster for the whole planet. After this, he persuaded me to call you there. If you are willing to, we shall go. He did not pick you up earlier because apparently you had not spoken to your wife for a long time, as was told to me. A trivial reason, I thought at first. But later I found out that it was actually necessary," he continued.

"The NIC databases can be handled sir, but you have the opportunity of being one of the chosen ones. It is ultimately your call, sir" he said, leaving it up to Shukla to decide.

"But what happens to things here?" asked a confused Shukla.

"Sir, do not worry. There are other people who can take care of things here. NIC has other people. But the teams up there are benefiting the whole planet, not just their species."

"So this is the meaning of higher order, as stated on the phone, aye?"

"Yes, that is absolutely correct," Vineet replied.

"Okay, let's go!" said Shukla, thoughtlessly, not knowing the effects of him going there. Although he had his reservations, he was convinced that he would have to give in to these people. And Vineet could be believed, he thought.

"Yes sir, we will go straight there."

"But wait, I need to be at home first, then at office. I have a lot of unfinished work at office. I have to give the daily report about the NIC intelligence wing. Apart from this too, there is a lot to be done. I simply cannot leave everything and go away."

"Certainly not, sir. I am sure that other people will take care of these works, and your home will also be notified, I suppose." He indicated something to the driver which Shukla was not able to see. The driver started to slow down the car, and looked around to see if anyone was watching them.

Shukla could sense that there was no point in arguing with Vineet, it looked as if the journey had already begun, so he submitted into going forward with it.

It seemed the three other people, the ones who had accompanied Vineet earlier, were following them in another car, which popped in front of them as Vineet nodded. They got down from the cab, and were escorted to the other car, which was not at all a God-vehicle, as was imagined by Shukla earlier.

In this car now, Shukla could see the other three clearly, and was just wondering how all this could seem so normal to them. None of them seemed as huge as a bouncer or a bodyguard. By looking at them, Shukla could surmise that they were normal, office going, and typical IT people, except one. This person had the perfect look of a college professor, erudite and disciplined. He seemed to have an experience in teaching of about 10 years. Shukla's stare was so disturbing that he just chuckled- "Sir, don't ogle so much. I feel shy."

All the people in the car smiled for the first time. The windows of the car were all tinted, so Shukla couldn't see much of the outside.

By looking through the front windscreen, he could see that they were still in the city, but were fast approaching an egress to the city. He tried to build a path from the place they were picked till this exit. When the car was out of the city, as was visible through the windscreen, the speed of the car rose to about 100 kmph initially, and was steadily rising.

One part of Shukla was still not completely convinced of this whole concept of God's database. His mind was full of suspicions. His experience and instinct told him that this was some terrorist group which had been targeting him and Jai. Jai for the hack, and him if they needed to control it, or perhaps because he was the first person to whom Jai had explained it to. To him, both of them were just being used. But then, why did he agree in the first place if this was the case? Was he being hypnotised? Had Vineet done something that made him agree? He kept thinking.

But the people in the car seemed rather friendly. The radio was switched on, and the latest Bollywood tracks were audible. Vineet got into a talk with the person riding pillion. Vineet and this person had a bet for the time it would take Vineet to convince Shukla to agree to him. Vineet had won the bet by a huge factor.

"Does it mean that if I had refused, you would have seriously left me there?" Shukla just had to ask.

"Yes sir, you might think that we would pressurise you, but you had the choice till that moment. You chose to do this."

"Does it mean that I can go back now?"

"Sir, we are almost there, what is the point of returning now?" Vineet continued playing his mind games.

The car was now moving at wild speeds, and making sharp curves. But both of them felt somnolent, and they dozed off.

CHAPTER

MISSING LINKS

Mr Shankar Shukla was worried for some time now. He had not heard from his son since the day he had left him and his wife. He was considerate at first as he knew that the amount of work Shukla had would not have given him the chance to. But Shukla's wife, Kalpana, had been in constant touch with Shukla's parents. Of late, she was worried and had told Shukla's parents about his erratic work timings, the tension that was always visible on his face, and the constant calls that he used to get. She had heard from Shukla that this was his most important mission in life, and was in support of whatever her husband was to do.

On the day when Shukla was to reach Ahmedabad, she had a call from Unnikrishnan in the night. She had already spoken to Shukla in the afternoon, and she knew that the next time she would speak to Shukla could take a day or two. Unnikrishnan wanted to reach her as Shukla's phone was unreachable at the moment.

"This is very important Mrs Shukla, please let me speak to Shukla," Unnikrishnan had said.

"But, what is the matter that you want to discuss so urgently? Can you wait? I do not take any official calls for him, and he is not at home at the moment. He might be in office, please contact him there. Okay?" Kalpana replied.

Unnikrishnan wanted to discuss why he was involved, and how his name was dragged into the matter. He was apprehensive about discussing it with Kalpana first, but later he told her everything about Shukla's current work, not knowing that it was a secret mission. He also told her that he wanted to help Shukla in every way, so he wanted to talk to him desperately.

Being the stubborn lady she was, Kalpana at first thought that this was nothing more than a spam call. Shukla had a lot of those, and she was not new to such a call. Often, she chose not to bother Shukla, and would deal with them herself. But this one felt highly magnified. She had an inclination to believe that this time Shukla was involved in something very big. She just wanted him to get back home safe now. She knew of the situation in which Shukla had visited his home in Gwalior earlier. Shukla was tensed for the past few days, and the story that Unnikrishnan had told her reverberated in her ears for quite a long time, before she was convinced that it was really true. She reported the matter to Shukla's parents now, worrying all of them.

This was the prime cause of his father's concern now, and he wanted to help him in all ways he could. The first thing he did was to contact the NIC head office, to talk to David. David told him that there was nothing to worry, and it was a normal but important mission. He had assured him that Shukla was capable enough to handle such missions. So there was no reason to be so concerned. David also called Kalpana, and tried to assure her the same. But the call did not pacify her at all, and she thought that David might be giving her a false impression.

Unnikrishnan needed to report to Shukla that he had been contacted by some person the day when Shukla was to go to Ahmedabad. But he could not reach Shukla's phone, and that's why he had called his home, only to reach Shukla's wife. Shukla's cell phone was not reachable, as he was in the car having a journey of discovery, where something new appeared on every corner.

A person had contacted Unnikrishnan informing him to stay away from the matter, while Unnikrishnan was near the tea stall. He had also given a clarification for the involvement of his name in the matter. The reason why Unnikrishnan was involved in the matter was a result of a random pick-up from Shukla's call list, as told to Unnikrishnan by the other person. But this was hardly convincing to Unnikrishnan, who had been frightened for life a few days ago when Shukla had told him of the possible consequences. The reason was trivial, as opposed to the threats that loomed upon him when he met Shukla at the NIC office. Unnikrishnan tried to identify this person very hard, only to conclude that he had never seen him before. But he noted his appearance, thinking it could be beneficial to Shukla.

"That would be all, Mr Unnikrishnan. I need to leave now. Thanks for hearing me out," said the other man and went towards a car waiting for him. The car sped away on the street opposite the stall, as Unnikrishnan waited there, thinking what to do next.

Unnikrishnan grabbed the pen hanging in his pocket, and took a piece of paper from a newspaper that was lying on the road, to write down the whole appearance of the person. He refreshed his memory to check if he had seen him ever in his life. He noted in points:

- Height about 5'10" or 5'11"

- Brown skin

- Moustache with straight sides

- Clean shaven

- White formal shirt with blue checks, black pant, nothing particular with the pant

- Sleeves folded upwards

- Hair unkempt, but not ugly looking

- Paused a lot while talking, drank water from a bottle a lot of times

- A rigid voice

- Around 25-30 years old.

Although the list was not organised very well, it certainly had every element that he had noted. It looked as if Unnikrishnan was trying to build his sketch while the person was talking about other things.

He called Shukla again and again, six times precisely, and then tried calling his office phone. But he soon realised that it was a Saturday night and Shukla must not have gone to office. So he called his home, finally.

After the call with Kalpana ended, he did not know what to do with the list. He was sure that she would be of no help with the matter, and had not told her the details of the list. But foolishly, he had told her everything that could blow up Shukla's mission. He put the list into his shirt pocket and started walking to the tea stall. He enquired if Shukla had been there, to find that he had not. He then decided to have a cup of tea, and sat on the same table that later Shukla would occupy waiting for Vineet.

The NIC building was visible to him now, and he thought of checking if someone was there. But later he thought that it should only be Shukla who should know about this person. He was confused about what would be the right thing.

To divert himself, he sipped his tea, and started a casual conversation with the tea stall owner. While he was talking to him, his mind was thinking about what to do with the list. They talked for about fifteen minutes, during which Unnikrishnan had bought a cigarette from the Pan stall adjoining the tea stall. After the discussion, Unnikrishnan walked to his bike parked on the opposite side of the road. But he decided that he should rather tell the people at NIC. Maybe they could find out who this person was, and hence walked towards the NIC building.

Meanwhile, Jai's mother had not moved from the temple in her house. She had been praying to God the whole time. Jai's father had been searching and contacting each one of Jai's friends to find if he was there. Although he knew that it could be in vain, he continued doing it. Apart from his missing son, he was also worried about the discovery that his wife had made-Rita, Jai's girlfriend. Although he had hints about the matter, he had not let his conservative wife know about it, for he feared her breaking down, as had happened. But he could think of nothing at the moment that could help his son, as he did not know where he was. He had to raise hopes for his wife that her son would come soon. Mrs Goyal, Jai's mother, only wanted to see her son, she was ready to accept any woman as her 'Bahu', only if her son returned home safe. Although the situation was gloomy, they were always hopeful that Jai could be at home any moment from there.

Rita was too worried to be able to sleep, and kept thinking about Jai, sobbing profusely. This was the first time that he had not called for such a long time. She partly blamed herself too; she did not leave him alone when he wanted her to. But she knew that this was not enough for Jai to take such a drastic step. She decided that she should do something about it. She called Jai's father, and decided to go to Jaipur to be with Jai's parents. His father instead told her to wait there, as he was coming to Delhi the next day. She also spoke to Jai's mother for a long time. They both shared their grief.

"All good, for when Jai returns, his mother would be ready to accept Rita," smiled Mr Goyal. The three of them decided to meet the next day in Delhi, to see what to do.

Meanwhile, Unnikrishnan reached the NIC office and met someone by the name of Mr AB Khan. He explained to him what had happened. Khan, on hearing that Shukla was involved, reported the matter to David. David, who was busy with his developer team decided to meet Unnikrishnan at once. Shukla was not in the office at that time, as he had left for his journey. Unnikrishnan explained the whole situation intricately, and also described all the elements of the list in detail.

Both Khan and David were stunned to hear the description, and confirmed it thrice before considering it to be true. David then called up the NIA to see if he could get a sketch artist. One of the investigators that was assigned by the NIA was a sketcher himself, so his skill was put to use. The sketch artist was called upon, and he drew the sketch exactly as described by Unnikrishnan. It took about an hour for the sketch artist to complete the sketch, noting each minute detail that Unnikrishnan stated.

"Are you sure this was the man?" asked David, realizing that the description matched the sketch accurately.

"Yes, I am perfectly sure."

It was Vineet Singhal's sketch.

INFORMATICS OF THE HEAVENS

As his eyes opened due to the cold wind troubling his eyes, they saw a huge gate, probably not built of steel but something much heavier. Completely green, the driveway had a picturesque canopy of trees. "Huge", said Shukla, captivated by the beauty. The person driving the car now slowed down to 60 km ph, at least that was what the speedometer said. The car kept driving at a constant speed, and Shukla was just awestruck by the beauty of this place. "Man, this place is not what a notorious group would have," he thought.

"Singhal, what is this place called?" he asked. His voice was relaxed for the first time since they met. "Sir, this happened to me too in the morning. Isn't this too good?" Passing by were giant orchid trees, with multi-coloured flowers. Butterflies were flying all around in the greenery that looked omnipresent. Further ahead, Shukla spotted a big pond on his right, which he could barely see through the trees. "Look, flamingos!" he said spontaneously. Shukla spotted deer all along the road that the car was driving, and in a few places some peacocks made for a visual treat. The whole place seemed to be a botanical garden, curated with the utmost attention. 'Organised chaos' he thought. He tried to guess the place by the look of it, certainly not possible on the earth, he concluded.

The car slowed down further, and far away, Shukla could sight some more flamingos. The cool air that was blowing into the car was a result of all the greenery there. The driveway was not made of concrete, it just had stones that were levelled, and there hardly was any car. The only two vehicles that Shukla could see were a caravan-like minibus that seemed to be the vanity van of some superstar and a BMW sedan which was standing opposite it. 'A film set!' Shukla thought, and here came one of the wildest thoughts in his mind-"What if all that was happening was an April Fools' Day prank?" But he knew it was not to be.

Apart from the 4 other people riding in that car, there was no one visible in the lush gardens, and the sound of the car was the only cacophonous sound, disturbing the natural sounds of the nature. Shukla lay there in his seat mesmerised by all this. He was wondering why they would use the car, the only entity in that place that could pollute the atmosphere. He had a lot of thoughts running through his mind. Vineet had once been through this driveway, but he was still equally interested in exploring the place.

After driving for about 10 minutes, the car slowed down in front of a mid-sized steel gate. The gate opened wide enough to let the car in, but did not reveal the other side yet. This time, the sceptic Shukla tried to tell the credulous Shukla that all this was a sham and there was actually something else happening inside.

The car now slowed down further, eventually coming to a halt once it had entered the gate. The three men got down, opening the doors for Shukla and Vineet.

Building 3

Informatics-Planet earth.

Shukla read it, trying to believe his eyes, telling himself that the place might actually exist.

"Seems like the effect of English has penetrated even here," he tried a bit of humour. One of the three answered, "Sir, the people here come from different places, so the Brits rule here too", he added, making Shukla burst out. "Ohh Britishers I see, I thought it must be the Americans, aye?" The banter continued. "Sir let's talk on the walk, this could be a bit long,"said he. "Okay, but where are we headed? And where is Jai?" Shukla asked. "You will know everything sir."

And so this odyssey on a path through a miraculously beautiful and ornate place began. "But how can all this be so perfect?" he asked Vineet. "Sir, humans on earth make errors, not the people here."

Shukla started talking to the person who was bantering with him-"Where are you from?"

"Sir, I am an Indian American. I stayed in Florida, working as a sound engineer for films. My career was at its lowest before I got a call to come here. I had struggled for 6 years building and modifying soundtracks for animated films, but most of the films were low budget. Last year, I had started with a solo album with a known composer, and I had given it everything I could have. But, the music flopped, and we could not find any distributors. I was broke, and had started having suicidal tendencies."

"Ohh. Interesting story. How does it feel to be a part of the chosen ones?"

"Actually, I feel that I am being rewarded for being truthful to what I loved doing in life."

"That is so nice. Tell me how you were picked up."

"Sir, I cannot tell you the whole story, but can give you some information." Shukla nodded, eager to hear whatever he was about to say.

"As I said, I began having suicidal tendencies, and when that happened, I felt too alone on the earth. I had only some amount of money left with me, enough for me to survive for another 2-3 months. I was in desperate need of a job. To sustain, I decided to go to some place where it would be cheap to live, and at the same time, I could find a job easily and work on music as well. It was the toughest decision in my life to move to India."

"India. Well I guess people here are recruited only from India. Is it so?"

71

"You will find out in some time sir."

"Okay, what happened after you came to India?"

"You might wonder how there is a need for sound engineers here. The thing is, I have been selected for the knowledge of modern sound types, and the necessity is that the music here is in the process of up gradation to electronic music. So I was chosen as the chief music architect. But why me?"

"Yeah exactly, even I wonder."

"The reason for choosing me, as stated here was that I had extensive knowledge about my field, enough to help in the transformation process, and also I did not have any primary projects at that time. They say here that the person who has finished with his duties on earth is called here. So that is the reason that people like me are given a chance."

"Do all the people here have similar stories?"

"Yes sir, almost everyone here has been recruited with a very specific job waiting for him."

"Okay, tell me about the others."

The conversation moved to other people who were working there, till Vineet interrupted to tell Shukla that they were almost there. After walking for about 15 minutes through this beatific place listening to a wonderful story, a building appeared in the distance, camouflaged by the trees and flowers. "Sir, the destination", said Vineet, pointing to the building. But the building was not that close, it was reached only after walking for another half hour.

As they reached the entrance, a young, cherubic lady came to greet them.

Krishnakant Rao, the person who was having the conversation with Shukla, asked- "Next assignment?" with his eyes fixated on the girl.

"Rest for the day," she said. All the three nodded, and left.

"Hello Mr Shukla," she said, in a clear French accent. Shukla recalled the dialogues from the movie-The Pink Panther, and replied "Bonjour, Madame!" She smiled. All three of them moved inwards, along the path which was covered with sand. But on the edges of the sand, there were blue fluorescent lights that glowed all the time. "I am Nicole, the assistant manager here." Nicole asserted.

"I will take you to the head of this unit." They walked towards the main entrance, which had a big door in the middle, again green on the borders. The door was richly polished and of wooden brown colour. It had a big board that read- "Welcome".

As she opened the door, a big hall emerged. All around, people could be seen happily engrossed in their activities. There were no computers around, only screens dropping plumb from the ceiling. "Giant, foldable, and detachable," said Nicole, as Shukla stared at one of those. "They are resizable screens, making this place the most flexible office," she added.

"The screens out here are assigned to people, just like computers in offices, the main difference with these screens being that these can move with the person all the time, in the form of pocket screens, just like you have smart phones. The screen is an all-time partner of a person, and can perform anything that the person wants. We call them keepers here." Nicole started describing.

"There, on your right, you can see the geographical IS, responsible for all the geographical activities. It also records the events that · happened due to undecided events. All the geographic history is recorded for a certain period of time in this database. Sadly, I don't know that database very well." Shukla was all ears when she talked.

"You can think of it as GPS maps, with access restricted to this place only. But it does not allow as much functionality as the navigation systems on earth, just that this one is very good at pinpointing locations. It is also linked to the genetic information system, which we are going to see in some time. The combined effect is the exact location of an organism at any point on the earth. This gives us the precision required for timing deaths." They walked past the geographical IS, as she continued.

"Once you are in here, you are allowed to do most of the work, leaving, of course some administrative works. This allows any person here to assist anyone else, through an easy peer to peer interaction. There is only a three-level hierarchy that is followed here. But we do have a lot of departments."

"Now as you can see, this is the Genetic Information System", Shukla could see the big direction sign showing the same. "This all is for the earth. So similar systems for all the planets, right?" Shukla asked with his eyes wide open. "I guess that question is very much unnecessary," she replied. A giant screen in the front flashed- 'English movies night! Tonight, main theatre.'

"Ha ha, here too?" chuckled Shukla. "Oh that, yes yes! Entertainment is taken care of very well here. And the people here are grateful to the people making the movies. I mean it. We have people like Krishnakant to whom you were speaking earlier for this part of the job. We cannot overwork our people. After all, these are people who perform all the work, the most important work."

"Can I go tonight?" he asked. "Oh yeah, sure," Nicole mocked him, reminding him that he had a very important task at hand.

"Now let's get to the point. We are specifically looking at one information system here, as that is the most critical one. So tell me one thing, how do you think every living being on the earth is managed? The death cycles, the profile of every kid that is born, and the period for which he lives?" she paused.

"Vineet must have explained to you what is really happening up here. There is actually a lot more than that, but it would take long to explain everything to you. I will not give all the details right now."

"Okay madam." Shukla nodded, as he tried to digest the information.

She explained to Shukla how the whole process began.

"The process or the cycle of life is very complex. We need to take utmost care to determine evolution of the organisms, otherwise it could lead to stagnation of the systems here, and evolution would ultimately collapse. Let me tell you about some species in particular. Should I start with humans?" she asked, and continued to narrate as Shukla nodded.

"When an individual is born, the genetic database is the first one to note the change to the ecosystem, to include the genes the child has inherited from its parents. Now human genetics is very complex, and to note the changes that happen due to evolution, utmost precision is needed. In the case of humans and some other organisms, we also need to consider the genetic modifications that you people have started doing, which has increased the work here manifold. After the genetics database, the geographical IS makes a new pin for this organism on its map, which is used for tracking. Then, the death time of a person is calculated using a formula which I cannot share, as I do not know it. The formula has a lot of randomness to it, and one particular information system, the Calc Base, is used for the calculation of the lifetime of each organism. The Calc Base is one of the most active systems here. The Calc Base is maintained by an elite maintenance group, which does not fall under the normal category of people here. I cannot tell you more about the Calc Base."

"Okay, still all this is too fascinating. Actually this is a lot of information to take at a time," Shukla interrupted her.

"Yeah it is. Now, after the Calc Base has calculated the death time, the biological information system is updated accordingly, and the death time is recorded. All the above things are done instantaneously. But I explained this for humans. There are other organisms that are different from humans, and all the organisms have different types of categories and criteria."

"What happens of those organisms that do not die, for example amoeba?"

"What can you think of Shukla?" she asked, with her ears eager to listen to the answer.

"No death calculation?"

"Simple, isn't it? No it is not. When the binary fission occurs in amoeba, the details about the parent need to be updated to note that the parent is no more alive. But this has to be done at multiple locations again, which necessitates a careful coordination and control," she said.

"Okay, looks like a lot of sophistication to me."

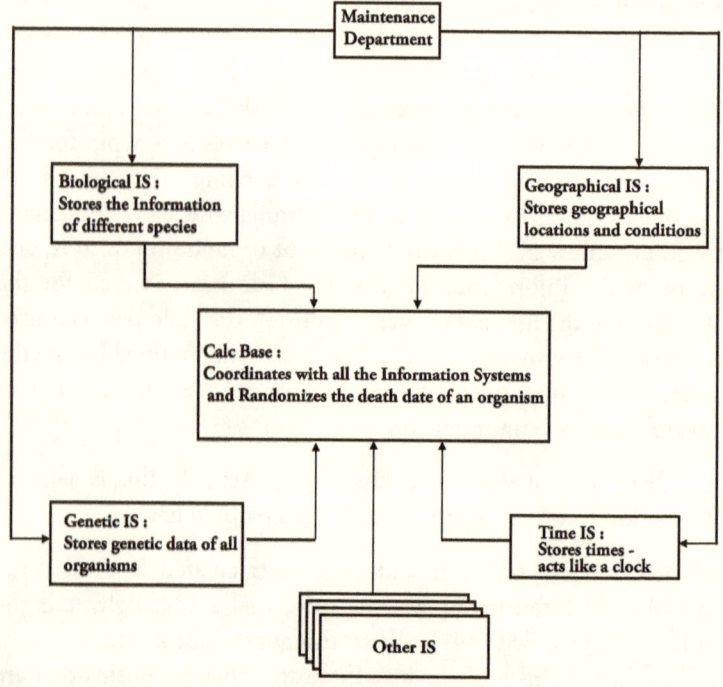

Building 3 Structre

"Indeed it is. I have explained the process to you for only two species; now imagine the same for each flora and fauna species present on the earth. For each of them, the information systems are doing the work. If you as a human look at a bigger picture, you think that the world is utter chaos. But look from here, you could see how magnificently it is being coordinated. And the earth is just another planet in the universe. Think of other galaxies, parallel universes and all that you can imagine," she went on.

"I understand it now. When I first heard that such an information system exists, I was baffled to imagine the size. But now that you are explaining all this to me, I am all the more confused, but at the same time I have a clear perspective now."

"But where is the storage? I see only screens. And the processors?" he suddenly wondered.

"Oh yeah I forgot to tell you that. The verdant walls you see around, serve the purpose. "What?" retorted Shukla. "The walls here are covered with vegetation, and these have special trees, with their leaves having storage spaces enough for species in small numbers. For larger numbers, there would be a larger number of leaves required. The climbers you see are for the protection of the actual storage leaves, hidden inside them. These leaves would not be visible to you. But, this is just the primary storage. Where is the secondary storage, can you imagine?" she paused.

"The forestry outside?" wondered Shukla, even though he could not imagine such a thing in reality. "Partly correct. The woods outside are made for the buffering and padding of the core storage which lies inside. There is no need of any external cooling system in such a scenario. The padding greenery makes it cool automatically. A special species of shrubs called the Datree is used for the storage. These shrubs can withstand many external calamities that are known, although the risk of a calamity here is too small. The leaves of these form the units of storage, and a normal 4 ft. shrub is capable of holding up to 64 TB of data. But sir this might leave you wondering. How such a large storage is searched so fast, updated so fast and summarized so fast? This happens using the crawbats, which are bats that reside on trees enclosing these storages. The crawbats, or you can say enhanced crawlers are vigilant and through their infrared vision can see the signals sent by the computers in here, thus making changes or responding to queries. As this data is being used not for customers, summarization happens every midnight, and updating happens frequently."

Nicole went on- "The Datree and Crawbats are indigenous to this place, and they were made specifically for this job. Now please do not confuse the Crawbats to be actual bats, they are named so because the bats on the earth have been gifted the features that Crawbats have- their ability to find their target precisely even without vision. Their most important ability is the ability to not collide among themselves. The Crawbats ensure that any crawbat carrying a request is out of the danger zone of the other, similar to a cloud of bats flying together."

Shukla was just amazed at the beauty of how bats were inspired by something that was related to information systems. He tried to find synonymous species-the ones who were here and perform some task very well on the earth.

Just as Nicole was about to say something, he asked-"Do you have something similar to pigeons?"

"Oh yes Mr Shukla, we do. And you guessed it right, we used them as messengers. But the communications using pigeons have become rare today, right? So we have made them obsolete, they have a new purpose now." She stopped.

"And what would that be?" Shukla asked.

"Let us leave that for some other time, okay?" Nicole replied.

Shukla could afford to wait to know each feature of this place completely. He was exhilarated by the wonderful things he had heard. It was the best day he had ever had in his life, he was convinced. A wide smile was clearly visible on his face. His anxiety to know more was higher than ever. He wanted to ask many more questions, but he held back his curiosity for the time being. He thought that he would know everything once his job was done.

Nicole was silent for some time, after which she said- "Sir, now we are approaching the boss' office. I can go on explaining about this place forever, but we need to stop here."

She knocked the door of an office, which read 'Mr. Hans, Senior Mathematician and Manager, System 3.' Shukla knew at once that this person was one of the highly crucial people there.

The door was opened to welcome the visitors.

REALISING THE REAL

"Hello Shukla," said Mr Hans, seated in his chair on the far side of the room. "Welcome to our abode," he continued in a jovial tone. Mr Hans was one of the main persons at Building 3. Along with his unparalleled administration, he was also responsible for framing the policies for recruiting people there. These policies were used in other buildings similar to Building 3 as well.. He had been a big fan of movies, and always tried to fix the screenings of the movies at times that were suitable to him. Shukla inferred that the man was about 60-65 years of age, his calm countenance spoke of his not being stressed. There was no sign of stress anywhere near Mr Hans. His office had a pleasant odour owing to the fresh flowers kept near a large window, which overlooked the greenery outside. Shukla saw that the screen in front of Mr Hans was constantly popping messages to him, as he read them carefully. Mr Hans finished the latest message that had arrived on his screen.

"Thank you Nicole for getting Mr. Shukla here. Can you please give us a few moments?"

"Sure sir," replied Nicole to Mr Hans and she left.

Shukla and Vineet walked towards Mr Hans as he asked them to sit down on the office chairs lying there. "Sir, by now you must know about this place well enough, and I can certainly say that you would have made your inferences too" says Hans. "Yes sir, to an extent," replied Shukla. The craving to know more about the place grew as he said this.

"Shukla, as you might have seen the size of this database and the complexities involved, the risks too have become big. But here, risks management is not very advanced as there is hardly any threat from human viruses or attacks. This time around, the system is at risk, perhaps a very big risk. We need your help." he explained.

"Sure sir, my pleasure," replied an eager Shukla.

"When this place was built, the prime consideration was to be able to do such a humongous task. And while building it, risks of the stature of a human virus were not considered, as we thought no threat could reach this level. Of course there are certain internal attacks from time to time, but we are able to mitigate them. So when we see something alien like 'ashtray' coming our way, we are perplexed thoroughly. We know the methods of controlling things, but for such a large database, the initiation of these methods could take decades in some cases, I think you can understand. Let me tell you what happened last week."

As he said this, a large screen dropped down from the ceiling behind him, starting a sort of presentation, which was more of an animation sequence. It clearly showed a graph of the activity and the sizes of databases. The graph filtered out to show only things related to Building 3 as Hans was about to start. The screen read, 'Attack 1'. Shukla prepared himself now knowing that there was another overdose of knowledge and realisation about to be showered upon him.

"You might have seen 2 or 3 information systems' offices on your way here. This place has a total of 13 such systems, which work in complete coordination to give us the desired effect, which Nicole might have explained to you. As a routine, every day at 6.00 am local time, we check the database and run safety tests. The load on this database is not much as it handles querying very well, but the data stored is very important to make birth and death related decisions. So on 31st March, we saw some unusual things happening here. As the check-up and tuning were being performed, the system power went down for a span of 2 seconds." Mr Hans' face turned pale as he said this.

"But since the generators were in operation, the backup system was somehow kept running. Why did this happen in a place where there is no restriction on power? Thank god we had the generator here, else a disaster would have been impending. Throughout that day, I was busy investigating the cause. Turned out something foreign had managed to reach the boundaries that guard the entry to this place, where there are additional barriers for such external threats. When the foreign data was identified, it was found that it was some stray data spamming again and again for a span of 30 seconds. The buffers barely managed to hold it. When this was found out, we added additional buffers, which are statically charged leaves, preventing stray bits from entering. It took us a long one hour to add the additional buffers before we could think of restarting the original system. Because of the heavy operations, our backup system was about to give-up. The maintenance department, as a result had to construct a new backup system. So the problem was mitigated for some time."

"Sir I can relate to what is happening till now," said Shukla.

"And that idiot fellow Jai thought that he had Ashtray under control when he made the test attack on the NIC system. Idiot, a big one!" Shukla thought to himself.

"Yeah. Now begins the important part. When we touched upon the issue, the data was coming from someplace where you reside, and hence we had to dig deeper. Normally here the stray data that arrives is from nearby places, that is, from the buildings similar to Building 3, but the data is generally not harmful, and it is blocked straight away by the buffers. But the data that day stayed longer than usual. When I searched for the address of origination, it turned out that the address fields were blank. The rule of addresses here are a bit different. We here do not use IP addresses like on earth. Since we have machinery which is not going to grow, we can afford to have fixed addresses for each system. Since we do not use an IP address, we thought that we would be able to find at least the address of origination. But as it turned out, no address! And let me tell you-cyber wars are not 'common' here."

"Sir, if this is what I think it is, it was ashtray as the DDoS is powerful enough to overheat the machinery and disrupt the power. It seems to be perfectly logical. But the address part is still tricky to me. I am not able to guess how this man has disabled the ways to reach the address of origination. There must be some way of finding the address."

"Yeah... We did some snooping to find out similar activities on the planet, and were able to see that something was happening with the Indian Governmental databases as well. The search proceeded lead by lead, ending up on Mr Jai Goyal, who is just about to reach here," Mr Hans said. There was a knock on the door as Mr Hans completed his statement.

In came a man whose very appearance spoke of a computer scientist. A tight fitting red tee, combined with blue denim jeans, spoke of the trite clothing sense of the youth. But this lank, tall person carried it well. Checking his wristwatch, which had been set to the local time here, Jai entered the room. His black hair with intermittent strands of white clearly showed the strain he was going through. He removed his spectacles very carefully, as Shukla noticed the broken frame of the spectacles. His eyes appeared worn out from lack of sleep and his tired face told the rest to Shukla. 'This man is the creator of Ashtray!' Shukla wondered.

"Hello sir," said Jai, in his croaky voice. "Mr Goyal, meet Shukla, the one whom you were destined to meet that day."

After exchanging regards, they came to the point with Mr Hans starting. "Jai, you need to completely explain to him whatever you have been working on. And, I need not introduce you both. You both must have researched well about each other. So, let the work begin." With that he told Jai to leave.

He then turned to Vineet and discussed his opinions about the matter. Vineet agreed with what Shukla had said till now, and added very little to it. Mr. Hans continued-"Both of you, Vineet and

Shukla, have to include Jai in your team and do all that is required to protect your civilisation and your planet. The information systems in this building are essential to the existence of biodiversity on earth. So tell me your plan of working."

"Sir, for that I have to discuss the matter with Jai first, and only then can I hand over a plan to you. I believe you can understand."

"Yes Shukla, I can. Also, you might want to know about the various departments working here, so you must pay a visit. But I should warn you, this will be a very time consuming affair."

"Yes sir, I will need to know a lot more than I currently do, if I have to safeguard this place. But it seems that taking a tour is not an option now. Does Jai have an understanding of the working of the place?"

"He knows the place superficially. Similar to you, he has not had the time to do his research."

"Okay. Sir, will it be okay if I send over Vineet to the most important department here. He could learn the working of the place there and then assist me?"

"Fantastic, that can be done. In that case, I should assign you to the maintenance department Vineet. This is the most important department here. Okay?"

Vineet politely nodded and took Shukla's approval by giving him a glance. Mr Hans offered a cup of coffee to both of them already sitting on the table, and took one for himself. Nicole arrived as he pushed vineet's cup towards him. She checked her keeper while they both sipped the coffee. "Social media here as well," Shukla wondered looking at her busy with the keeper..

Mr. Hans asked her to take Vineet to the maintenance department after they had finished sipping the coffee. Nicole and Vineet left for the maintenance department. Mr Hans continued his conversation with Shukla.

"Shuklaji, I have carefully observed your past activities and I do admire your capabilities. You certainly deserve to be here, but this time is not the best."

"I wondered the same. They said that the time for your recruitment here comes when you are free of your duties on the earth, and have not much left. So please tell me why I am here so early. I still have NIC to work for!"

"Shukla, I guess you will figure that answer out. It is self-explanatory," he continued.

Shukla tried to ask the same question again, but his voice was suppressed under that of Mr Hans, who changed the topic.

"While you are here, I want to tell you that you should get acquainted with some rules and conventions here, they may make your life much simpler here. Nicole will be explaining everything to you. She has built in a plan for you to work. Any queries, anything you want to know, she is your go to person. I maybe on this seat, but she is the one who coordinates all the departments," Mr Hans paused as Shukla nodded. "But let me tell you one thing that no one knows, not even Jai, or Nicole."

"This place has only one way, people only come in. That too, specifically by invitation. Egress from here is determined by replacement policies. One cannot control these rules. Because of 'little' work, you cannot have people coming in bulk here, as the system has to have a fixed set of people working on it. But, to adapt to modern times, we do make some changes. Now to bring in one person, we need to vacate someone else. There are certain rules based on which this 'someone' is chosen, to make way for a better cause. All of this happens in good spirit, and it is a routine event. But with you coming in right now, your exit from this place should be happening, if at all, only after 39 years. So, in this current lifetime of yours, you will not be able to visit your loved ones. But you do not have to worry, because your lifespan will be compensated by somebody else's."

Shukla's ears widened as he heard this. He started panting. "Sir, what do you mean I won't visit family? As far as I know, the people invited here are already dead, but I am not." As soon as he said this, reality struck him. He could not believe that it could have happened, that he actually died so soon, and without any pain. An array of pictures started flashing through his mind now, he started thinking of his son, Raghav and his wife. After a few moments, he somehow gathered himself and said, "Sir, I know that I am not dead, and I am going to leave, for this manner is not correct. I cannot believe all this. This place is nothing but a grandiose movie set, nothing else," he talked in sheer panic and disappointment.

Hans tried to explain to him the same thing again, but to no end. He then said:

"Do you know the reason you got that call from some person regarding your father's health? It was to make sure that you visit them one last time, as we had found out that day that you could be needed here. So as a precursor to picking you up, we wanted you to meet your parents."

"But is this the way? You were trying to be sympathetic by allowing me to meet my parents, I see. Well, that did not happen, you do not have any sympathies from me. And this method, it is just not done, please let me return home. I was not even told that I cannot go back. You yourself said that my case is not similar to the normal ones, so please allow me to return!" pleaded Shukla.

"That's all that I have to tell you, I have a meeting now, so I am leaving," said the boss, leaving the conversation to an abrupt end. "What do you mean? Okay, enough of the drama, please make arrangements for me to leave, else I will call the authorities. Sir, are you listening?" he could do nothing but watch him leave as his eyes became wet. It seemed as if Mr Hans was trained to deal with such situations with ease.

Outside the office where Shukla was about to shed tears, Vineet reached the maintenance department along with Nicole. On their way back, they talked a lot about the maintenance department while Vineet thought about why Shukla had not included him in his team. Although he knew the obvious reason that Shukla had given to Mr Hans, he knew there was something deeper, and was trying to get that. This was apparent because when Shukla was told to put Vineet into some other team, it felt as if Shukla did not want Vineet in his team at any cost. He was able to think of multiple reasons. After all

Shukla had a reputation to stay furtive about his plans most of the times.

"What if he thinks that I have been turned and this place is not genuine? Let time do the talking now, I am done convincing," Vineet thought.

Mr Hans left. Shukla still kept wondering what had happened? Was he in bad company? Was this some April 1st joke? Or was it a new agency in some national or international intelligence wing? He sat in that chair, as tears started coming out of his eyes. He kept wondering about all the possibilities. If this was really something superhuman, would it not have happened with the ideal principles, which avoided his coming here in the first place? This guy Jai, was he turned? All that was here, was nothing but a big farce, he thought. The real deal was to keep him away from the NIC, so that these people could destroy the place, and hence the country, and perhaps the whole globe's computers and thus, economies. This would ultimately collapse the civilisation, and a new order will be set, as is shown in some movies, he wondered.

But what about his family, was he really never going to return to them? He had so many plans with them. His son was just in school. And what about his parents? He saw the time on his wrist watch, and while doing it, he thought of calling his home. But he knew that this would be of no effect. His thoughts and his hands were working contrary to each other it seemed.

He removed his phone from the pocket, and dialled the first number on his speed dial, that of his wife. There was no ring, no "The number you are trying to reach is currently unavailable", neither was the call busy. He now sensed that this was a lot more serious than he had thought. But in his mind somewhere, there was the thought that he was now going to work for some secret spy company, which would spare nothing to get secret data using ashtray.

He tried calling the second number in his phonebook, then the third, the fourth and so on. He dialled up every single number starting with A in his phonebook, and realised that he was alone. His brain was not working to be surprised that his phone was left with him, even though the place was highly secure. He went on with the calling process, which he knew would be in vain, but just did it for his satisfaction. Out of frustration, he threw his phone on the table, just to find that he was not even able to break the phone. The silence spoke loudly to him now- "Alone you are, and you must learn to stay alone always." He sat motionless for ten minutes, after which he started to reason the whole process.

He thought of the way he was picked, in a normal car, with a normal driver, and normal people around him. There was nothing that felt godlike there, neither was the office of Mr Hans a top quality office. Shukla wondered about the place where he was.

It struck him.

He hastily picked up his phone, and assembled the battery which had been thrown out of the phone because of the impact. GPS was his solution. He knew that if all the possessions that were here were so world-like, he was certainly on the earth and he would certainly find the location. As he made an effort to connect to the satellites, his phone switched off. He tried doing it again, to get the same result.

All was in vain, he knew now, and started to accept what had happened. His heart had been pounding loudly all this while, and he himself was thinking that he was about to have a heart attack. After some more time, he could finally feel a bit silent. The chaotic atmosphere in his mind was pacified, as it turned to memories that he had with the people he loved. He checked his phone for photos, and looked at each one of them, watching his family, his friends from college, work colleagues and many others. All good memories were forming a cinema strip in front of his eyes now. The strip changed from sad to light hearted, then to intense and sentimental drama, till the climax was reached. The climax of this movie was the photo that Shukla had asked Mohan to take a few days ago, when Shukla was appointed the advisor to the security committee. After looking at the photos, he sat there for a few moments, to find himself dizzy. His head slowly dropped to the table in front of him. As he put his head down on the table, someone knocked the door.

PLACATION

On the other side of the door stood Nicole. She managed to enter the office without disturbing Shukla, whose head lay on the table. She first attended to her pocket screen, checking a popup that had just arrived. Next, she turned her head towards Shukla. Nicole remembered leaving Shukla intrigued and hungry to know more about the place. But what she saw on Shukla's face now was complete opposite of that. "What's wrong, Shukla?" she enquired.

"I was just told that there is no returning from this place! I will never see my family," he paused before retorting, "But, but why am I telling you all of this? You are one of them after all," replied Shukla dispassionately.

"I didn't understand? What do you mean by no return? And who am I being grouped with? I feel worried for you Shukla. Please explain," said she, feeling guilty at having done wrong with Shukla.

"Yeah, do not pretend to be caring and consoling, I don't need any sympathies now. And, if you still don't know, I am not going back to my people, is what I just came to know. My life has ended, and since you are a member of this place, you know that you come here after your jobs on earth are over. That is, once you die." With that, tears again started dropping from his eyes to the floor.

"I am so sorry to hear that, Mr Shukla. And believe me, I did not know any of this. And I am not lying when I say that. Had I known, I would have hinted long back. One thing I hate is tears dropping from someone else's eyes. Please, believe me," she defended.

"Okay, whatever. I see no point in blaming anyone anymore. The point is, I am not going back, and my family must already be devastated. My son is still in school, and it will be tough for him. As for my wife, she will be fine after shedding a lot of tears. My pals, my office, my parents, my car, bike, driver, degrees, phone, laptop, and what not, all taken away so deceptively that I could not even think of it."

"I am so sorry for you Shukla. I did not know that your case was different from us. I thought you were a regular one, who is informed before he comes here that he does not go back. I empathise with you Shukla. I so want to do something for you right now. Only if I could do anything…" Nicole tried. "Just take me back! I want nothing else!" was the prompt and arrogant reply. "But sir, that is not in my control, nor do I see it happening. You will have to stay with that feeling," was the caustic yet true reply, which almost burnt Shukla.

"Take some time off, that's the best I can do for you. I will leave you alone for some time. Meet me in my office once you are ready. Just step out of this office and you will be able to find my office. I will then assign you your role and show you your workplace."

All that Shukla could think of was whether he was working for some enemy force. Similar thoughts found their way into his brain for some more time. All these swings in his mind were just not dying, as he sat there thinking. Only after a lot of pondering did he realize that he didn't have anyone to complain to. He realized that all this could eventually be for a good cause. Thus, he tried to get himself to get up from the chair, and walked towards the door. After opening the door, in a weird and whimsical way, he screamed to grab the attention of everyone, "It is for a good cause, you will be remembered," and laughed hysterically.

As he stood on the other side of the door, he realised that he did not know where Nicole's office stood. As he looked around, he could not find her. He remembered that she had told him he would be able to find it, but the office was not visible.

In front of him was a big wall, on the other side of which stood an auditorium, the place where movies would be screened. On the left side of this wall, Shukla saw a moving walkway, as is seen in the airports. Further left was the way from where Shukla had come here, and on his right was a door which read- 'Exit'. Looking at this signboard, Shukla's heart again filled with emotion, and he thought of just following the signboard. He was about to open that door.

He looked in all the directions to ensure that no one was approaching, followed by looking at the door's knob to check if it was locked. If it was, there was no chance that he would be allowed, but it did not look to be. This increased his resolve, as he moved towards that door. It was hardly ten steps from Mr. Hans' office, but the journey seemed to be a mile long. As he walked, adrenaline was gushing in huge amounts to his muscles and all his senses were alert to see the slightest movement, He could listen to his breath. He reached there.

As soon as he lay his hands on the door to push it, a big screen on his left vibrated. He almost jumped out of fright. It read- "Please hurry" and was sent by Nicole. Nevertheless, Shukla opened the door, and stepped to the other side. He was anxious before pushing the door, but it turned into complete sadness as he looked on the other side. It was a toilet. Shukla was baffled, why was the 'Exit' sign placed there? Why? He wondered.

But he had to make do with the fact that what seemed to be an opportunity to him was not actually there, and he decided to return to Mr Hans' office. He reached there, just to remember he did not know where Nicole's office was. As he was about to go sit in the office to wait for Nicole, he observed a mobile-phone like device.

There was a dock on the wall opposite him, and in it was a pocket screen, which blinked 'Mr. Shukla, the family guy!' Shukla now knew that he was helpless and had to accept whatever was coming his way. So he picked up the screen from the dock, which now said- 'FOLLOW THE TILES', and a tile diagonally on his left turned light green. Seeing this, Shukla was in awe of the technology as a tech-enthusiast, but at the same time he also wanted to go in just the opposite way, and to search for a road that could lead him out. But, he did realise that it would probably be of no use. So he decided to walk the path. The path was different from the one he had used while coming here the first time. He tried to visualise the path from which he came and found out that this was the exact mirrored path. Anyways, it did not bother him anymore. So he walked passively.

After walking for about a 100 steps, his screen prompted him to get to the moving walkway that was now visible. The walkway did not seem to have an end, as far as Shukla could see. He travelled over it to the other end, without thinking about the distance and the direction, remaining nonchalant all the while.

At the end of the walkway, Nicole was waiting for him. She escorted him to her office, which was right opposite the walkway, and offered him water to drink. A hungry and thirsty Shukla had not had anything for a long time now, apart from the coffee in Mr Hans' office. As he gulped it, Nicole spoke, now speaking with authority of being the project manager- "I believe that you have regained your composure now and are ready to work," she said. "Lunch is being served as we speak." She took the empty glass and filled it again. Shukla again gulped it with the same thirst. "Need more?" she asked. "No that is enough," he said. So she invited him for lunch, which was to be served in the dining hall, diagonally opposite Nicole's office. While on their way, she had already started talking about the project and what she exactly wanted from him.

As they were about to reach the dining hall, Shukla's taste buds were already preparing for the ultimate treat, as they had been resting for a long time now. Shukla did not feel like eating anything out of remorse, but his stomach growled, stating otherwise. The dining hall seemed to be a small place, until Shukla's eyes saw through the glass façade. A big dining table sprawled, with about 100 seats, which had names of the people there attached to them. In the four corners of the room were smaller tables, with six seats each, which seemed to be for visitors (although there would not be many, Shukla wondered). Nicole took Shukla to a table in the near right corner, and told the person waiting there something in French. Then this person turned to Shukla.

"Sir, what food do you want?" he asked Shukla. "Dal chawal milegi?" (Will I get rice and lentils?) Shukla asked. The multilingual man replied- "Haan." After about ten minutes, the food arrived. Shukla, although having asked only for dal-chawal, got to see tandoori Nans, Veg. curry, and a lot of salad. The aroma of the food was so tempting that Shukla knew straightaway that it was going to be one sumptuous treat. Nicole had ordered a plate of salad, nothing else. Shukla ate his meal, and for the next ten minutes, there was absolutely no talking, only the sound of Shukla munching his delicious food.

Meanwhile, Vineet also arrived at the dining hall for his meal. He glanced at Shukla and waved to him, but Shukla did not respond back. He could sense that something had gone wrong with Shukla. "He is not feeling well, probably," he wondered. He reached the table where Shukla and Nicole were sitting, and started talking to Nicole. They both chatted for a while, before he ordered food for himself. Shukla asked for the bathroom to Nicole, who showed the direction by pointing behind her. Shukla left, realizing he had probably overloaded his stomach.

Nicole wanted to know if Vineet was brought there in the same manner as Shukla, and she even wanted to tell him the truth in case he did not know. She asked him about his recruitment to Building 3. He started telling his story, when Nicole's keeper beeped. She was reminded of a meeting with the head of the maintenance department in a few minutes, so she had to leave for some time.

Shukla came back looking a bit more relaxed and started talking to Vineet.

"Where did she go?"

"She had a meeting, so she left. But she said that she will be back here soon."

"Okay. Vineet, I have a very important assignment for you. Please, please do not let anyone know about it."

"Okay sir. Tell me what to do."

"It is a simple assignment. Make it a point to note down every detail of the maintenance wing, and try to befriend as many people as you can. Just do this for now."

"But sir that is what I am doing, right?"

"Yes, you are. Just be careful and watchful now. There are a lot of things that we have to do here, I cannot tell them to you yet. So, be vigilant."

"Okay sir," said Vineet, looking perplexed at Shukla talking so hazily. Nicole returned to the dining hall in some time and waited till Vineet finished his food. She told Vineet to finish his recruitment story, and found out he did not know that he was not going back. But she resisted telling him yet. If he was not already told, perhaps it was for a reason, she thought.

After Vineet was done, Nicole took Shukla back to her office and took his pocket screen from him. She connected it to her screen without using a wire, and tapped on it a few times. Then she disconnected it. "I have fed in the route to your accommodation, which is near that of Jai, whom you will be working with," she added.

"The nerve centre of all the databases is located behind my office, but you would not be able to access it if I am not here. Do not even try to get in. You will be in a lot of trouble if you even try. Whenever you need anything, just say my name to your keeper, and I will be there for you. I will be available for any assistance that you need. Your activities here are not monitored, but the activities of this keeper are carefully logged into the system. Oh, I forgot to tell you, in some time, the big screen will be showing some Bollywood movie. Turns out it is a big hit out there. You might want to watch, you have my permission," she explained. All this while, Shukla remained a silent spectator.

"Jai will be here in some time. In the meantime, you may get some sleep. I have some work to do, and will be back after about an hour. Bye," and she left.

Shukla now, although not knowing why, started thinking about the food he just had. He realised that he had food in the dining hall of the creator. Whoa! It would be one thing that he would want to brag about somewhere. He thought of the person who had been standing by the table while both of them were having their meals. He had seen him talking to Nicole in French, to another passer-by in German, and seemed to know all of them. 'Polyglot' -he remembered the word he had read in the newspaper while explaining its meaning to his son. And suddenly, all those memories came back again. But this time, Shukla had realised that he was here to protect all of them. And he now thought of the job at hand, "to protect all of them, to save the planet," he thought, and chuckled- "as if it were some sci-fi movie, where I am the hero."

He got a message that Jai would be a bit late, as he was having his food. He decided to roam around the place and looked at his keeper for the direction map. He wandered around Nicole's office for a while, and then decided to take a look at the auditorium which screened movies. So he requested his keeper to take him to the auditorium. The tile in front of him again blinked light green. The child inside him jumped on the first tile, then on the second and so on. He reached the auditorium just in time to watch the climax of a movie, after which the movie Nicole had mentioned was to start. He took the seat in the last row and started watching the movie, undisturbed and full of resolve now. He took a look at the theatrical auditorium, which looked like a perfectly normal theatre, and was very small as compared to today's theatres. He realised that he did not like the movie a lot, and decided to leave. Taking a look at the Information systems that Nicole had shown him earlier in the day, he ordered his keeper to take him to the geographical information system first.

He observed whatever he could. Unfortunately, that was not a lot. He would need Nicole's permission to access many places, but he decided not to bother her about it, and moved on to the next IS that his keeper showed him. In this way, he visited three information systems, before he got a popup message requesting him to get to Nicole's office at the earliest. He duly followed the instructions. He had started to believe now that the place and the people were not fake. Slowly, steadily, it had started sinking in that he was never going back.

He reached Nicole's office to see that Jai had arrived, and both started to discuss work. Not before long, Jai needed to leave for some work, and said that he had to report that day's work to Nicole, and would be back in about ten minutes.

Shukla had nothing to do for those 10 minutes. So he decided to take a nap. He dozed off on the chair itself, not even bothering to find a bed.

Vineet watched the working of the maintenance department carefully. He had a close look at the protocols that were used in the making of the backup systems. He saw that the team had a very small membership, but it certainly was the most powerful team that was present there. He also tried to involve himself with the team. His job was simplified when he found that Krishnakant Rao, the sound engineer, was also there. He wondered why. Why would he need to be in the maintenance department? So he asked him the question.

"Hello Vineet. To answer your question, I am involved with the porting of movie formats and similar stuff, so for that we also need to make the movie auditorium a modern one. We need better storage facilities, better processing systems and a lot of other requirements have to be addressed. I am working with these people to make the theatre better. By the way, did you get a chance to see the theatre yet?"

"No, I have not been there yet."

"Okay, make sure you do sometime later. You should see how people enjoy being there."

"Sure, I will do it."

Krishnakant introduced Vineet to a few other people there, and Vineet got involved with the team with their new assignment of making yet another backup system, a stronger one. Vineet still kept thinking what Shukla could have meant when he said to be vigilant always, because Shukla spoke as if he was in some danger. But the work on the backup system kept him busy enough and he decided to just follow what Shukla had said. He gave his own inputs on the backup system.

"Let us increase the size of the backup structure. What say?" Vineet stated when he had a brief idea about the current system.

"Yes, we can do that, but considering the time frame which we have because of this attack, it would not be possible," said a person from the team.

"If you let me do it, I can do the work within the time limit, if it is okay with the team."

"Yes, why not, please try doing whatever you can. And please let us know what you need."

To increase the size of the backup system was just an excuse for Vineet to look into the system properly, and learn how exactly it worked. If he knew the working of the backup system, he could easily decode the working of the main system and the storage. He involved himself in the work completely and whole-heartedly.

BACK AT THE OFFICE

Back at the NIC office, David was too worried to do anything. He felt like just sitting down in his office and wanted all this to end as early as possible. But at the same time he had to monitor the work of the Investigation team-team 1, as he call them. The reports from the teams were not at all good. A disaster was impending. Not to mention the fact that he would have to explain what was happening to the families of Shukla and Singhal. Above all, he had to tell Jai's family. He had to deal with emotions and feelings of relatives, which had always been hard for him.

Reporting to Shukla's and Singhal's families would have been a simpler job than reporting to the family of Jai. He had no clue that Jai's parents had already reached the city and were hunting for their son. They had lodged a police complaint and the investigation was proceeding according to protocol. This sounded troublesome as the news could be made public any time, and the people would try finding out reasons unknown to anyone at NIC. David wanted to keep the affair a well-guarded secret. So he called up Amit Joshi and told him about the police investigation. Amit set up a meeting with Jai's parents and Rita on the next day. The police were told not to report anything to the media, and the case was handed over to the NIA. David let Amit handle the matter for him.

The next day, Amit and David met Jai's parents as scheduled. All of them discussed the possible reasons for his disappearance. Mr Goyal even mentioned Shukla's coming over to his place and telling him that it was a matter of national importance to find his son. He also told them everything about his son's skills with computers and his introverted nature. David knew that Shukla had gone to see Jai's parents at Jaipur, but he had not gathered any substantial information there.

Rita arrived for the meeting shortly. She had her own inputs to be added. David's assistant had been recording everything that was being spoken. David had asked about the nature of work at his office, to which Rita replied the obvious- "He was always particular about his job, and he loved to be at the office, just that the last few days he would go home early, unlike earlier, when he could stay in office for as long as needed." This was enough to confirm that ashtray was the cause of all the trouble these people were facing.

David wanted to meet Jai's office colleagues, and was tempted to go there. But Amit told him that he had the reports of his team's questioning at the office. On returning to office, he not only checked the report of the questioning, but also read all the reports on Shukla's investigation. It took him a while to do the job, during which team-1 prepared their plan to save the databases and the system. They were almost ready to present their plan to David.

But the presentation had to wait. David was right now focussing on getting his people back. Someone in team-3 told David that Shukla had left on the 4th of April in the evening after receiving a call. He also mentioned that Shukla seemed petrified by the call. All this was accumulating the burden on David. But David was not someone who would go down easily, all this was just increasing his curiosity to know what was exactly happening.

He worked through the first half of the day deliberating how a new team could be brought into action. When a revamped search team to find Jai, Shukla and Vineet was formed, a few things were kept in mind. The search team was formed in such a way that no one would disappear this time. There were two teams, one moving parallel to the other, so that each team could watch over the other team. The NIA had initiated its own investigation, and had told David that their team would find them. Nevertheless, David had decided to send his own teams too.

Later in the day, the team at NIA reported that they had one Mr. Unnikrishnan who said he might know something about this and was being questioned. David was called over for the enquiry. After discussions for about 15 minutes, Unnikrishnan had given them all he had. He reiterated the discussion he had with David earlier when he helped draw Vineet's sketch.

"Sir, I shall tell you what has happened, and why was I dragged into it. It began on the 30th of March when Shukla was to leave for Gwalior and met me at the railway station." He narrated the whole story about his dilemma, and also the call to Shukla's wife. He told him how terrified he was when his name was dragged into all of it, and how Shukla had handled the matter with utmost professionalism.

He mentioned that he had told Shukla about a guy he found the other day at the tea stall who was discussing stuff related to hacking. Shukla had thanked him then for the news then. He also mentioned that Shukla had warned him that he could get into trouble.

"But why was Vineet the one who gave Unni the news?" questioned Amit, when he was talking to David over the phone after Unni left. "We at the NIC did our investigation. But Amit, sorry to say; it is very tough to arrive at any conclusions yet. All we have is conjectures," replied David.

"Let me see what I can do. One thing looks certain, this man, Vineet Singhal was acting as an agent. Now for whom he was acting as the agent, I don't know yet. Let me speak with my team about it, then I will get back to you. You guys should focus on the solution right now. Goodbye, David."

"Bye, Amit."

In the meantime, team 1 extended their plan to the other teams. As a result, all the teams came together with a comprehensive plan of action to resuscitate the NIC systems. Right now, the systems were working only partially now, considering the extra security parameters added to them due to the first attack of Ashtray.

After the discussion with Amit over the phone, David had specific instructions ready for the investigation teams. This time the teams from NIA and NIC were to work collaboratively, as individually searching for the same thing was redundant work. The teams, three in all, were now dispatched. One team headed for Gwalior to find Rajinder's parents. The other teams were to work locally, and were to grill the tea-stall owner now.

The tea stall owner was not to be found when they reached the stall, and the workers told that he had gone to his village. He was called back from there. But as expected, he refused to come back. The reason was pretty much clear-he had seen all of it happen, and was scared. After a fair share of convincing and a little bit of threatening, he was ready to come back. And, not to the surprise of the team, he arrived in an hour. He had never left for his village. The team from NIA was obviously infuriated with this behaviour. And these investigators had the reputation of questioning some of the most notorious people in the world. So the tea shop owner was questioned ferociously, and he had to answer them carefully and truthfully.

The shop-owner, Sitaram ji, spoke all about it. He told the team how Shukla had meticulously planned an operation. Sitaram mentioned the voice recorder that was with him. He told the teams that Shukla had asked him to keep it until Shukla returned, and hence he had not returned it to any of the NIC personnel. The voice recorder was found, but there was a problem. Nothing was recorded. Also, Sitaram could not hear much of the conversation that took place between Shukla and the other person. Mohan asked for the sketch which Unnikrishnan had helped draw earlier.

"And the person did not have any expression of fear or pain. He seemed normal, and was excited to meet Shukla, it seemed," mentioned Sitaram. "The two people got into a car, and I heard that they were going to the visitor's home."

"Is this that person?" Mohan asked, showing him the sketch.

"Yes, this is exactly that person. He took Shuklaji to a cab and they went that way," he said, pointing to the southwest direction."

The teams had their next place of visit planned now. So they left, as Mohan decided to go back to the office to try to communicate with either Shukla or Vineet. This whole episode had made sure that he would not be able to sleep until he could talk to either one of them. He tried calling each one of them-"The number you are trying to reach is currently unavailable" being said every time he tried. But he decided not to give up, and kept calling after intervals of about five minutes.

The episode which had Vineet as a primary element was worth noting, as Vineet was also mentored by Shukla, and would never do something that could be harmful to the NIC, wondered Mohan. He decided to do a background check on Vineet nevertheless, and started checking his records with NIC. After doing a solid check on Vineet, he was convinced that Vineet would not do anything that would jeopardise the mission. But then, why was he at the centre of all that was happening?

Next day in the morning, the investigation team reached Vineet's house, just to find out that he had not been home ever since he left for the airport that day, early in the morning. They had to explain the whole situation to his family who till now, thought that he was still in Ahmedabad. The team now contacted the car-driver who was supposed to take Vineet to the airport that day. But, he too had no information as Vineet had left for the airport even before he had arrived. So the team decided to return to their respective offices, and check on the other teams.

It was time now for Mohan's prayers to be answered. Mohan had already started losing hope. He had been making calls continuously for a long time now, and not a single one was responded. He was calling Shukla the whole time. Convinced now that it was of no use to call Shukla, he decided to call Jai now, maybe twice or thrice. So he did. Surprisingly, the call did not end: the phone was not switched off, neither was it out of coverage area. The phone rang for some time, as Mohan's heart rate increased manifold.

"Hello, who is this?" said somebody on the other end, stirring Mohan up. "Is it Jai?" the call was dropped as Mohan tried to speak more. His heart was pulsating at a fast rate as his eyes opened wide now, and he was convinced that he had established a link with Jai. He waited for some time, thinking that he would get a call back. He tried calling the same number again and again, to find no answer. The connection failed to establish, every time he called.

Mohan reported this to the teams and the whole unit sprung back to life. They finally could get a lead. The lead however, was found to be quite a deceptive one. It turned out that the call picked up could not be traced back, as the memory flushed while trying to calculate its coordinates. "Add more to my worries," said David on hearing this. His head had started pounding loudly now. The work was more complicated than ever before, but the team had got a reason to believe that Jai was certainly within palpable limits.

Mohan called up Rita and Jai's parents and fixed an appointment at 11.30 am. He met them and told them what had happened. They were so elated that Jai's mother picked up her phone straight away and dialled Jai's number. Mohan had to tell her that the phone was received only once, and he was not even sure that it was Jai speaking on the other end. He had heard Jai's voice earlier, but did not know his voice well enough to recognise him. He described the voice to them.

"It was a croaky voice, and somehow felt that the person was half asleep while speaking."

"That is my son, definitely. He is the only one who always seems sleepy." Jai's mom had insisted for a long time that Jai change his habits, and start living a healthier life. She had warned Jai that his voice was also affected by his lethargic behaviour. But she did not know at that time that this voice would today identify her son.

Although Jai's mom said so, Mohan would not believe her completely, as it was normal for people to feel that it is the person they are searching for. But he thought that it could be true. And with this in his mind, he reported it to David. David was sceptical about it being Jai. He reasoned by saying that someone could have just picked up the phone from Jai or he could have been robbed. That did not confirm it was Jai, though he didn't negate the possibility. He was certainly not ready to believe it with closed eyes, but earlier had not stopped Mohan from telling the teams as he could see that the whole unit was excited, and had found a new hope in the case.

David had a lot going on in his mind, and had not had any rest for quite some time. So he asked Mohan to leave and lay down on the sofa set in his office. He soon started snoring loudly, and all the officers could hear him.

That afternoon, the team that was working with David, team 2 finally made a presentation of a concrete plan to proceed with the construction of a secure system that was protected from any attacks like Ashtray. The plan was to build a new system from scratch, and then port the data to it, while the current system would be kept in quarantine. The current systems would be available only for basic functions, and advanced uses through which 'Ashtray' could penetrate were to be put to a halt. This was to result into slower loading of Governmental websites, and advanced data, such as biometrics would not be available. In the evening, the team explained to David that this was the only possible solution. David called for a meeting of all the teams at once and decided to discuss the matter with all the people, rather than taking a call on his own.

The meeting with all the people working in the investigation started at 8.50 pm in the NIC main auditorium, and David asked for permission from the people to go ahead with the plan. The meeting went on for the next 25 minutes, where certain new additions were made to the plan, and the NIA team had their concerns addressed. The NIA wondered if the same thing was needed to be done to safeguard their database, but team 1 representatives thwarted their fears by obviating such a process. It would lead to a lot of resource consumption, and there was no attack on the NIA database yet. The discussion continued till David made sure that he knew how all the 13 potential attack systems would be modified due to this operation.

The loopholes that the teams had found were not enough to hamper the new system. The teams had prepared a timeline of the porting of the databases to the new system, which took care of the basic flaws, although it was still vulnerable. But, this system was to include bigger and better 'safe mode' features, which could keep away the attacks. It could automatically go into a state of hibernation until the virus's effect subsided. This was to ensure that the system, if attacked, could perform limited querying with ease, and would not allow anything suspicious to enter and modify the database. The filters that were to be put into this system would not process any request which could remotely be associated to an attack of the stature of Ashtray.

The work would need another 7 days, with about 40 people working on it. The system was designed in such a way that the basic programs could be extracted straight from the old system. The construction of this system, porting of the databases and the testing were to be done in the short span of seven days.

All this while, the old system was still not under attack, and it seemed to be quarantined for no reason to the outsiders. The upper sections of the government were perturbed by what appeared to be a failure of the system to address the queries of people. One major failure was when the Ministry of External Affairs was not able to serve online visa applications for very important foreigners. This had led to the fury of the Ministry and David was held responsible for it. The Government wanted a lot of explanations from him. David had another job at hand now-to convince the Ministries to be supportive of him and his team.

Again, Amit Bhai came to his rescue. He told David to report to him all the happenings in a systematic manner, and he would take care of the rest. Amit Joshi had contacts in the Government at high levels, and due to his weekly briefings to the governmental bigwigs, he had developed a certain level of trust for himself. David was relieved to hear that he would deal with it, and breathed a lot more easily, now that some free space could be created in his mind. He directed both the teams to make detailed reports of what they were doing within the next three hours, so that he could compile them and send them over to Amit.

As was expected, the reports and plans were delivered to Amit Joshi in the afternoon by David himself. David was told by Amit to leave the communication with the higher authorities to him, as he was a frequent visitor at the Home Ministry. "Thanks a ton," said David as he left for his office.

As he reached his office, he gave instructions to the teams to go ahead with the project and finish it at the earliest. Forty-one people from the NIC, the best coders were to be picked up now. Mr A S Singh, a veteran hacker, who was a member of team 1 was handed the responsibility of the project. By the end of that day, he was done picking up his team of 41 engineers and started briefing them with the plan, explaining to them each aspect of the project. He made it clear that reporting and documentation was not to be given a priority while the project was incomplete. Normally, documentation would begin as soon as a new project started.

Singh was a man known as a martinet in the office, and he saying that documentation was to be given a lower priority was enough for the engineers to know the urgency of this project. Singh introduced the team to David, who briefed the team about the importance of the mission, and told them to begin working straightaway. He handed over some printouts to Singh, who glanced at them and started to explain to his team what was written in those papers. Mohan was not included in the teams, as David had requested for him to be kept out of the process, as he had been going through a lot of mental stress due to the matter.

It did not matter to him whether he was in the team or not. Mohan was tirelessly trying to reach the phones of all three of them-Jai, Vineet and Shukla. But, after that one call, there was no reception. He just seemed to know that there would be something important waiting for him, and there was.

SCIENTISTS AT WORK

April 8

"Sir! Excuse me, sir!" exclaimed Jai, trying to wake up Shukla, who was deep asleep. It had been almost two hours since Shukla had been sleeping. He was murmuring something to himself in his slumber. Jai had got busy with explaining his plans to the boss. Hence he could not return in ten minutes, as promised. Jai had to shake him up to awaken him, to which Shukla did not react very positively. He slapped Jai on his face, in an attempt to save himself from the cruel terrorist who was the main villain of the story in his dreams. The terrorist was planning a cruel attack on the governmental web sites, and he planned to burn every database in the world. Shukla was the hero of his dream, and he had just grabbed the terrorist's collar while the interrogations began. Shukla was the main interrogator there. He was too angry, and his anger was further aggravated when the terrorist spat on his face. He slapped the terrorist forcefully, creating a loud noise.

As his eyes opened, he found out that it was Jai, and he quickly gained his senses to apologise for the slap. Jai, who was actually quite embarrassed, pretended as if it did not matter to him at all. He offered him a glass of water, and sat in the chair beside him. "Sir, we better hurry now. I actually need you there for the job."

"Yes, yes, I understand. I feel like I have slept for ages, but I want to sleep more. How long did I sleep?" asked Shukla, turning his eyes towards his keeper. "Two hours? Seriously? You were to arrive here in ten minutes. What happened?"

Jai explained that he had to meet the boss and discuss his plan. He asked Shukla to come to his office cubicle.

Both of them left, and as Jai himself had turned up, Shukla did not have the opportunity to turn to his pocket screen for the directions. They again had to get to that long, seemingly endless travelator. The walkway this time was moving in the opposite direction. It was as if this whole place was revolving around Shukla. Whenever he had to go to a place, he would just have to stand on that moving walkway, which did the rest. Shukla was desperate to find its working, but this was not the time.

Exiting the travelator as it came to an end, they took a right. When they halted, Shukla saw Jai signalling someone to come over. He took Shukla to his cabin of sorts, and waited for the person to arrive. After he arrived a few seconds later, Jai started explaining. The problem was very much clear to Shukla now. Thus, he told Jai to skip that part, and come to the point. Jai decided against introducing the person whom he had just called, and continued with their discussion.

This was the first time that Shukla had a proper dialogue with Jai. Although he wanted to kill Jai for what he had designed, he was much more impressed with the potential of his virus. But he first wanted to thrash Jai to have claimed that the test attack was under his control. Shukla was sure that it was the test attack which had created all the problems.. Jai began talking, but Shukla was thinking along a different line. He was reminded of his visits to Jai's house, his parents, his office and every possible place where he thought he could get any information about Jai. As Jai was about to continue to blabber further, Shukla intervened:

"Do you know how much your dad values you? And your mother has also made amends with Rita. She wants you both to marry each other," he said, barely resisting himself from telling Jai that he would never be back for that day.

"Sir, I am glad that you have searched for me, but I could not help, I had to be here. How is everyone there by the way?"

"Worried about you, everyone!"

"I realise that sir." His face saddened as he missed everyone there. But somehow he condoled himself to keep calm and concentrate on the work. He was the only person in the whole universe who understood his work, and he could only wish that he was not. He wanted to get rid of it, as much as everyone else. His work had ruined his life for him, which he did not know yet. He was in love with what he had done. He saw Shukla as someone who could save the world from all the trouble now.

"Sir, I will see them when I get back," said Jai, filled with innocence. Shukla did not utter a word at this point.

"Okay, let's get to the point then. The main problem is, I designed it, but have no solution to stop it. It is apparently not possible to stop once it begins. In the letter to you, I had just given a brief description. The system is actually based on a chain reaction. It is similar to nuclear fission. One request splits into two, these two into four, and similarly the requests increase exponentially. While all this happens, memory can get flushed multiple times, causing the inability of memory to serve requests. Sir, if there is no second processing system, then it is sure that the requests will not be served. And even if any request is served, the databases associated with it will not be able to update the transactions, and no logs will be saved. This causes huge inconsistencies in the long run, and the only way to stop it will be to cut-off the system from the supply, port it into another system, but that too will be a temporary solution, as the new system will still be vulnerable to attacks. So, I am unable to arrive to a solution yet. The only thing I see working is to stop the processing of a large number of requests if Ashtray is detected. Ever since I arrived here, I have been searching for something related, and then I requested that you be called here. I am aware of your expertise and work in the field."

Shukla's eyes widened as he heard this. "No need to praise me at the moment. Let's see what you have done till now," he said. As the authorities here had picked Jai on March 31, he had been here for eight full days. Jai had taken the first four days just to see the depth of the problem, and was involved in a lot of grilling, frisking and interrogations. He was initially seen as a sinner who had just given reasons to believe that apocalypse was possible, although the databases here did not show anything of that sort. But after a lot of convincing and pleading, Jai had his way.

While he was picked up earlier, his laptop-the heart and the brain of 'Ashtray' had come later. The other man whom Jai had called picked up Jai's laptop from a table lying across the place they were sitting-Jai's cubicle. One could say by looking at the laptop's screen that it was tweaked for efficiency. The laptop's appearance spoke of the workload it must have handled. Although not very old, it seemed as if it had been under operation for the past ten years. The i key of the laptop looked crooked. The original key had broken, so to fix it, Jai had stuck to the keyboard a plastic cap and over it he had written 'i' with a black permanent marker.

Shukla remembered him noticing the sticker which said- "Never back down" in the lower right corner of the laptop lid. Shukla would never forget this machine in his life. Mohan had spent considerable time with that laptop. The laptop had test databases that Jai had tested Ashtray on, and these test databases were actually a danger if they were connected to other servers.

The laptop was picked up from Harish in the most normal manner. Shukla's trap for finding leads through the laptop was nullified without a problem. Jai himself had gone and picked it up from Harish, but Harish would not remember it, as he was inebriated with a special sedative which made him forget whatever he was doing then. It was a risky affair again, as only Harish should have spotted Jai. If anyone else would have spotted him, it could have created a lot of trouble for Jai.

After four days of continuous interrogation, Jai had now been working for the past three days straight without getting almost any sleep.

But, what work was Jai doing? He decided to check out if he could reverse the effects of the attack. He had made a plan according to which, he would just attack back the sender with the request. But, this was easier said than done. As was the nature of Ashtray, the attacker could not be found, as the addresses were spoofed in such a way that the requests appeared to be coming from the same network. So finding a reverse strategy was problematic. But, after all, if Jai could make Ashtray, he was capable enough to go a step further and find a solution to the problem, he believed. He had started off well, and his strategy seemed perfect on paper. He had explained this to Nicole and Mr Hans earlier, and it took him almost an hour and a half to explain his solution to them. But in the end, they both agreed to the solution, and gave him a go-ahead to think of ways to implement it.

His work for the past three days not only included looking for a reverse strategy, but also looking at the possible ways in which Ashtray could turn self-destructive. He was convinced that his first plan could be implemented, but it would take a lot of time, which was not permissible.

Jai told Shukla what he had planned. "What? That might just aggravate the problem. The fission reaction would also lead backwards, so what is the good point about it? Fission backwards is just going to flush the memory and will lead to multiple crashing of the systems, if that doesn't happen during forward fission," said Shukla, clearly showing his dissatisfaction. "Sir, I thought about it, but this is the best I could do. And, I have actually started implementing the first module. I have started looking at the reverse fission part quite seriously. Believe me, it could work. I can contain the flushing of the memory. Just give me some time," replied Jai.

"No, but I know that you can do better than that. Think of something different. Back at the NIC, people must have started implementing something better than this. I know your work, and know that you can think better. You have been with a company which has some of the world's best thinkers, and I did not expect this from you. Please, find something better. The first part of your solution is done, okay. We can use it somewhere else. But look at something else. This solution, I know even you believe, is not going to work." The manager within Shukla was doing his job. He convinced Jai and filled him with an energy to find a solution that could prove to be better. He told Jai to explain to him details about Ashtray and focus on the loopholes that he had found. Jai explained every detail to him.

Shukla's habit was to note down details in a notebook, which he would usually carry with him. He preferred carrying notebooks to tablets and other digital gadgets, simply for the reason that they could never be hacked. But this time, he had no notebook, and was forced to use his keeper and a stylus for the purpose. It took Jai only half an hour to explain the code to Shukla, who was meticulously taking down his notes. This was for the only reason that the code was only 476 lines. "Now that is a feat!" Shukla thought in his mind. After Jai was done, Shukla saw that he had noted exactly six points about it.

- The scale of the system
- Particulars of the fission concept (given in the code)
- Training of the system (Parts of AI used)
- Line 146-157(Code for fission)
- Line 171-251(Watch out-something might be possible here)
- What would NIC have done?

After they were done, Shukla went to the washroom near Jai's office, and was surprised to think that he did not have any bowel movement for the past three days. He chuckled- "I had always dreamt of this day!" He washed his face, tucked his shirt in, and moved towards the hand dryer, which actually read- "Use napkins instead! Don't act so human," Shukla laughed. He stayed there for a couple of minutes, and then returned to Jai's place. With him, he brought a few sheets of tissue paper, and took out the first sheet, wrote all the six points on it using a pen he borrowed from Jai, and kept it in his pocket. He then deleted the points from his keeper, and once again touched the papers containing the material. He then looked at Jai, who was looking at him in a confused way. "Yeah, it is my habit to do that," said Shukla.

"Okay, sir," was the reply from Jai, who finished the matter without heeding it much.

"Sir, we had the premiere of a Hindi movie yesterday. You were asleep and I did not want to wake you up. Today, there is some Charlie Chaplin movie. You want to go? I will take my laptop there. Please do not say no," said Jai, his eyes already red because of the lack of sleep.

"I guess you should get some sleep first. Look at your eyes. I prefer you sleeping rather than watching the movie. That could also clear your brain to think of something new. Please, sleep."

"Yes, I am not working tonight, it is my night off. I will be sleeping tonight. Don't worry about it. But, will you go to the movie?"

"Okay, let's go! And yeah, I need a laptop, I cannot work on these screens. They are just too advanced to be used for our purpose. I won't be able to adapt to these." The man who stood by them earlier had gone by now to his original place, and Jai again waved at him. He told the man that Shukla needed a laptop. But, the problem was, there were no more laptops available anywhere in Building 3. All the people had moved on to keepers which were much better systems. The man said he would have to talk to his seniors for the same. And so he left.

After the man left, Shukla discussed with Jai a wide range of subjects, from his childhood to his getting a job. He actually admired Jai now for his qualities and wished that he had some of them. He also discussed Rita's and his mother's crying the other day, when they came to know that Jai was missing.

"I even met your parents and Rita. They were all together searching for you. I spoke at length to your dad about you, and you must know how proud he is of his son, and so is your mom. Rita also mentioned your days at the college, your teachers, friends and everybody. She also told me about the company you work for, and how you had left almost everyone baffled with your recent lifestyle. I must say, please be careful from now on. Do not ignore phone calls from the people you love. Get it?"

"Yes, sir. I will keep that in mind."

"Okay, now tell me how you were going to port your solution to the other information systems. I believe from the biological one, it could penetrate into the others as well. So tell me what your plan was originally?" Shukla asked, ridiculing him again over his solution.

"Sir, I have already thought of a way to contain ashtray from one system. I believe that if the solution can work on one system, it will definitely work with the others as well. So please understand what I am saying, and believe in my solution this one time." Jai was vexed with Shukla's earlier negation of his solution. "Please, just take a look at the implementation of the first part once, you will know what I am doing."

"Oh yes, I will look at it right now!"

Jai showed him whatever he had implemented till that time, and showed what he planned to do ahead.

"Okay, I understand that you have put efforts into it. But you need to understand that there are serious drawbacks with it, so please try thinking of something else as well. I will also try to think of something. You actually have the lead to finding a proper solution, but it would not be this one, certainly."

"Sir, I shall take some rest and then start working on it, okay?"

"Yeah do that, you need it."

Jai left the cubicle to go to his room which was besides his office. He was visiting his room for the first time since he arrived, as on the earlier days, he was sleeping in the office itself. Today due to the negatives he got from Shukla regarding his solutions, he did not want to be in front of him. He went straight to the bed that was lying in front of him, without looking at anything in the room.

Shukla also took some time off to think about Jai and his style of working. He looked again and again at his laptop, and got a strong hold of what Jai was implementing. Although he had expressed dissatisfaction to Jai for the solution, he knew that getting to that solution was the first step towards achieving a more convincing solution. He sincerely appreciated what Jai had done till then. He felt guilty at having spoken to Jai in that manner, but he knew that it was required.

His mind wandered to some other topics too. He was looking at the code while he started wondering what the recruitment story of Mr Hans was. Mr Hans was a man whose appearance spoke of him being a no nonsense person. Shukla wondered whether he had been the same throughout his life, or was he being so only to Shukla. He also thought of Nicole, and had some funny thoughts about her appointment to building 3. He was looking at the contacts that his keeper had while he was thinking all this.

'Vineet Singhal' appeared. Shukla swiftly swiped the screen twice or thrice before he had sent the message to Vineet, which read, with every letter written in capital-

BE VIGILANT!

It was about 7o'clock in the evening now. Shukla started thinking about the system and Jai's first part of the solution seriously now. Jai's technique to find the address was to poll each neighbour of a system which could have sent the virus. Then some instructions and decisions would determine the sender. But till now, Shukla was doubting the efficiency of this technique. He started thinking of a technique to improve the solution.

This time, he was picturing the whole system and Ashtray: a swarm of cockroaches, trying to reach every corner of the system to lay eggs. These cockroaches had started growing, and their number doubled every instant. Soon there was a colony of cockroaches, who wanted to go to a new place now. The brainpower of one of India's best information scientists was just starting to come into action.

RAAKH 1.1

April 8,9

At the NIC building, the teams had begun working on 'Raakh 1.1', as the project was now called here. Mr A S Singh had taken it into his hands now to see that the work was completed before the deadline. The whole team, the bunch of 41 people, was rotating in shifts of day and night, and all the members were working almost double their stipulated times. The teams had strict instructions and were not allowed to discuss any part of the project with anyone outside the team. These people were chosen carefully by Singh and were trained for expediting solution implementation, as opposed to the normal staff, who were trained for finding efficient solutions. They all had been trained by Shukla in the past five years in different ways, and this was the opportunity for them to give back to the excellent mentor that they found in Shukla.

The process of protection looked so simple, yet it was about to have one of the best safe modes. It was this system on which the whole nation's existence stood. The people were to work in conference room #3, the place where Ashtray was first discussed. The 41 people sat on the round table that could easily occupy 50 people. Mr Singh himself was hooked onto his laptop at most of the times, looking for something new popping up always. Everyone was alerted not to discuss anything that happened on this side of the glass wall that separated the conference room from the outside.

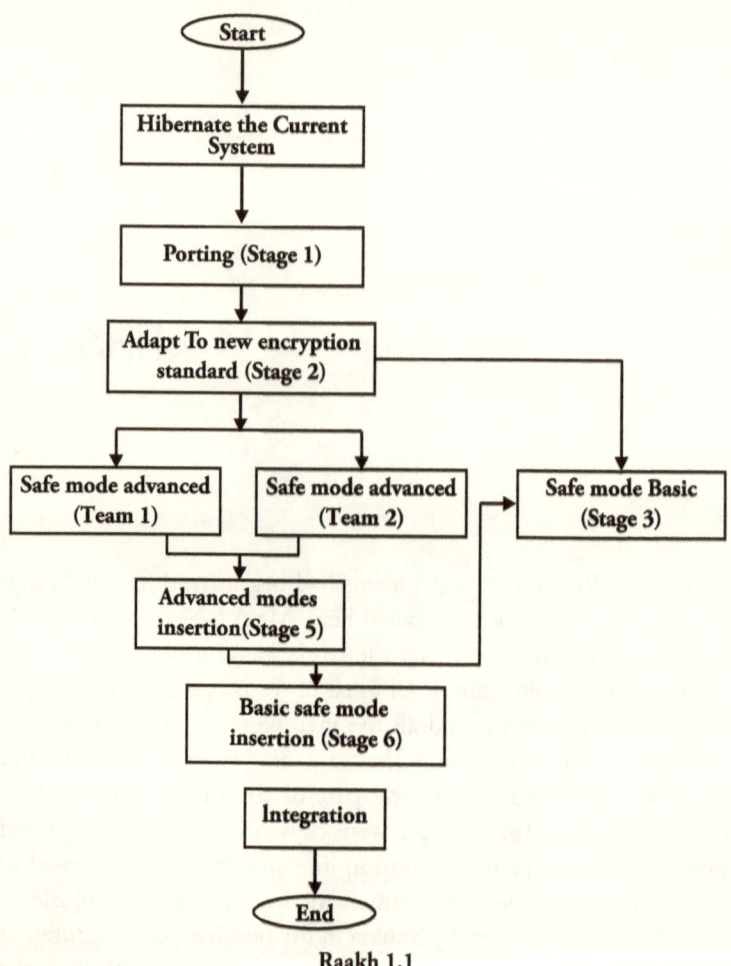

Raakh 1.1

The work began at 7.30 in the morning, after the last person who was included in the team reported to work. Singh had to call back many people who had left for homes late last night. As the work began, a round of discussions started. The instructions that had been given to the teams before they reported had been very clear. Also, the team members had been given an intimation that they could be needed to work for days at a stretch.

All the food that they needed was also available. Singh had estimated that some people might not leave that room till the work was complete, so he had a coffee maker installed there. Although it was a small gesture, it made sure that people felt that they had whatever they wanted, at their disposal. David had even put the menu cards of all the nearby food home delivery joints on the table, so there was no need to move out of the room. The only basic need that could not be taken care of was that they could not shift the washrooms.

Conference room #3, which was normally reserved for high profile meetings, was also playing its part in getting the systems running back properly and to get its hero, Mr Shukla back.

The main concept that was being used for safeguarding the system was this: Stop all the requests from entering the system and hold them in a queue for a while. Check if the queue is flooded with requests in a short span of time. If it is, then flush the queue. But the queue could be flushed repeatedly. In such a case, stop access to that queue, and block all similar requests. This could be done, because the requests would not have started to have their ill effects yet, as they were still in the queue, and not into the system.

At 9.30 in the morning, the stage one of the implementation, which included identifying and using the existing system's safe code snippets and modules, was complete. This was a rigorous process, as the codes that were identified by the teams earlier to be 'safe' were to be checked and tested to ensure that no gap was left at all. After this process was over, the team took a half hour break and decided to resume with the next stage. Meanwhile, David asked Singh to have a look through those bullet points that appeared to be the stages of the project, written on a piece of paper. David had an idea of what was happening, but wanted to know the specifics. "Actually do one thing, go write these on the whiteboard, everyone might want to see this," he added. Singh nodded and proceeded to write the stages on board. David tried to contemplate each stage himself.

Stages:
1. Port the safe code snippets.
2. Adapt ported stuff to newer encryption standards.
3. Safe modes-Basic (to be inserted after stage 5)
4. Safe modes-Advanced- accessible from any point in the program (minimum loops)

5. Advanced modes insertion-pointing
6. Basic modes insertion
7. Integration

Singh and David had been up all night now, and it was time that they took some rest, when the team started working on the second stage written on the whiteboard. In the small break that the teams took, someone had switched on the projector, which now displayed in a crisp and bold font: 'Project Raakh.' "Please let us do this for Shukla," was what everyone was saying in that room, and the dedication to the purpose was very high.

After the first stage was complete and the teams were ready to begin again, Singh changed the order of work a bit before going to get some rest. Two teams of 4 people each were made and deployed for the implementation of the basic and advanced safe modes straight away. They would be joined by the others as soon as other people were done with the earlier stages. The main motivation was to expedite work in any possible way. These two teams were chosen in such a way that one team always worked on implementing something, while the other team did analysis and research of that method. They also looked at multiple ways to make sure that the transition was a smooth one, and the whole data would port to the new system without substantial trouble to the team. Since there was another team that would follow their work, these people had to document whenever necessary.

The other team, the people not included in the two special teams, started with stage 2-the adaption to newer standards. This process was particularly important because the older system had not been adapted to the newer encryption standards, which could have led to loss of integrity of data. Although the earlier standard was capable enough to defend the integrity, this new standard would have reduced the chances of data being stolen to a minimum. The stage was actually mechanical, since the same work was to be repeated for all the snippets that were taken from the older system. This was perhaps the easiest of the stages of implementation. The team was split up to speed up the implementation of this stage. The work lasted only four hours. Although it appeared that it took only four hours, it was a lot more work than was expected of this stage. Another reason why the teams were separated after the first stage was to reduce the load of those two teams of four members each. Their best was needed in the later stages.

When the work on the second stage was completed, Mohan prepared the report of the team's work. Although Mohan was not directly involved with the project, he had been appointed to document all the stages as David had guessed that he would need to report to the Ministries over the matter sometime soon. Mohan was ready with the reports of the first and the second stage now, and mailed them directly to Amit.

By this time, both David and Singh were up from their rests, and Singh started looking out for any snippet that had been missed in the process. He expected to find some anomalies between what he wanted and what he had been given. But, as it turned out, on analysing the process for about an hour, he could not see any discrepancy. The system had only got better because of the smart team.

This was probably the first time in his career that he had seen his team work so effortlessly and at the same time meticulously. The rest he took had refreshed him enough to begin working with the first of the two teams working on the third stage. "Team One," he called them, and sat with them, discussing the implementation of codes for safe modes that the teams had planned to make. He worked on a sub-module of the third stage for a while, and then received a call from Amit, saying that he had received the report of the first and the second stage. For a moment he was furious that the report was sent without his authorisation.

But he realised that the situation was not one where he could afford to argue with someone, and so he went on with his work. He did make a note of Mohan's behaviour somewhere in his mind. The reason why he wanted to check that report first was clear enough-he did not want to disclose more than what was needed.

It was now time for a shift change, and the people working all this while were to get some rest. The new set of people had just joined, and within minutes got an overview of what had been done. This team consisting of 11 people was a part of the 41-membered team initially planned. Overall, there were 22 people working in the first shift and 11 people in the second. The two special teams of four members were to work there and rest there itself. At least, this was the plan Singh had in mind. But Singh knew that this arrangement of shifts would not last long, as the main stages would approach.

The new team started working, and joined the two teams working on the safe modes. These two teams were not officially allowed to take a long break, but could rest whenever they felt mentally fatigued. All these teams now had to get through the toughest part of the task- building of the safe modes. It was decided among the teams that these two teams would continue to work on the advanced safe modes, while the other people would try to finish the basic safe mode as soon as possible. The new people started and chalked out a strategy according to which they were to finish coding the basic safe modes (stage 3) by noon on 9th of April. While this was to be done in the third stage, the insertion was to happen later, in stage 6. The reason for this was, they first wanted to check the system's response to the advanced modes, and if needed, they might have to increase the size of the advanced modes. Hence, the basic modes could be compromised or enhanced, as needed.

Singh briefed David about the change of plans regarding implementation.

"I am perfectly fine Singh, but give me a timeline and the deadline."

Singh replied, "Sir, we are on track regarding implementation. You know how much time it could take. The team is working at its highest efficiency."

"Tell me specifically when you will finish the work, and along with that, give me a time line."

"Sir, the work will be finished by the 13th of April, I can surely say. But it could be done earlier as well. Regarding the time line, sir, we do not have the details to explain the time of completion of each module. But I can assure you of completion by April 13."

"I am okay with you not giving me specifics. But the problem is, I need to report it to Amit."

"Sir, actually Mohan sent him the reports of the work till now. And I was not even asked before they were sent. I wanted to go through them to change a few things. I hope you understand. Please tell him to show the reports to me first from now on. Could you try and make that happen."

"When did he send them? Even I wanted to check them out before sending to the NIA. I will talk to him straight away. This will not happen again, don't worry. I will talk to him. You may get back to your work now. Best of luck once again."

As planned, the work on stage three was completed by these teams at 11.45 am on 9th April. During this time too, there was a shift change, and the rotation was again done seamlessly. Up till now, Singh was impressed with the teams performing so well. Now these teams had to check the work done by the chosen eight on the advanced safe modes, and they also had to get it tested.

The daunting task of this stage was to ensure that the virus-repelling part of the code was accessible from any other part of the program, which was a serious measure if quick action was needed in case of an attack. The teams till now had worked up on a new algorithm to avoid writing redundant codes, and this was a big plus. The other teams now just had to proceed with the implementation, and while implementing, the redundancies would automatically eliminate themselves. This was, of course, customised for the security purposes here. The advanced stage of safe modes was to be completed by the 11th of April, to have more time for the integration stages. They would take a lot of time. Thus, if this stage got delayed, there was a very high chance that the team could miss the April 13 deadline. Missing this deadline was not at all admissible to David in any case.

All the 41 people had been working with these things in mind. Singh himself was testing the work done on the earlier stages. The work was to continue for the next 70 hours approx., that meant six shift changes. So the teams were told to stick to the plan, and not to implement something new, causing problems for the further shifts. The plan that Singh had developed without thinking for long was turning out to be a very good one. David visited Conference room #3 to check on the work and to motivate people to work harder for Shukla.

Although this was redundant, David kept doing it every now and then, and took care that the ones who were tired got enough sleep.

The second team consisting of four chosen people, Team Two, had been working tirelessly now on the advanced stage, and they did not have Singh with them, unlike the first team. As a result, the whole team was too tired to work anymore, but they somehow managed to keep themselves up. When Singh realised this, he immediately ordered all the four people to rest, and told the other team to rest once this team was up working again. But the team members decided that they would not rest until the current sub module was completed.

Singh replied, "In that case, I shall request Alok to rest for a while, just look at him. He is hardly able to open his eyes." He pointed towards Alok Desai, who was sitting in the chair on the other end of the table, munching on chips and drinking coffee as he looked at Singh.

"Alok, you better go and sleep for a while. I will do whatever you are doing. Tell me what to do and leave."

Alok thanked Singh and explained to him the research that he was conducting on his computer. Singh took over from him as he went straight to the men's resting hall, where only one bed out of the five was vacant. He went to sleep without bothering to change.

While the teams were working in full swing, on the 10th of April, Mohan got a call on the office telephone.

"Mohan? Keep…!" spoke the person at the other end, and the phone went off.

It was twice now, first Jai receiving his call and this time it was Shukla who had called Mohan. Mohan clearly recognised the voice on the other end. Mohan promptly reported this to David. "What did he say exactly?" asked David. "In a frail, almost breaking voice he said my name and then there was a lot of disturbance. But he was trying to say something through the disturbance. I could hear 'Keep', but don't know what. Then the phone was off. I could clearly sense that he was tensed, and seemed like he was falling to the ground."

David ordered the investigation team to trace the call. But, this time too, the attempts turned out to be futile. Mohan noted that both the times, the call had not ended abruptly due to a connection error. It was deliberately ended. He wondered about the call for the next hour, sitting in one place, absolutely still.

David shook him and told him that the investigation team was heading out to Ahmedabad, to interrogate the hacking group people again. Some leads to the hacking group had surfaced again.

As he was wondering, something struck him. He was certain that Shukla had a message to deliver to someone. "But who? Jai? No!" he wondered. He was trying to complete the sentence Keep... What could it have been? Keep it up? Keep up the good work? Keep a sharp eye? Google Keep? Keep your calm? Keep the system working?

"No, it must be something related to retaining something. Keep the system working? Probably, but which system? Keep the old system working? Yes, the old system might need to be kept alive. I wonder why," he said to himself. While thinking about all this, he fell asleep in his office chair. He woke up about half an hour later, and again started thinking about it. After thinking for a while, he convinced himself that Shukla wanted him to keep the old system alive. He thought that Shukla must be having something of his own that he wanted to implement. And this was the only logical thing that he could think of that related to 'keeping'. He kept thinking of the possible ways in which Shukla could assist the NIC.

"It might be that he is with Jai, and knows the solution. Let's do it, let us keep the old system," he thought.

He rushed out to the teams and made sure that the old system was not destroyed till now. He had inferred that this system was always to be kept alive, even if the new system was ready. He tried convincing David about it, but the story seemed too much about one individual's perception and was hard to believe. But still, David told Mohan that it was still 4 more days before the new system was to go live, till then the old system would be alive. And he told him to wait in case some other message was to arrive from the other end.

Meanwhile, the implementation team was busy with the fourth stage, which looked good to meet its deadline.

SOLUTIONS-THE FIRST STAGE

April 8, 9

As Jai and Shukla started to individually work on their own strategies, a message popped on Shukla's screen that a laptop had been arranged and he was requested to collect it at Nicole's office. He again had to take that long travelator to her office. As it turned out, they had decided to retrieve Shukla's laptop and had to pick it up stealthily from his house. Again, this was all done very swiftly. Shukla took it from Nicole, who had instructed a person to make some changes to the laptop. This person was the same man whom Jai had ordered earlier that Shukla needed a laptop. She had also asked him to add the essential security layers, and to make sure that the laptop had only restricted access to the system.

Shukla walked back with a smile on his face, happy that at least he had something tangible in his hand. All the things present here seemed too good to be true. Also, his laptop was where he had done most of his coding, and he would be able to refer to them, if needed. Travelling back to his and Jai's office, he decided not to take the travel at or, but to walk beside it. He wanted to check what the actual distance was, and how was the travelator's end not visible for a long time. But he soon had to curtail his plan. As he walked, newer travelators originated in front of his legs all the time. Although he did not get on the travelators the first 4 times, the fifth time he had to surrender. He decided to take the travelator. He again was not able to find out the working of this travelator, and where it actually took him. But he reached his destination.

He first reached his cubicle to take a look at his own laptop, and to check if there was anything left on it after the serious security drill it had undergone before reaching him. Also, he wanted to check if the compressed version of Jai's hard disk was still available. Mohan, while creating a replica of Jai's hard disk had made a compressed backup of the hard disk on Shukla's and David's laptop. He then replied to a popup message from Vineet, who had been too busy to meet him here. The message read-"Sir, things under control here, everyone is fantastic at their work. But why do you want me to be vigilant?"

Shukla replied- "Do as I say, BE VIGILANT." He then messaged Nicole to thank her again for the laptop, for which he was truly happy, like a kid who had got his first bicycle.

He reached Jai's cubicle in some time. It was 2.30 in the afternoon. Jai started to explain the way in which he thought that his method could be modified to get a better solution. Shukla said after hearing the solution- "Yes Jai, you are getting there. Think more on these lines, I will also look into the solution now. Give me some time to get my laptop running, post which I will do whatever I can."

"Okay sir, I will continue what I am doing as of now. I think I might even look at a possibility of building a filter for the machines here, which will thwart the effects of Ashtray. Let me look into this first, then I will check the requirements for the filters."

"Filter? I was just thinking about something similar. These filters would have features that the people at NIC were including, that is queueing of requests. Jai, I have even looked at a very remote possibility of a filter, but I guess you should know the problem. How do we take the filters to each and every machine on the earth, and of course, here?"

"I guess we can here, because everything here is linked to a central repository, you see."

"Even if it is, our job is to secure each information system. And I guess you know the number of information systems present here. So porting from the central repository to each IS will be tough."

"Sir, give me some time to think over it. I will make notes about it, and then you can show me the problems you could see. Just give me some time." Jai started working on his laptop again and sipping coffee from a cup sitting on the table in front of him. Shukla went back to his table, which was beside Jai's cubicle, and looked at his laptop.

After some time, Shukla was completely taken aback as his ears were alerted. Jai's laptop started to make a croaky sound. It was a ring tone. He had managed to hide his phone emulator in his laptop in such a secure location, that it passed the frisking that the laptop might have gone through earlier. Jai first silenced the volume and answered the incoming phone. He was about to say something but suddenly he decided to drop the phone. "Sir, it was Mr Mohan calling." He said. "But, but how is your phone working here?" asked Shukla, perturbed.

"Sir, I have designed something that could destroy this whole place, is it not easy to design something so that my phone breaches the security layers? Haah!" he gave a witty laugh.

"I see, so you think you can do anything that you want to do? You think it would not be noticed? And do you mean to say that you are the smartest person in this world. Let me remind you that all that is happening is because of something that you have done," said Shukla with his face turning expressionless.

Jai soon understood that Shukla was in no mood for banter, and apologised. "Sir, I did not mean to hurt anyone. And by the way, my phone might have been detected by now and turned off. So nothing can be done. I am sorry sir."

"It's okay... By the way, did Mohan say anything?" Shukla realised that he could be in contact with the NIC whenever he wanted. He just hoped that the call was not detected and he would be able to do it again.

"Is it possible to do it again?" asked Shukla.

"Sir, it is possible, but not likely. Although I can try if you want me to."

"Okay! Let's get back to work," said Shukla, leaving the call aside for now. And so they did, with Shukla now having his laptop on Jai's desk, constantly looking for any calls on his phone. His hopes of being in contact had just been rekindled.

By now, Shukla had been working on discovering the nuances of Ashtray, trying different combinations of changes to the code and testing their effects. As was visible in his notes, he had now correctly understood what the system was going to do exactly. The fission concept that was used was particularly interesting, he saw the code for it. He was trying to see the ways to break the loop, and check the number of fission reactions that could take place.

He had made new notes for all this. He then went through the Artificial Intelligence that was used by Jai, who had termed this virus the 'smart' virus. Now, this was a challenge. The design was such that the fission would continue to find newer nodes (machines) and this process would go on until the network ended. Jai had made this process 'smart' by making use of heuristics, according to which, the system could train itself to find the node that would have the highest damage, and this information would be saved for further uses. "Intelligent! Aye," said Shukla, astonished at the depth of the virus. Shukla continued for the next 3-4 hours, with breaks in between for food and using the restroom, but otherwise he was only working on this 'smart' concept, trying to break it. He had lost all his sleep. All his concentration was on the work that was in front of him.

Jai intermittently thought of filters and even approached Shukla twice or thrice regarding their implementation. Shukla had deferred it each time, as he still needed more time to understand the system completely. Each time he ordered Jai to continue with his work and not bother about the filters currently.

As was ordered, Jai had to stick to his plan now and improvise it- to try and reverse the action of fission; that is, to redirect the requests that were arriving to the originating machine instead. Of course, the original proposal that he had given to Shukla was nullified, but a stronger proposal would have Shukla's approval. Jai had been breaking his head over this problem. He had cleared the initial hurdles now, and had Shukla's experience with systems there to help him with finding addresses. Shukla who was initially not satisfied with his work, was now supportive of him.

The problem was certain to encounter a deadlock, from which there was no return. There were two main reasons for the deadlock situation:

- The situation arose because a node would attack its next nodes, and at the next instant, its next two nodes would retaliate, and this process continued in an infinite loop, causing huge complexities.

- The program for reversal of the attack had to originate at the end system that could be a part of a big database such as the one at NIC. A big system would take a lot of time to initiate the reverse action. But this would be a problem for the earlier nodes where the virus would have caused harm in the meantime. These systems would not revert to being unharmed once they were harmed.

Jai had been trying to find a solution for the deadlock, and this was eating up his brain. "Tunnelling of vision," he thought and reported the problem to Shukla. Shukla was still working on the smart features, and had somehow deciphered the code. He was now trying to break it into pieces that would have no significance individually. He had found the code's anomalies in three hours, flat.

When Jai reported the deadlock to him, Shukla was initially not moved, as he had expected that such a deadlock would arise out of the fission reaction. He gave Jai a few more reasons why the method won't work in the current state. It needed a lot of modifications.

Shukla had also made a plan according to which each device that was connected to the internet would have the filters that they were planning, regarding which Jai had approached him repeatedly, but this was a solution which was very, very long term. What about now? The effects of this attack were already noticed when the system was down. Shukla told all this to Jai and ordered him to look at different possible ways to incorporate a global solution like his and at the same time be implemented quickly. "But, sir! The task at hand is to secure the informatics of the heavens. Since the systems follow the same protocols and the tiers in the hierarchy are less, I think we can find a way to build filters for each device. Let me think over it as of now. The global outlook can be incorporated later, right?" he said and got back to his laptop. Shukla nodded in partial agreement.

Jai started working on the filters right away, neglecting the deadlock for the time being. He contacted Krishnakant Rao, asking Rao to give him a plan of the maintenance department, and the lists and specifications of all the information systems.

Krishnakant replied saying that it would take some time, so Jai asked him for the architecture of the biological Information System first. It took half an hour for the architectural diagrams to reach him. He analysed the parts individually and the relations between individual parts.

"Sir, it is going to be a daunting task. We will not be able to do it so soon. Unless there is a way to make a plan where the maintenance department says that it would be able to port the code."

"Okay, how many components are to have filters in the biological IS?" asked Shukla.

"I have counted the 28 processing elements, and along with these, the Datrees. The Datrees are allocated dynamically, so we will not be able to do it IS wise. The work needs to be done collectively. Right now, I am thinking only of the biological IS."

"Okay, ask Nicole if she can help with it. I have Vineet working in the maintenance department, and he would certainly find out anything that would be needed. But before that, please talk to Nicole once."

Shukla went back to what he was doing. He had a look at the next bullet point, which was to check the code for fission. He did this to refresh his mind, which he thought had been too involved with the 'smart' system. He checked over the code and could infer within minutes that the simplicity of the code was what made it truly a genius one. It had come to his notice earlier while Jai had explained the whole system to him, that the code for the system was too small to be true. He searched for loopholes in this code now, putting checkpoints wherever he thought he should have them. After this, he had to go to each checkpoint and create a code that would expose that loophole. He did this multiple times at the same checkpoint to see the various permutations of codes. It was a great habit he had built, and he was this efficient at this job because of it.

Nicole came to the office to see what was happening, and why the architecture of the biological IS was requested. She was concerned about exposing the architectures to novices. Jai explained the process of building filters to her. Although the solution was ideal, it was to take too long to implement, she inferred and told them to look at alternative solutions. She then talked to Shukla about Vineet.

"Sir, your companion, Vineet, is very efficient at what he does, I must say."

"Yes, I know that."

"He helped develop a new backup system while at the maintenance team, and he seems to have coordinated well with the team there. All of them are working simultaneously on a new project."

"Ohh, good to know."

"Just that, what does 'BE VIGILANT' mean?"

Shukla's eyes widened now. He managed to reply- "Yeah, if he is vigilant, he would know the system well. He could also learn the architectures and how they are maintained. Once he knows the maintenance of one system, we can use his knowledge, you see."

"I hope that that is the only reason."

"Yes that is the reason. You should not worry."

"Okay, I trust you Shukla. Jai, please give me something positive on this method that you explained the other day, so that I can talk to the boss about it," she said, facing Jai.

Jai replied, "I will need some more time."

"Okay. You both may continue with your work, I will leave."

Shukla vowed to never send messages that could create questions. What he meant with 'BE VIGILANT' was for Vineet to look out for loopholes in the systems, so that he could try for a possible return to earth. At the back of his mind, he was convinced that he had a chance to be back with his family if he was able to use Ashtray just enough, that is, alter the field of death against his name to some day later. He would be back, he had thought.

But that was not to happen: once a person was brought here, the administrator of the building had to make sure that the entries against that person's name were erased very soon. Even if this was not done yet, it would be tough for Shukla to locate his entry, as the name used in the database was not "Rajinder Shukla", but something that these people used here. Rajinder Shukla was a mere alias here. His true name was a unique random sequence generated by an information system.

Both of them continued working for the next few hours, before Shukla decided to get some sleep. Jai had almost fallen asleep by now, and both of them decided to call it a night. The next morning, Shukla and Jai both did their morning activities, and were ready to work in an hour. This day too was no different with both of them working, collaborating and doing their analysis. Jai reported to Nicole that he was currently working on the new solution Shukla had thought of, as the earlier one had a lot of shortcomings.

By that afternoon, Shukla thought he had found a few loopholes, which could collectively work against the virus. But soon after, he realised that they would not work because of the artificial intelligence. Since the system had its smart features, these loopholes could not have been used against the virus, as the system would learn from these small anomalies, strengthening itself to act better in the future. This was just adding to the problem. It was as if they would act as vaccines to the system, increasing its immunity to the diseases yet to come.

And although Shukla thought that these small loopholes could help arrive at a solution collectively, there was no proof of it, and the risk was not worth taking, he thought. So he got back to the next stage, to repeat the analysis and formulate decision making strategies for the problems. This was what he thought could go on as an endless process, until he was ready to take some risk. But the risk of testing against small loopholes was too big to be taken. So he was seeking alternatives.

Around 5 o'clock in the evening, Jai reported his new plan to Shukla. He had made a plan to build the safety filters into every system that was present in Building 3. Surprisingly, the plan was implementable within hours of its initiation. This plan included some risks, but if done the correct way, they could be mitigated. He had been thinking about it the whole time, and had plans for its implementation too. Just that, he would need many permissions from the higher authorities, and would need people for the implementation. And he was right in thinking that getting permissions would not be a problem, as Shukla was with him. He had noted down the implementation details, and had estimated that it would take about 10-15 hours for it to be done. It would prove to be a big boost, and could reduce the effects of Ashtray at least, if not destroy it.

Here too, his hacking acumen was his biggest strength.

THE CALL TO INDIA

April 9, 10

Jai had decided that he would use his weapon to perform the task. He planned to make a fission based antivirus similar to *Ashtray*, and then port it out to all the devices. Because of fission, the antivirus would quickly spread to all the devices here. This plan was fool proof, as the fission methodology would be able to penetrate every system. He meticulously planned his workflow for the same. But there were a few problems with regard to its implementation. Shukla was completely engrossed when Jai pitched his solution. Excited, he sent a message to Nicole straight away, and told Jai that he would look into the problems.

Jai knew only a small part of the standards of security of this place, he had no clue about what would be needed to optimize the antivirus to fulfil all the standards. At the same time, interaction between different components such as Crawbats, Datrees and processing systems would be a different problem. Also, Shukla was now sceptical about the idea, as he somehow was convinced that the higher order would not allow them to tamper with the security. If it was played with, the system could actually grow more vulnerable to Ashtray, and it could create havoc. Shukla understood the implications very well.

He started explaining these to Jai, when he got a message from Nicole informing him that she would be there in a few minutes. Shukla told Jai to try and first think of building a quarantine, and then try something out. They both discussed the stuff that could well have worked with the systems at the NIC, but had no clue if it would work here or not. Quarantining would probably not work here, as the number of systems was too big a number. The maintenance team had been developing a backup system, so Shukla and Jai thought of incorporating it into their plan.

This was the appropriate time to contact Vineet, or the maintenance department, Jai thought and informed the same to Shukla. Shukla told Jai that Vineet was not yet ready and he would need some more time to get a holistic knowledge of the working of the maintenance department. Before moving ahead, Shukla wanted to confirm with Vineet that he was ready and had a complete understanding of the systems. But to communicate with him, he would need to write a message to him, which was to be avoided. He had no other way but to tell Nicole, other ways would have raised speculation. Hence he sent another message to Nicole, this time requesting her for permission to talk to Vineet. The reply asked for reasons and the nature of the talk that he was going to have.

"We shall discuss the matter when you come here to discuss the filter antivirus' process," Shukla replied.

Nicole arrived as promised, and heard out the whole filtering solution as Jai narrated it to her. She was at first terrified to hear that they were going to attack the system, and calmed down only after they explained the whole idea to her. But, the reason for the terrified look on her face was not just the mention of the word 'attack'; she knew the systems here very well, and had a reason to believe that this solution could signal doomsday. In case it worked this time, it was still not guaranteed to work against future attacks. The whole thing was actually going to blow off the data nerve centre, was what she thought. Nicole specified the reason which Shukla did not think- "Sir, the systems are interconnected, and when you will try this out on the biological IS, the other ISs will have to pay the price.

The biological IS will throw the virus to another IS, as it would not serve many requests. So the requestor will try to route them through other ISs. Unless you find a way where you release the filter to all the ISs without any delay, this method would not be effective."

"And Nicole, I believe there will be a problem with the crawbats as well. This is a pure guess. I think so because the bats do not receive changes very easily. Am I correct?" This occurred to Shukla's mind on hearing Nicole's reasons.

"Yes, you very much are. The crawbats would not receive the changes very well, and they would need a lot of convincing. You will have to modify their behaviour to reach the filters before they reach the main areas of the Information Systems. Plus, there will be the danger that the programs for the crawbats might get modified as well. These are the problems that I could see straight away. Let me talk to my back-end team as well," Nicole replied.

"Oh, yes. Sure. But may I speak to Vineet. You see, I need to discuss the working of crawbats with him in detail, so may I talk to him?"

"Oh yes, go ahead. I will be there when you meet him."

"But…"

"Let's call him to my office as soon as we finish discussing this. You both be there in 10 minutes after I leave, he will arrive by then."

Shukla's attempt to convince her that he wanted to talk to Vineet privately had failed. Nicole turned to Jai to discuss his solutions. Shukla tried to reintroduce the topic, but he failed again. Nicole was certain that Shukla had something of his own in his mind, and he would end up discussing that, and avoided the topic any time it came up.

All three of them discussed some alternate possibilities, Jai doing most of the talking. Nicole was hardly convinced, and Shukla was in partial agreement with her over the solution. "For the quarantine thing, we can actually use the second nerve centre (the back-up one) that was used the day when it was under attack, but it could only last for maximum 10 minutes, it would crash as the power source goes off. So it would not be feasible either. I hardly see your plan working in those 10 minutes. If you could build something that could do the job in those 10 minutes, then it is worth trying. Otherwise, a big no!" Nicole said, her face clarifying her stand.

"Apart from that, I believe the issue with crawbats that you mentioned, Shukla, can be handled by the team. You should not worry yourself over it. Please improvise upon your solution at the moment," she added.

Jai and Shukla started discussing the possibilities of speeding up the fission work. Nicole sat there listening to the conversation for some time, but decided to leave, noticing they were involved in their own discussion.

"Will you excuse me?" she politely asked Shukla, who did not hear her the first time she asked. He nodded when she asked the same question the second time, and she left.

Jai had started thinking about how the various nodes were visited again and again. He could flag the ones visited, to make sure that each one was visited only once. This reduction of redundancies caused by repeated strikes of the antivirus would lead to a reduced time, he thought. He also thought that if the attack was not launched from one place, but launched at the same time for the different nerve centres present here, it could just work. He got to his laptop, and started to calculate the time complexity, albeit for the first time in his life. Normally, he would delegate the work to a junior.

A few minutes after Nicole left, Shukla was summoned to her office. Shukla mentally prepared himself to meet Vineet. He had to deliver the message to Vineet clearly, yet it was to be given to only him, and no one else. So he thought about how he would say it. He wanted a clear understanding of Vineet's work, as well as wanted to tell him to look at the databases in a way that he could think of an escape plan. After thinking while walking to Nicole's office, he finally saw Vineet. He could sense that Vineet was deeply involved with the maintenance department, as was explained by his ongoing dialogue with Nicole. Both of them were in a detailed discussion about something related to a backup system that Vineet wanted to change, but Nicole was not granting him permission.

"Good, he wants to alter something. That means he knows where the faults are. These people would never allow alterations. My job is more than half done! Yes!" Shukla thought to himself, and laughed in his mind as he saw them discussing. A smile came to his face. Nicole observed this and thought that it was the affection for Vineet that Shukla had which showed on his face.

"Yes, Shukla, you both may talk now. Let us discuss the solution that you are considering with him."

"Yes, Nicole. Vineet and I shall discuss it now. But, can we do it in private?"

"Shukla, what is it that you want to discuss, now I definitely want to know!" Nicole exclaimed, smiling wittily. But Shukla took it in a wrong way.

"Okay madam, we will not discuss anything. Goodbye."

"I did not mean to offend you Shukla. Sorry. I will leave." Nicole said and left.

Shukla smiled at her full of wit. He then started his dialogue with Vineet.

"Vineet, I hope you are following what I told you."

"Yes sir, I am being vigilant."

"Good. You must know a fair deal about it by now? Don't you?"

"Oh yes, I do. I certainly do a lot in the maintenance department."

They started discussing the principles over which the whole system was built, and how the main idea was always to be able to read every time from the databases, but write to them only a few times. Because of this, a lot of trouble regarding writing to the databases was avoided already. Vineet told Shukla about his own project and how it was going to affect the current system. He then told him about his next assignment-"Sir, I need to build a replica of the geographical IS, which would include enhanced security features, extracted straight from your solution to the biological IS. I need to work on integrating the current IS into the new one and to build a new data porting method till then."

"Seriously, they assigned you to make a replica?"

"Yes sir, they did."

"That is very good. Keep up the good work." Shukla was happy that the people there trusted Vineet more than him. He thought this was the perfect time to pitch his idea about escaping after finishing the work to Vineet. He did not notice that Nicole had come back and she was sitting behind him, when he started.

"You know what vigilance means, right? We need a plan."

"Yes sir, I am working on it."

"You don't understand. I want you to observe ways to…" Shukla paused to gather his thoughts. Nicole's keeper beeped to break the silent atmosphere that had been built around Shukla. Shukla was terrified even to look behind. He sat there looking at Vineet with wide eyes, and then finally continued.

"Well, that's what I want. Be vigilant. I will be having work for you later." Shukla stopped short of telling him the real thing. Nicole knew there was something in Shukla's mind that made him think of a possible exit. But she was confident that it was not possible, and thought it best to not bring the issue back. She thought that if it was keeping Shukla going, it was for the best, and kept ignoring Shukla's thoughts.

When the meeting was done, Shukla requested Nicole if he could have tea with Vineet. She readily agreed, and the tea was brought in a few minutes later. They both had their share, talking about nothing in particular. Then Vineet asked her permission to leave, which she gave. Now she wanted to talk to Shukla. She began-

"So, how was your meeting? Did you get to talk enough?" she asked, knowing that the time was not enough.

"Yes, yes. The main point was to be able to talk to Vineet, you see I will need him for implementation purposes at a later stage," Shukla hastily replied.

"May I go back to work?" he asked.

"If you want to, please," she replied and showed the door to Shukla. Shukla left her office, and realised that he would have gotten into a lot of trouble, had Nicole's keeper not rang. But he wondered, what if she intentionally beeped her keeper? What if she knew what Shukla was going to say and the beeping was a way to stop it? Perhaps it was, and this was the reason why Shukla needed to be even more cautious now.

All this while, he had forgot to mention Crawbats to Vineet.

He reached his cubicle, and observed Jai staring at his laptop screen for some time, "What is the matter, Jai?" he asked.

"It's nothing sir, I have been trying to do something about our discussion. Till now I am getting nothing."

"Do one thing, take a small break. I guess you have been here for a long time. Go and eat something."

"Yes, I think I will do it. I will go now," he replied, and left to go to the dining hall. Shukla turned his eyes to Jai's laptop to see what he was actually doing, and he was amazed to see how Jai had been working on the solution. Shukla was assured that the solution to this problem would be final very soon. Jai had worked on his original Ashtray, so that a deadlock would not arise. He was now working on a way to prevent the deadlock with the already existing version of Ashtray. This was the first step to finding a final solution.

Jai went to the dining hall, and found Nicole already there, having her snacks. He went to her, to discuss what happened in the meeting between Shukla and Vineet.

"Nothing in particular, they discussed whatever you have done till now, and then left," she replied.

"Okay, I didn't find the time to ask this to Shukla, that's why I asked you. I will find something to eat now."

"No problem Jai, you can always ask me."

Jai asked for a sandwich at the kitchen and waited for it to arrive, talking to Nicole about what he was doing. He ate his sandwich when it arrived, and left again to go to work.

Shukla was thinking on a different tangent now, he was wondering what the people at NIC might be doing to safeguard their system. He could clearly think that a new system would be on the cards, and that the old system would be abandoned after a new one was built. He was thinking of what all would have been included in the new system, as he was sure that the work on it would almost have been completed. This was when it struck him that the old system could just be used to repeat Jai's plan of introducing filters into each device. This system would act as the starting point of filtering process. The old system would be of no use, and all the data would be ported. He knew that the NIC would destroy that system as soon as the new one was ready, and would make backup plans for the new one. He desperately wanted to prevent this now. He thought here of the whole of humanity, and not just the NIC. The old system could send the filters all over the world, if needed. He desperately needed to send a message, and to the right person, but how?

Jai had earlier received a call; could he make one? Jai politely refused when Shukla requested this. Jai explained that it was not under his control anymore and the matter would have to be taken with the higher authorities. But the situation demanded urgency. And Shukla soon found a way to lure Jai. He promised Jai a job at NIC, although he knew that they were never going to be there. He just had to make up something, and Jai too was convinced very easily. Even Shukla wondered how Jai was convinced so easily. "Let me look into the matter, I will do it if I can, but I can't say for sure that a call will happen," Jai said.

"No, but you have to make it happen, it is very important, and our life hangs over it, I want it to be done straight," said the bossy Shukla. Jai started making some amends to the filter that he had bypassed the last time, when he received the call from Mohan. When he had received the phone call, his phone might have passed through a complex network. He knew it would be very tough to bypass this network, which he called the spider network. But he was sure the same hack which had helped receive the call would work this time as well, with a little tweaking.

This time he tried to route the call through the other informatics centres, by making a huge looped structure of routing the phone call. While looping (as in the spider web), his plan was to just keep the detection mechanisms busy so that they would be exhausted and the call could then be made through the normal interface. Although he did not know the exact routing sequence after the final barriers to this place, he had decided to transmit the signals to the closest possible satellite, which could just do the job after that. But it was going to take him a while. The soonest he could be done was by the evening. Shukla was forced to wait, hoping that no one in the meantime had shut the old system at his office.

It was not possible to locate a satellite directly, as Jai had no clue where he was, so he had to use a method where he would pick the satellite that would respond to his requests fastest. He did not have enough time at hand, so he sent a 'hello' message to 10 satellites randomly, and the one which responded the quickest was chosen.

It was 5.33 p.m. exactly when the call was made. The looping trick actually worked, and the satellite could catch the signal to transmit it to the NIC office. The message was delivered, loud and clear. Shukla wanted to speak more, but before he could do anything, the call went off. The reasons for restricting the calls at Building 3 was the secrecy that had to be maintained at any cost.

Shukla was certain that Mohan would decipher his message correctly and he was sure that the old system would not be destroyed now, unless it already was, which was highly unlikely. His screen popped, requesting him to report straight away to Nicole's office. He was scared to some extent, but was breathing easy as the most important job of the day, according to him, had been done.

"What is the matter with you? What is with all the calling? There was a call two days ago, then today! You think you can get away with this? No, you won't. In other times, there would be an action taken against you, but right now you are needed. That does not mean you are freed of the breach. After the job, you have some serious answering to do." Nicole fired at him straight away.

"No, I would not have done it without a reason. I have done it for a good cause, and am ready to answer anyone who asks me. Should I start with you?" was Shukla's blunt reply. "I actually spoke with Jai just before you reached here, and was informed that you offered him a job at NIC? That goes as another charge against you," she replied, stinging Shukla this time.

"I am sorry for that, but I can explain," Shukla said, in an apologising tone. He then explained why the call was made and tried to convince her. She was not interested in his apologies and told him to get back to work at the earliest as they would have to resolve this later. Shukla was perfectly happy with that, and went back to Jai.

SMALL ASHTRAY

April 10, 11

The fourth stage of implementation was under progress while Mohan was still pondering over the call. "Why had Shukla asked to keep the old system alive?" he kept wondering. He had been thinking for a lot of time now, and he had started feeling dizzy for this reason. He decided to go wash his face and freshen up a bit, so that he could wait at the office, as he had no plans to leave for home. In the washroom, David met him and told him to take the day off, but he didn't listen. He thought that there was a possibility of another call, and if that happened, he had to be there. Nobody else at NIC understood Shukla the way Mohan did. Shukla was not just his boss; he was Mohan's role model since his early days at NIC.

The rotation policy that was taken for changing shifts was still alive, to David's surprise.

Singh and the two special teams were the only ones left now who had not gone home for the past three days. On one of his breaks, Singh was taking a nap when Mohan came up to him, waking him up. "Singh, I could see something here," he said.

"What are you talking about? The old system?" asked Singh.

"Yes, I have a clue as to why he called not to shut it off. It maybe that Shukla has found some solution to the problem and needs this system to test it. He might actually be with us on this."

"You think Shukla won't communicate that straight if he had a solution?" Singh replied.

Singh did not even try to believe in the message that Shukla had sent. He explained to Mohan that the system his people were building would be ready in the next 4 days. There would be no way that they would keep the old system alive after that, as they could not take the risk of it getting attacked.

"Singh, but it could be true. Give it a thought, if Shukla wants to test some solution, where would he do it? It has to be the old system, under quarantined conditions. This would give him the results that he wants to see, and check if his solutions work."

"Mohan, we do not even know where Shukla is, whether he was taken by some terrorists, by some hackers or God knows who! And for me to believe that he wants to keep the old system awake is just not possible. Bring me some evidence, any small one. And I will consider what you are saying, but right now, you are just making speculations which do not lead anywhere," was Singh's befitting reply.

"Okay, let me think over it. You carry on with your break," said Mohan as he left.

Although David knew Shukla very well and was a good friend of his, he would not take the risk of leaving the old system up for even a fraction of a second after the new one was ready, as that could be just the required time that Ashtray needed to penetrate. Mohan was convinced now more than ever, and his frustration showed on his face.

On his way back to his cubicle, he tried to explain the same thing to David, who was unperturbed. David told Mohan that Shukla was certainly a person to be believed, but what Mohan was thinking was just a wild guess. Inevitably, after the next four days, the old system had to be scrapped after all the work on the new system was completed. But David reiterated that the old system would remain untouched for the next four days at least, or till the new system was ready. Mohan still believed that that would not be enough.

Mohan was already anxious thinking about why Shukla gave the message, for he needed some evidence to prove to others. It was night by the time all this had happened. So he decided to go home, and come back early the next day. He did not want to stay, as no one seemed to believe his theory there. His going home was a risk; if another call was made, someone else would receive it. But he was sure that he would not want to work there at the moment when no one was believing him. Also, he thought that David's view might change, if he was not there. In case any call came from Shukla, others would take care of it their way, he thought. He got into his car, only to find him not able to drive. So he decided to just take a cab instead. He slept well that night as a result of all the mental fatigue.

The next morning, he came to office at 6.30 a.m. David was already there, as the implementation teams had begun the last leg of the fourth stage. The deadline was 12.00 noon. David was himself supervising all the work these teams were doing. Mohan reached for the fax machine, as he could see some papers coming out of it. "Report 1 from Ahmedabad" it was titled. He understood that the teams from Ahmedabad must have reported their findings to David by now. He went straight to him and asked him about it.

"The teams are already on their way back. They did not find anybody there, perhaps, the hackers must have come to know that the teams were coming again, and might have left. But since the hackers have left, it might be the case that they are involved in the disappearance of Shukla and Jai. Or, they might just be scared of investigations," David replied.

Again, Mohan started convincing David that Shukla would not disclose the data to anyone, and he would not take orders from anyone. "He is the one who orders," he said. David was again partially convinced about it, and said-"I know, but we do not know these hackers, they could take anything out of him. I understand your sentiments, but let us all have some patience and wait for some more information."

Mohan went to his desk, and read the whole report that had arrived on the fax machine. He noticed that there was nothing substantial that he could get out of the report, and almost threw it away in frustration. He decided to work rather than focus on only one thing. Projects at the NIC had been delayed due to these sudden mishaps, and there was a lot of pressure from the upper sections of the Government to complete them on deadline. So he decided to walk up to David again and ask if he could take over the project on which Singh was working earlier, when he didn't have Raakh 1.1.

David was a person who knew exactly which persons were required where and at what time. When Mohan asked him for the job, the reaction was a placid "No". David did not want to give any project to Mohan at that time. He knew that Mohan was frustrated, and this could have resulted in a new project going bad, if he lost his cool. Mohan had by now lost all hopes that things could change by explaining. So he decided to just go with the investigation team that was going to head out that day for finding leads to Jai and Vineet. He left with the teams early in the morning.

They were going to Jai's friends first, they had two of them on the list. After that, they had to be at one of Vineet's social groups, which he would visit every weekend. Then they had to go to Jai's office, and check his computer there. They already had the data on Jai's laptop, and his office computer was the last thing that they had to look at regarding him. They took the whole computer with them to the NIA headquarters from Jai's office, and analysed it thoroughly. But before that, the investigation teams had to first be at NIA headquarters, to report their findings personally to Amit.

Mohan had remembered hearing from Unnikrishnan about Vineet's involvement. The team had been on the lookout for any leads to Vineet, as he was the target man who looked to be an agent for an enemy agency. Plus, to others, his solitary life seemed to be perfect for being an agent. Vineet hardly left his home, and hardly had any acquaintances nearby. His neighbours did not know much about him, only that he worked at NIC. All of them thought that it was a part of his job to be secretive about his work, and would not broach such subjects with him. But there was an anomaly as well. His neighbours did not know him very well, but he had joined four social groups, each in a different area in the city. Was the obliteration of NIC's databases planned in one of these groups?

Mohan realised that the investigation team was actually getting nowhere with the investigation, so he thought that it would be best if he explained what had happened, the call that he received, to Amit. Not just that, he also told him how no one believed him, and that he was sure about what he believed. But he was not certain why Shukla wanted to preserve the old system. Fortunately, his attempt to convince Amit was not in vain. Finally, someone was ready to believe him.

Amit, though not convinced completely, thought of it as a possibility. But the story was far-fetched, he thought. He reported this to his team, and they made it a point to consider it as a part of their further investigations. He knew that the NIC would have done the initial investigations regarding the call, and went with Mohan straight to the NIC headquarters to know what they found. He also wanted to know why he was not informed about this before.

He headed straight to David. David clearly knew what was coming as he saw him enter with Mohan. He prepared himself for an explanation. Mohan left Amit at David's office, and went to his desk. He began looking here and there, trying to avoid attention, but Singh came up to him, and gave him a stinging tirade.

"Are you out of your mind? We are not to let anyone know about this. The NIA cannot know because that would lead to a formal investigation which will trouble us, nothing else."

"I see no wrong in Mr Amit knowing about it, so let him discuss it with David now. It is not for me and you to discuss the matter anymore. So let us work, the both of us. I will make the report of the third and the fourth stage once it is complete. Tell me if you have any other work for me in the meantime," Mohan ingenuously replied.

"Certainly I do. Keep your mouth shut, which is all I want of you," Singh said, unable to control his temper. He left towards the conference room, staring at David through the glass wall of his office as he walked past it.

David openly discussed everything related to the call, about Shukla's voice and everything. But he also explained that a large group of people at NIC believed that it was a hallucination for Mohan, who was deeply affected by Shukla's departure. This was because the call records did not indicate anything that would lead them to believing Mohan. They both discussed Mohan's nature, and David was naturally not supportive of Mohan, although he told Amit that his integrity was not to be questioned. To explain this, he had to tell Amit about the letter that Mohan had sent to him.

But Amit convinced David that he be included in whatever was being planned by NIC. David called Singh to his office, to know the progress of the project they had undertaken, and give him a briefing of the further stages to be implemented. The meeting turned out to be one where Singh brought up the subject of Mohan being mentally ill. He tagged him 'retarded', which Amit disapproved of at once. Amit told Singh to involve Mohan in every step of planning, and to not reject his hypothesis already. They had no proof that he was wrong, if they did not have any proof of his being right, he mentioned. The meeting lasted for an hour. David and Singh were convinced by Amit that he would not let the higher authorities bother them, and that they had his full support.

When David had just finished his meeting, at about 11.35 a.m. on April 11, the old system was showing some abrupt movements, such as denial of access to the database, and the server appeared to be shut down, as if its memory was flushed constantly. Meanwhile, the team working under Singh had almost reached the completion of the current stage and they had already started to think of the integration stages. The two special teams were working on the basic and advanced safe modes and were beginning to feel the heat of implementing such a large system in such a small time.

David was quick to observe the abrupt movements to the old system. "Quarantine? What happened to that?" he uttered in a clear sign of displeasure. The teams that had used the standard procedures for the safe-zoning of the system were recalled. This abrupt behaviour in the system ended within a few minutes, but on checking the databases it was found that only a few rows were altered. It was as if someone had deliberately attacked the system, but not using Ashtray. At first he thought that the attack was a warning sign given by some terrorist group, but he altered his thought on careful observation.

This was something else, much smaller and was some kind of a hint, David inferred. He thought about it for some time before he came to a conclusion. But he was sure about it. Spontaneuosly, he called Mohan back from where he was. Mohan was interviewing Jai's girlfriend Rita. In the meantime, he told the Raakh team to continue the work, and finish it before 13thApril if possible. At this point, the team did not have to know about this small attack, and it would be best if they finished their work at the earliest. He met Singh in his office, telling him what he was about to tell Amit as well. They both were wrong in not believing Mohan, he was convinced.

"Mohan babu! What were you saying yesterday? I think we have the proof that we needed to believe in you," David said to Mohan when he came back to the office. "Sir, I knew it! But what happened, you look disturbed."

"A small attack happened on the old system, and we have good reason to believe that the attack was conducted by Shukla, as the damage done proves that," he said.

"Actually, the data was infected in such a way that only the redundant data was corrupted, and everything useful was kept alive. And since the system was quarantined, it was safe from outside attacks, which would have been known to Shukla. He was the only one who knew that the quarantine could be shut off in case intentional damage was required. And that is what has happened. Also, the stature of this attack was such that it very clearly was a toned down version of the Ashtray description that we have. So, it is also evident that Shukla is with Jai and they both are doing something," explained David. He now called Singh for a meeting, telling him everything about it and clearly ordering that the teams should not destroy the old system even after the new system is ready.

Singh looked dubious about it. His thought was valid, what if Shukla had really been turned by some terrorist group, or secret service of an enemy nation, what would happen? He wanted to believe in whatever David said, but he did not want to completely leave aside the possibility. And so he spoke to David and Mohan, who almost convinced him eventually that it was Shukla they were talking about, and he was the most bankable person in such scenarios.

"Singh, what if Shukla and Jai had planned out some secret mission and were in the process of completely overhauling the security components of our machines? I think Shukla could do it, and he has Jai with him."

"All we have is beliefs and conjectures, sir," Singh mentioned. "Let me work on my job as of now, and we will look at other possibilities later, okay?"

"Yes, you must be very busy with your work, I won't burden you any more at this moment. So let me think about all this. Go back to your work." Singh left, leaving Mohan and David discussing what was happening. David was waiting for the report by his associate who was analysing the attack. He read the report once it arrived, and handed it over to Mohan, impressed by the details. Mohan read the report partly, and started-"Sir this was exactly what I was trying to explain, I guess now you can believe in what I was saying. The old system is needed by Shukla, and let us do him a favour. Not just him, all of us."

"Yes, I agree with what you say Mohan. I will tell the teams not to destroy the old system for some days after the new system is ready. Let me decide the time for which it should be kept alive."

"Thank you so much sir, any job for me?"

"Yes, do whatever you are doing, but keep trying to contact Shukla always."

"Oh yes, I will. Thank you very much." Mohan left, looking at his cell phone and dialling Shukla's number. He dialled five times, before leaving the phone aside for some time. He then looked at the report on the advisory committee meeting that had just arrived on his desk. He had to handle the work in Shukla's absence, and had already opened the envelope which had big red letters stamped on it,- "CONFIDENTIAL". It did not bother him.

He hastily made a document summarising the recommendations of the advisory committee, and signed the document on Shukla's behalf, approving every recommendation that was stated in there.

The implementation team had completed work on the fourth stage by now and were readying for the final integration stages. Of the team, some people would continue testing the fourth stage, so that new problems didn't arise later. Singh reported to David that the fourth stage was done and left for his work. David had clearly explained to him to leave the old system on for another two days, and build some additional features into the quarantine, if necessary. David had ordered him to do so, whether he liked it or not. Singh discussed all this with his team.

Meanwhile, the TV screen across the David's office flashed news that 31 jaguars had suddenly died in Brazil and Venezuela, though the cause of their death was completely unknown.

BREACH

April 10, 11

After the call was made, Shukla and Jai went back to what they were doing earlier-finding the perfect strategy. Jai was working out a better strategy to reduce the time taken while Shukla was still on his theory- 'Filters for the world', he called them. He was formulating methods to set up a channel to the NIC's old system. Jai did not know about it, and this theory was the reason for making that call to NIC.

By now, Jai had discovered places in the antivirus code that could be avoided, and places where extra code would have to be added. He wanted to make the code faster, even if it meant writing redundant and repetitive instructions. Infact, he added a lot of repetitive instructions to make sure the code ran faster. The code was executed in a lesser time now, but there was a cost involved, in terms of the space required for the code. Jai decided to do it anyway, assuming that the space required would not be a problem here. The prime consideration currently was to execute it within the window given to him, just 10 minutes. Unable to reduce time till now, he contacted Nicole to check if the window size could be incremented to a further extent. But every time he did, he got a negative from her.

Shukla, at the same time, was constantly thinking about saving the world from Ashtray. It was almost midnight now, but hardly did he notice the time. His stomach was growling, but the voice was not heard by his ears and mind.

He first thought about a few more things to be taken care of, then he thought about how to use the NIC's old database (which he thought would still be existing) for the initiation of the fission. But as he was thinking this, it struck him that the people at NIC might want proof. There was a possibility that Mohan might not have received the message correctly, raising speculations. He thus thought of doing it: a dummy attack onto the system, to send a clear message to the people at NIC. This attack would prove to the NIC that he was involved in the matter. It was time to consult Jai again, again try establishing a contact to earth, which could again lead to confrontation. But Shukla did not care. He was sure that he was doing the right thing, and was ready to face the consequences.

On the other hand, Nicole now felt that she should have listened to the whole conversation between Shukla and Vineet that took place earlier, and blamed her keeper for being so loud. She could have also convinced Shukla there itself that whatever he was thinking was not possible. But she could not, courtesy her keeper.

She was to meet Mr Hans to discuss the work that was going on, and report her recommendations to Shukla and Jai. She prepared a note to give to Mr Hans describing all the work that Shukla and Jai had done, but she did not mention Shukla's meeting with Vineet. Though she had guessed what Shukla was trying, she decided not to give it away, as it was of no use. Mr Hans would probably call Shukla into questioning at once, which she did not want. Shukla's time could not be wasted at the moment.

Shukla ordered Jai to perform the task. The task was to design a small dummy Ashtray, developed in such a way that it had a subset of the essential components of Ashtray, and it would stop after some time. To develop this, Jai had to rewrite the fission code, to limit it to a certain depth. Also, he had to add components to attack only the redundancies in the NIC database, as it was enough to deliver the required message to the teams at NIC. Shukla thought that this system could be easily developed, but in reality, the system was developed only on the next day, the 11th of April.

The last step was to finalise the route. For this, he needed the working of Datrees and Crawbats. Jai got the complete working model of Datrees and Crawbats from the maintenance department. He was not surprised to know their functioning, especially the crawbats. He analysed the Datrees who were strikingly similar in working to the normal Hard Disk Drives used today. He needed time to tweak the program he developed, to accommodate the advances that crawbats and datrees provided. He ensured that all the components of this small Ashtray were working properly and the route designed was perfect. Three hours later, Jai was done verifying every detail, thus he reported to Shukla that the system was ready to be deployed.

Shukla, by this time had messaged Vineet that his real job would start now, and again advised him to be vigilant in whatever he was doing. Vineet was still working on the backup system. Vineet ignored his message this time, thinking that Shukla had become paranoid due to some reason. But after sometime, a message from Nicole arrived on his keeper. It read-"Be ready, Shukla might need you." He finished the work at hand, and rushed to Nicole's office.

"I heard Shukla needs me. Can you tell me where his office is? I haven't been there even once."

"Yes, but he does not need you right now. You will have to wait for some time. I don't know what they are doing, but it might be best if you ignored what Shukla's messages are constantly telling you."

This was the point where Vineet realised that there was something serious about the message that Shukla had been sending again and again. Faithful to his boss, he was now going to be more vigilant than ever, he thought. Nicole had thought that her talk with Vineet could be taken the wrong way, but the chances were low.

"Okay, and why do you say that?" asked Vineet.

"The thing is… Shukla has not been in the best frame of mind, you know he is burdened with Ashtray right now, so please do not pay heed."

Although Vineet thought earlier that he would see to it that he keeps his eyes open at all times, the reason that Nicole gave was convincing. It took Nicole no time to turn his thoughts around. After all, Shukla had not given him a single reason to believe in his messages. Now confused what to do, he took the middle path. He assured Nicole that he would not heed to Shukla's messages; at the same time, he started looking around at everything with suspicion. He decided to be alert at all times, unable to decipher what 'Be Vigilant' meant. He had to stay awake any ways for a lot of time, as the replica system was under construction.

Nicole then told him that Shukla would call him directly to his office, and his keeper would show him directions. Vineet then returned to the maintenance department, to try and finish the replica system work at the earliest, and wait for a call from Shukla.

Now, since the dummy Ashtray's system was developed in full, it was ready to be transmitted through a medium. Jai knew that if Ashtray could cross the boundaries of this place to come in, it could go outside too, provided the communication worked as he had planned. He had to make sure that the external barriers, which had handled the original Ashtray earlier, would not be affected by this virus. When dummy Ashtray would move out, there was a slight risk that the barriers would fail to block the bigger Ashtray. This could happen if this smaller Ashtray and the original Ashtray were to clash at the barriers, then the barriers would not curtail the bigger Ashtray. They would be inoperable for that split second when this virus was transmitted outside. The Datrees closest to the barriers could be affected because of this. The data in these datrees, the ones close to the barriers would be modified as a result and the system would collapse, eventually.

Shukla asked Jai to finish the work of adapting his code to crawbats at the earliest and straight away deploy the dummy Ashtray, without any delay. The system would work like this-It would first try to bypass the barriers, within the short span of time. Then it would move to the NIC database through a path specified by the call that was made earlier. The same channel was to be used to communicate this time too. After the virus reached the NIC old system, it would assess the damage that it could do, replacing only the redundant fields, and printing pre-specified messages in the spaces. After identification of the fields, it would start its operation.

Since Ashtray was based on the concept of fission, stopping this smaller version from spreading was extremely important. And to assure the people at NIC that indeed it was Ashtray, the logs of the operation of the virus were to be printed too. The fields that were modified were to be made conspicuous, as in a large database all the modified fields might not be noted. Shukla left it to David and his team to decipher the further complexities of the system. The system looked ready now, and Jai had tested it on a dummy database that he built on his laptop earlier.

They both knew the risks. If the operation failed, it was certainly doomsday. There would be a profound imbalance affecting everything on the earth. They sat down for some time silently, praying that nothing of that sort happened. Jai went to the washroom once before beginning. While returning, he met Nicole on the way. Unable to resist, he called her to his office at the earliest.

Nicole had to finish the task she was working on, and arrived at their office in half an hour. Shukla had earlier thought and decided to proceed without telling Nicole, but this time, Jai straight away reported everything to Nicole. He did not bother what Shukla said. Shukla had tried hard to convince him to do it without her consent but he resisted. Of course, this was trouble for Shukla. It looked to Nicole like Shukla was not dealing with the job at hand, but was doing something bizarre. She started criticizing Shukla once again, and this time all the anger about his meeting with Vineet was also reflecting.

She was giving him a lecture when Shukla screamed- "I know; I know what you are saying. But this is equally important. If tomorrow we are able to develop filters similar to the work we are doing here, we need a gateway to the systems of the earth. From my understanding, there are no systems that could be used that way, except the one that caused you trouble the first time-the old system at NIC. The reason for this is very simple-this system was perhaps the origin of the attack here. The design of that system might have tried to prevent itself from damage by deflecting the signals initially, to diverse systems so that it remained unharmed. This could be the only possible reason to have caused the jeopardy here. Because the attack here might have originated there, a communication channel already exists. So, please…" he paused for a moment, and began again- "Also, nowhere in the world was it reported that a Governmental database was under attack, except us, when the attack first struck us. We were unprepared then, so the people at NIC might have quarantined it. They might have already built a new system. Of course, all this would have happened if they followed the standard procedure. They would destroy the old system unless someone tells them to keep it alive. And that someone is me!" Nicole and Jai looked in astonishment at the revelation that Shukla had just made, and were curious to know what was going on in his mind exactly.

"This could be our best chance at protecting all the databases on earth. If they are protected, we can safely say that attacks like Ashtray would not be able to reach here. So we would need to make sure that the gateway is not destroyed." Shukla looked towards Jai condescendingly.

The path to the gateway was clearly available to Jai and Shukla, and it could be easily reached as the path could be searched with ease. Jai had already noted the route to be taken. Shukla explained all this to Nicole, making this the smartest statement that he had ever made out to anyone here. Both Nicole and Jai were still not able to respond to him, and kept looking at him. After a few moments, Nicole finally broke the silence.

"Okay, but is it our only way? Work with the engineers here, and see if there is any other gateway out there," she said.

"I have full faith that the engineers would accept this. No matter how advanced this place is, my considerations are based on sound facts, and above all, we do not have the time. If another system has been developed by now, the people at NIC might already have started the destruction of the old one. And it doesn't take much time to destroy a system, you see," he answered spontaneously. Nicole submitted and asked him to wait for a few minutes, and told Jai not to do anything until she got the consent of a few people. She said she would be back, while she was typing something on her pocket screen. She hastened out of there and got onto the travelator.

After she had left, Jai screamed out- "At your order sir!" and sat down in front of his laptop. But this time, Shukla told him to just keep everything ready. "Let's wait for her orders this time. I guess she will get the permission," he ordered. Jai had everything ready, all the variable values were fed in, the limit of the fission depth was set, and the system was ready to fire. In a few moments, Nicole arrived.

"Alright, here is the thing. We cannot risk exposing our barriers to Ashtray for a long time, although a short time could be harmful as well. Nevertheless, the management has decided that we should allow a very small window through which you could make it pass. I hope that is alright. And regarding the filters that you were building for this building, the management asked why it could not be done before this work. I had to explain a lot, but handled it." Both of them nodded.

Nicole had to explain to Mr Hans why this was the only way of doing it, and why Shukla should be trusted on this part. She reminded him of Shukla's impeccable record at the NIC.

Later, while she was talking to Vineet and Shukla, she got a message from the boss- "Please tell Shukla to meet me at my office whenever he is free. Just tell him to message before coming." She continued before telling Shukla about this message.

"Your friend Vineet has almost completed his assignment there, and he has been allotted to the window opening and closing task. His allotment is only a formality. He is a part of your team now. He is well accustomed to the barriers, and can do the job for you. So use his help. He will be here soon. And, best of luck," she added.

"Thank you," said both of them, looking content.

"And Shukla, you have to meet the boss at the earliest possible time. Please text him before you go."

"But, what is it about, should I worry about anything?"

"No, certainly not. I guess he wants to know the complete procedure, I did not explain the specifics to him. So he might want to know. But be sure that you do not make him wary of your plans in any way."

Shukla wondered why Nicole did not take any action about his talk with Vineet the other day. He had an inclination to believe that she had been a spectator to the conversation that was taking place between them, and it was she who precluded the conversation from moving any further. He thought that she understood his sentiments, and might support him in his venture. Or there could be another reason. She might think that Shukla's plans did not deserve any attention as they were futile. But of course, this was all speculation, he realized. It might have been otherwise too. Shukla ignored all this to focus on the work.

Nicole left the place and after a few moments, Vineet Singhal arrived, as promised. Both Shukla and Singhal smiled and winked at each other, and got to work straight away.

"Vineet, did Nicole tell you what we are doing here?"

"Yes, she explained that you need me to operate the barriers on the outer boundary. But I do not know anything else. Can you please give me a brief overview?"

As he said this, Jai jumped in, explaining his plan to him, and why Singhal was so crucial to it. After properly hearing what he had to do, Vineet thought of the way in which he would do it. A few minutes later, Singhal explained the procedure to be followed to both of them. He first explained the standard procedures to be followed for the barriers, and then explained what was to be done in this case.

Vineet pulled a keeper hanging on the wall, and calculated the window that could be available for the virus to pass the barriers. This time limit was estimated at 1500 microseconds. So, he decided to open the window for exactly 1400 microseconds, and started inputting the values of time limits into his keeper. The idea was that by shutting it off at 1400 microseconds, the risk of being attacked would be further lessened. The time was too small for the original Ashtray to cross the barriers. And the barriers were capable enough to pull back the viruses already penetrated, if they at all did.

The only condition to this was that the barriers could not work both ways, that is, they could not push away new attacks and pull back viruses at the same time. In such a case, it was important to know if Ashtray would have kept on attacking the barriers periodically. If the barriers were not under constant attack, they could easily pull back already penetrated viruses. And in such a case, the damage would be practically negligible. If they were under constant attack, it would be hard to pull the virus back.

Shukla had almost forgotten that he had to meet the boss. He got a reminder from Nicole, to meet Mr Hans urgently. Shukla messaged Mr Hans that he would be there. On reaching there, he saw Mr Hans seated in his chair, watching at a screen which stated the report of the performance of the Biological Information Systems. Shukla started explaining what he was doing exactly while creating the small Ashtray.

"Are you serious? Do you not see the risk involved?" asked Mr Hans.

"Sir, I am aware, and I assure you that nothing is going to happen, as the window size that we shall use will be too small. We have fixed the time at 1400 microseconds, and the probability of Ashtray penetrating the system is too small for this window size. So, please let us do it. We are ready to deploy it, provided you approve, sir."

"I am aware that Nicole has given you permission. If the window you are planning is so small, I don't think there should be a problem. But do recheck your basis of ashtray time estimation."

"Okay sir, I will do that."

Shukla was elated when he came back to his cubicle.

Jai was ready to go when Vineet was. Vineet did a final check of his values, and then sent a message to Nicole saying "ready". A similar message was sent to the maintenance team, which by now would have known the plan, as Nicole had gone to explain them. When everything was ready, Shukla gave the final call, and Jai initiated the address search. Within a matter of seconds, the address of the NIC's old system was found out. It was time to send the virus to that address. The barrier opening time was perfectly synchronised with the virus transmission time, which easily managed to move out in the 1400 microsecond window. All of this happened too quickly for the people to notice any attack. The process was completed as planned.

The barriers were back to work after the brief hiatus, just to find a breach.

INTERACTION WITH THE INSIDE

April 11

The barriers were giving out a red alert to the maintenance department. The department soon got into action, and started checking what had happened in those 1400 microseconds. They had to look up to see if there were any breaches, and had to take measures to undo the effects due to them. This was the first time when the maintenance department had been so involved in the functioning of the barriers. Due to the very small number of attacks from outside, the maintenance team's interference was hardly required.

And they soon found out that Ashtray had penetrated the system. The small Ashtray and the original one had met on the barrier. In the process of throwing out the smaller one, the barriers could not stop the original one. They checked to see what all had been affected till now. It was a relief to find that Ashtray had only reached the border Datrees till now, but had not damaged any. Jai reasoned that Ashtray would find the best computer to reach for the first time, and then fission would activate. After this, there was no going back. But while they were checking the initial few Datrees, they could see that the fission had begun, and the effects could be seen.

The logical barriers had to now quickly calculate the location of each node that was reached by Ashtray, and stop its operations. But, since the fission reaction was too fast, developing a plan was really tough. The plan would have to ensure that all the nodes reached due to fission were completely stopped. This was a tough process, as the nodes were penetrating deeper into the hierarchy. The first level of Datrees was showing the effects now. It came to the notice of the maintenance team that something abrupt had started happening, a typical characteristic that Jai had told them about. Values in some fields were altered, which the maintenance team reported to Shukla straight away and initiated a crash control procedure.

When it came to Shukla's notice, he actually thought that someone was joking. Because the operation of sending out the message was carried out meticulously and Vineet had calculated the time period so accurately, anyone would have thought similarly. Only after viewing the alerts on his keeper, which he had hardly checked ever since he got his laptop, was he convinced. Now was the real pressure felt by Shukla. He checked with Jai to see if he could temporarily do something to halt the fission. But it was not in Jai's control, as the virus had entered and the fission process would have started. By this time, exactly 15 fields were modified, and now it was the turn for 16 more fields, in accordance with the fission rule. This rule said that the affected numbers would be a part of the series 1, 2, 4, 8, 16 and so on.

It was time for Mr Hans to look into the matter. He dropped at Shukla's cubicle to see what exactly was happening. Shukla himself was confused at the way it had happened. Vineet was busy talking to Krishnakant Rao on his keeper, and the whole maintenance department was baffled. Jai was looking at his keeper, waiting for the maintenance department to do something. He could think of nothing that he could do at that moment. Mr Hans waved at him as his eyes looked lost. Jai looked at him, nodded, and looked at his keeper again. Nicole too arrived there in a few moments.

All four of them; Mr Hans, Shukla, Jai and Nicole started discussing the prospects of the filters in the present state. It was something which looked positive, just that it had to be implemented on a large scale, which needed a massive, time-consuming operation.

And Jai still had to complete the essential parts of the filter code. He had designed the system, but not yet developed it completely. Also, the ten-minute condition was not taken care of yet.

The maintenance team decided to shut down the main system, and initiate the backup system. But later it suspended the plan as the attack was on the databases, not on the system. So instead they decided to hibernate the system. And, they stopped the system from accessing the affected section of the database. The effects of hibernation of this system were going to be profound.

There would be no deaths as the fields of death time would not be accessible. At the same time, to compensate for no deaths, there should be no births as well. But births were not under control here. This would result in an imbalance. This could lead to the ultimate, untimely collapse of the earth's biodiversity and the ecosystem, deserting the planet. But, it was strictly against the rules to allow alterations to the death date fields, as there was a lot of calculation involved while arriving at the death date of a person. The maintenance team was hence left with no choice but to do it- hibernate the system. But the positive side of it was that Jai would have enough time to send the filters to each system. The ten-minute time limit would be relaxed.

It was time for action. Shukla took a look at the filter code that was already developed, to check how much time it would need before deployment. He told Jai to get this code to all the Datrees surrounding the barriers first, as they were the ones directly under attack. Vineet knew the complete architecture of storage, and he was capable of incorporating the system into the Datrees.

Shukla then told Mr Hans that the filters would first be deployed to the bordering Datrees, as it would be quicker, to which Mr Hans hastily nodded in approval. Nicole raised a doubt here- "But Shukla, what if this current attack penetrates the inner sections while the filters are being installed on the peripheral Datrees? I think you should start from the core system and move towards the peripheral parts, don't you agree?"

"I would have agreed with you Nicole, but the ones on the periphery, the bordering Datrees need immediate attention. That part is not accessible for querying anymore."

"Okay Shukla, I will not interfere with your work. But tell us, how much time will be required? And Vineet, you must know the safety procedures for the other systems and Datrees by now, so please initiate them if you have not till now."

"I have already done that," s aid Vineet.

"Boss, what do you think? Should they work the way they are, or am I thinking right?" said Nicole, still not convinced with starting on the peripheral Datrees first.

"Let them do what they have to do, I don't care about the methods used. I just want everything to be safe, that's it," was the befitting reply from Mr Hans.

"Shukla, you must get started. Jai, do your work!" ordered Mr Hans desperately.

"Thank you, sir." said Shukla.

"Jai, let us start, tell me the status of the filters. I guess you just have to build the remaining code and test it, right?"

"Sir that and a bit more. It will take a while before it could be ready. I don't think we can curtail this attack, hibernation might not work for long. The main system will eventually have to run."

"I am positive that we will stop it. Just finish the code and give it to me. Do not test it extensively. Just give it some basic checks, and be ready for the next job."

"But sir, what about the time reduction?" Mohan With jai asked.

"Let us not worry about all that right now. I give you 10 minutes, please finish writing the code. Till then, let the maintenance team take care of disabling the systems."

After about 5 minutes, Jai told Shukla that it would not be

possible for him to finish coding in those 10 minutes, so he would instead do another thing. He would separately insert the code of fission into each possible node that he could, and spread the antivirus from there. He would do this after the filters are inserted into that system. He had it all planned out brilliantly.

"I guess that is alright. But it means additional work for you. And you alone will not be able to do it, do you need somebody else?"

"I guess I will have the maintenance department with me, so I can coordinate with them regarding what to do. Okay?"

"Yes, let us work then."

"Okay sir, can you tell me a way to reduce the time required?"

"It does not matter! Just go out there and get to these systems first." Since there was no estimate made yet, Jai was unable to decide as to which systems he should insert it into, and how many he should start with. This number was important as the spreading of the filters would start from the Datrees and systems in which this code would be present. He looked at the layout of the system in his keeper, and was drawing statistics about this building.

He consulted Vineet on what to do. Without thinking much, Vineet took Jai straight to the Maintenance wing, where his team was waiting for orders. Vineet ordered the team, which only had four people, to gather as many people as possible to do the work which was physical this time. The work involved contacting each of the Datrees, reaching them and initiating the filter program into them. Jai was baffled with his idea, but on thinking, he could infer that this was their only chance. The first Datree was to be the one that had been directly attacked, and Jai demonstrated using his screen how to initiate the program into the databases, so that the filters were embedded. The people had to make sure that the system was connected to the nerve centre at all times, so that Jai could do the tweaking that was required for the program to spread to others using fission. That is, he had to insert the code for fission into them.

The four people were busy texting and talking to almost anyone that they could get to through their keepers. They managed to do a humongous task-to gather almost anyone present in the building.

About 100 people had gathered there after some time, almost everyone from Building 3 had arrived there in less than 5 minutes, barring Shukla, who was overseeing the whole operation from his laptop. All these people brought opened screens and stood in a circle around Vineet so that every screen could be viewed from the middle, where Vineet was standing. The ring of screens did not allow anyone from the outside to view all the screens. For the people on the other side of this ring, there was a big screen on the north end of this big hall. Shukla was still in his own cubicle, viewing the proceedings on his keeper.

Shukla had to ensure that no storage device was left to chance, and only the ones that were adjacent to the attacked barriers were to be covered first. This was to ensure that there was no extra work done here, as Jai had the fission planned for all the other devices. As soon as the people had gathered, the maintenance team laid out the instructions for initiation to each one of them. The Datree numbers which were to be altered by them was on their screen. They just had to open the code of that address. But for this, it was important that they physically reached each Datree whose number was shown on their screen. After this, they had to insert this piece of code, maintaining the existing linkages, and dynamically create new ones. After this was done, they had to reconnect the system to the nerve centre, where Jai would add the latter part of the code.

The operation was to take some time, as the number of Datrees to be covered was about three hundred. This was only the number of Datrees that had to be reached by these people. The total number of Datrees was much larger than that. Shukla had a visual picture of the whole architecture on his screen by now, and was pinning each Datree that was being modified. He was in constant communication with Vineet, who was out on the ground, directing people to different Datrees.

Shukla was joined by Mr Hans and Nicole, for whom he put up a screen on the wall in front of him. Both Nicole and Mr Hans sat there staring at the screen, and heard Shukla's conversation with Jai the whole time. After watching the operation for some time, Mr Hans was convinced that he had recruited the right person for the task. Approving of the operation now, he left the place so that he could carry on the work of reporting and logging whatever had happened.

Jai in the meantime had started making a procedure that could be included so that the neighbouring Datrees would not attack the current one again. This was exactly what was to be dodged if Ashtray was to be kept away, apart from curtailing the fission. He was able to do the work even before 100 Datrees were tagged by Shukla, and started copying the code into each one of them. He had to ensure that the system did not accidentally start unless this was completed. Shukla started putting a double tag on the Datrees that had the latest procedure installed onto them.

Shukla's keeper beeped.

"Sir, please tag faster, the hibernated system is about to fall apart. I don't think there is much time left now," said Vineet.

"Vineet, ask the people to work faster, I am doing my best. Tell Jai to transfer the code to me, I will do the insertion of the final piece of code if needed. Tell him to do only the fission one, I shall do the other one."

"Okay sir, I am telling Vineet to do it. Let us work faster now."

"Oh yes." And Shukla kept down his keeper.

In about half an hour, the first 150 devices were pinned by Shukla. The work looked on track to be finished in an hour's time after Jai had finished inserting the extra piece of code. Overall, it seemed to be a loss of about an hour, the period for which the data would not be accessible. Shukla was constantly keeping track of this time, as a message had popped up saying that 1 hour was the threshold. The system could collapse if that time was exceeded by even a minute.

Shukla had ensured that his screen was projected in the maintenance centre the whole time, so that anyone could see what work had been done, and how much was left. To speed up his work, Jai called in Nicole too to just copy the codes and put them into the addresses of the Datrees that were already pinned once. Vineet was in the centre of the hall, and was just pointing at screens in the air, and saying the number of the Datree that was to be pinned. It seemed that he was at the centre of the whole world.

Shukla managed to pin 287 Datrees by the time 59 minutes and 30 seconds were gone. They had no time left, so Vineet turned up the main system again. But there was a problem. He had double pinned only 276 Datrees. 11 were left, so it was upto Jai to do the work in the next 30 seconds. These Datrees were still not turned up by Jai. Jai initiated the procedure for the first one. Vineet, standing on his right, watched it being double pinned. He brought a keeper near him, and inserted the code into the second one. Jai started again. By this time, three Datrees were done. Still, 8 were left. All of them decided to do the work simultaneously, at least the insertion part, which was more of a mechanical job. 14 seconds had passed already.

Jai, Vineet, Shukla, Krishnak ant Rao and 3 other people from Vineet's maintenance team, made 7 people who would take about 8-9 seconds to insert the code. The last one was to be done by Jai himself, but Mr Hans took control of one keeper and helped with the job himself. He was relieved to be a part of this grand operation. These 8 people finished the insertion in 23 seconds, and Vineet turned them on after that. Nicole was thankful that she had the right resources for the job.

The fission procedure of the filters was completed on time too, with all the Datrees in the vicinity of the building secured in time to avoid havoc. It had been tiring work for all those 100 people who had been running from one Datree to the other on orders from Vineet, who felt like a king for some time. But there was no time to be tired, all these people went back to their respective jobs after the operation was termed a success by Mr Hans himself. But the relief was short lived.

The work was completed on time and the systems were called back to life. The maintenance team now started an inquiry into what had actually happened when the virus struck. The database entries of 31 jaguars, whose death dates varied from a day to another four years, were altered. Thus, they were found dead. This was before the hibernation of the system.

This had created an imbalance now, and in an attempt to balance it, the computation system decided to alter the dates of all the animals and plants in the food chain before these jaguars. This was the biggest problem. Although the team knew that it was happening, they could do nothing about it, as it was necessary to maintain the balance of nature. Mr Hans' face was pale, and he was not able to digest it. This was the biggest disappointment that he ever had in his life on earth, or in building 3. He just felt so helpless. But it was not the time to weep now, he ordered the maintenance team to see what could be done, and told them to shut the system down, if it ever came to that.

All this was too disturbing for Shukla, who felt guilty at having given the orders for the shutting down of the barriers while sending the dummy Ashtray. The whole centre was in shock at the statistics. Although they knew that only 31 fields were attacked, they did not think that the effects would be visible so soon. Such was the power of Ashtray. Shukla although worried, maintained his composure, as he knew that there was a task at hand. He could not have just started sobbing there. There was no time for it.

Their next task was to conduct the live testing operation, which was to be done after a small break. Jai had been awake for long now, and his head had been pounding for food. They both sought Nicole's permission, and decided to take some time off. They planned to begin working at 8.00 pm, and went to sleep. Shukla dozed off in their office space itself, while Jai was still at the maintenance centre. Meanwhile, Vineet did some checks on the new filters that they had added to find any anomalous behaviour. And there were none. All appeared to be working perfectly.

ONCE AGAIN

April 11, 12

The news on television was hard to bear, and there were harsh reactions by animal rights' activists around the world. Everyone was blaming human exploitation as the root cause of the death of the jaguars. But the scholarly were unable to give a proper explanation as to what had happened. Nobody knew about it. The Forest Officials of the forests from where the Jaguars had gone missing were the object of stringent criticism, and one of them had even committed suicide. He was unable to see himself going down so badly even though he had no hand in it. Others were brave enough to face the consequences.

David was able to view the television from his office, but had hardly noticed the news until the same news was repeated about 20 times. He got irritated and went out to switch it off. The news hardly mattered to him at present, he had a task at hand. It did not even remotely occur to him that the news was related to Ashtray.

He spoke to the teams that had gone out to interview Rita, and was not surprised to know that she did not know anything about Jai's whereabouts since the day he disappeared. An engineer had just dropped off the report of the latest attack that had happened, and he decided to just go through it, although he had accurately estimated what was written in it. He understood the nuances of the attack through this, and came to understand that the attack proceeded in the powers of two.

One computer attacked two, these two attacked four and so on, he noticed. He could see its impact now. "The system would be very hard to inhibit," he thought. He then started thinking about reversing the effects of the attack, but he could not think of any significant solution at the moment. He gave a copy of the report to both Singh and Mohan, who were busy with their works by now. Mohan was trying to get the place of origin of the small Ashtray. He wanted just one lead to find Shukla, and was using all the knowledge he had to find it.

From the report David gave to him, Singh analysed the manner in which the attack proceeded to other computers. Since an already attacked system would be attacked again due to a reattack from neighbours instantly, it was hard to curtail. The expansion would be rather too quick, he guessed. He was still in disapproval of David and Mohan's thoughts about Shukla. The power of two rule seemed too good to be true. How could one design a virus with such capabilities? It was unthinkable for Singh. His scepticism refused to die.

Mohan was looking through the messages Shukla had sent through the attack. All the messages were reported in the report that was with David now, who forwarded a copy to Amit at NIA as well.

Singh tried, but was still unable to convince himself that Shukla was helping. What if this was a part of a bigger plan; to build confidence with the NIC people, and then use them to extract the contents of the system? Shukla would help do it, and sending a warning to NIC was the first step to doing it. It might be just to distract the people and do something bigger and worse.

He told this once again to David, who was now convinced about Shukla's intentions. Although David would have thought about all the things that stopped Singh from believing in Shukla, he would never doubt Shukla's fearlessness in dealing with attacks on his own systems. And Shukla was one person who would stay loyal, even if everything went against him. David, in return, tried to convince Singh that Shukla was really with them. But he would not believe.

"Okay, Singh. Let me make it clear. You believe in him or don't, I don't care. I just want you to follow instructions. Your opinions are welcome, but they are not binding on me. Get that?"

"But, sir…"

"You may get back to work," said David, showing him the door.

This was the first time that David had spoken in such a superior manner to Singh. He proved for the first time that ultimately he was the boss. Singh was now irritated with the conversation, but he had no power to do anything about it. This was the first time since this mission began that he felt powerless.

Nevertheless, he had a task at hand, and his team was working because of the trust they had put in him. After a few moments, he thought about the other side of it. He saw those 41 engineers who worked for him, obeying whatever he said. Maybe his boss also wanted him to be similar. So he stopped thinking about it, and started to work. He went to Mohan, and asked him to update the reports he had made to include the dummy Ashtray as well, and to mail it to David and Amit. Mohan had already started doing it. He finished the report soon, and gave it to David in person. David forwarded the report to Amit.

David thanked Mohan for believing in Shukla from the beginning, and putting forth that theory of his. But David also asked him to deal carefully with Singh, explaining the reasons. He then told him to discuss with Singh the prospects of including the NIA's local software group. Amit had mailed David saying that he wanted to include this group for the faster implementation of solutions to their systems as well, as hibernation was proving too costly. David had replied saying he would consider the proposal. But he left it to Singh and Mohan to make a decision.

The team working on Raakh 1.1 had started with the first insertion stage, the fifth stage. The advanced modes were to be inserted first, owing to their technical complexities and space requirements, followed by the basic modes in the sixth stage. Both these stages were to be completed by the morning of 12th April, so that the teams got proper amount of time for integration and testing-another critical stage. The teams that had worked throughout the fourth stage were now on a break, and new people had joined the others.

The two special teams could breathe peacefully now, as a major part of their job was done. The work on the fifth stage was planned in such a way that the most time consuming work would be done first. This was to ensure that there were very few complications later on, when the smaller modules would be loaded. It was a meticulous task, but was not as gruelling as the fourth stage. The work was in full swing and Singh was himself working on one module of this stage.

Whatever be his frame of mind about 'Mini Ashtray' and Shukla, Singh's job was clearly laid out to him. And he had the backing of his full team there. He thought that if his team trusted him so much without showing any apprehensions, it was time he trusted his boss too. He ordered one of his team members to take rest as he was about to collapse. He then ordered pizzas for everyone in the team, and left the conference room for a while. His mind was occupied with the talk he had with David, but he was focussed more than ever when he came back. Soon after, Mohan walked into the room.

Mohan and Singh discussed the possibilities of working with the NIA's local software group to secure the NIA system faster. Mohan was open to doing it, but Singh was opposing, as had become the norm. Whenever Mohan said something, Singh would hastily negate it. But Singh's consideration was correct this time, he considered the secrecy of their solution to be of utmost importance, no matter who asked for the solution. Only the NIC people had known it, and all were bound by an agreement not to disclose any details to anyone outside NIC. So, would it be right if NIA was involved completely? NIA could even challenge the ways used by NIC. And, another concern was regarding Shukla. Shukla could be trusted at NIC, but the people at NIA would not.

Once Again

As soon as he conveyed this point to Mohan, Singh just realised that including the NIA members could give his opinion about Shukla a much stronger case. So he went back on his opinion now, averring that he wanted the NIA team on board. The reason for Singh going back was simple; he would get a chance to give his opinion about Shukla to an unbiased NIA team, he thought.

But on careful consideration, Mohan understood the reason why Singh was now supportive of it, and rejected his opinion again. It was as if they were opposite poles-one would always speak the opposite of the other. The conversation lasted a bit longer, when David came out of his office to settle it. But he did not want to impose his opinion on them, so he was a spectator there, only to calm them down when they became too aggressive.

Eventually, they found a middle path. They decided that they would include three more people from NIC, who would go to NIA to help the team there implement the solutions. This way, they would not expose the whole idea of their solutions. Also, since NIA would be involved, Singh figured out that he might get a chance to interact with Amit regarding his concerns. In fact, he set up a meeting with Amit, and kept Mohan busy with some other work in the meantime.

Mohan by now had exhausted all his ways to find the exact location from where the smaller version had come the other day. He thought that the investigation agency might have some exceptional techniques which were unique to them. So he talked to David about it. David was positive about getting some inputs from the NIA and said that he would call Amit Joshi and ask for a meeting. But Amit mentioned that Singh was already going to NIA for a meeting. So David decided to go along with Singh.

Singh was summoned to David's office. David asked him his plans for the meeting that Singh was to have with Amit.

"I need to discuss the working of the local software group," replied Singh.

"I am coming with you."

"Sir, but I am capable of doing it alone. Wouldn't it be better if you stayed here, and I go?" asked Singh.

"I am going, say whatever, Singh. If someone is needed here, let's have Mohan here, and he can report to us if anything is required. Or better, even you should stay here..." replied David, realising the true reason why Singh wanted to approach the NIA.

Singh knew that his voice would be suppressed again if he tried to argue once more. So he stopped and accepted, believing he had lost his chance.

"We also need to know what has been coming down from the upper sects of the Government. Amit had promised me that he would handle it. Let us reach the Government and report the whole thing to them now," said David. He called Amit instantly and fixed an appointment for later in the day.

"Singh, I think you should come with me," David reconsidered his thoughts. Singh, as the project manager, knew each part of the project thoroughly, so he was inevitably needed.

"Yes sir, sure, I will," Singh replied, deciding that he would talk to Amit about his concerns, no matter what.

After this discussion, David went to the conference room to check the status of the work. The work had to be paused for a while, as a large sub-module was creating a lot of problems for the teams. David just warned Singh- "Please make sure it is completed on time!" and proceeded to see the status of the team members. He decided to stay there until the work on this stage was finished, and was motivating the team to somehow get this sub-module into the system. Singh himself was motivated when David got to a computer and started looking at the flowcharts. He checked the diagrams and made some changes to the proposed architecture. The changes looked trivial but worked.

This gesture proved to be enough, the sub-module was completed just in time to allow other stages enough time. From here on, the teams would not have faced much difficulties, they thought. They kept working zealously, as their goal was now within sight.

David waited there till a part of that stage was tested, and then came back to his office. He then switched on the TV. On a news channel was flashed- "Possible hand of excessive pesticides in the killing of Jaguars". Yes, the news was very disturbing to anyone.

"Why these animals, which are close to extinction? You could have considered humans, God!" David uttered in grief. But God had already taken two of his gems with him, and he did not even know.

The NIA team that was deployed to search for Shukla and others returned from their respective locations, and there was no lead on him anywhere, not a trace. But all this while, they had not noticed that Shukla's laptop went missing after he went missing. This was brought to their notice now, when they asked for his laptop to the NIC members. Mohan explained the whole story.

They thought that if the laptop could be taken from his office, it was possible that Shukla was somewhere nearby. Of course, they could not be certain about it. Still, the team checked all the offices in the vicinity. No trace of these people. Moreover, Shukla's laptop had not been synchronised with the NIC server for cloud backup and other facilities. This was to maintain the confidentiality of Shukla's work, which was paramount. But this proved to be a major setback to the investigations. Had it been synced, the laptop would have communicated something to the NIC system, but it hadn't. Tired, not knowing what to do now, the investigation teams aborted the operation for the day.

The development teams managed to finish the fifth stage by midnight, and decided to take a small break of about fifteen minutes. Shifts were to change, but no one left the centre, planning to take small naps there itself. Pizzas were flowing in now. People thanked the office mess for being closed. The teams were ready for the big thing. After the break, they started the sixth stage, and were positive that the insertion of the basic safe modes would not take more than seven hours.

Earlier in the day, David and Singh went to the NIA headquarters and met Amit, who had just finished his daily report to the Home

Minister. In the meeting, they discussed everything that the NIA local software group would do. Amit assured his full cooperation to the NIC, and wanted to know more about the dummy attack. Singh gave him a detailed explanation of all the events that had happened, starting from Shukla's phone call to the attack.

Amit was impressed at Shukla's perfectionism, and said he would want to congratulate him when he returned. But, all of them knew that it might not be possible. Amit also asked Singh to check the local databases of the NIA once, just to be safe that the data important for the intelligence was not altered till now, although it was highly impossible. NIC handled all the requests to this database too. Under quarantine conditions, the system was not vulnerable. But he also mentioned the need to expedite the process of recovery, as the whole data that NIA was gathering over the past few days was being handled solely on papers.

Now was the time for Singh to bring up his reservations about Shukla to Amit's notice. And he did that, telling him numerous reasons to not believe the others.

"Sometimes, we should believe in things which we hope would happen, my friend," Amit replied.

"Yes sir, but…"

"I know you are right about thinking of these possibilities, and I am sure that David has done it too. But the thing is, we will lose drive if we do not do it right now. It might be our only way to get them back. Do you have any other way, any other leads?"

"No, sir."

"I have spoken to David for a long time regarding this. You are not the first person who had these reservations. But this looks like the only positive way. I agree it is a gamble, but while gambling, you need to pick one option from the lot. We have just done that. Now don't think so much. Let us just work and get it done."

The meeting ended after half an hour. Singh realised that Amit must have considered all the possibilities. Only then would he have arrived at the conclusion.

The work on the last stage was not a complicated procedure, considering these top engineers had made this system in just 5 days. It was just a repetitive procedure, as the earlier stage was almost completely a larger version of this stage. The work was completed before time, just before 7.30 am on the 12th of April. Singh was now a relieved man. Again, there was a brief pause, and the teams started the integration and testing stage- the final stage.

As the work was on, something unusual again happened. The attack which had occurred the first time tried to surface again on the old system. But it was taking longer than it earlier had, which might be due to the quarantined state. But how could it be attacked? People knew that this time it would not be Shukla, as he had his message delivered loud and clear. Perhaps he had begun his work, whatever it was that he wanted to do with the old system, which would be good. But what if it was not him, but the virus hit again, as it had in the earlier times? With this possibility, the vulnerability was taken to a whole new level. Singh discussed with the teams about cutting down the integration and testing stage to just integration, and test the system after it was in operation. David gave a big thumb down to this, and said that he would rather turn the switches of the system off, if that was required.

"Test it thoroughly before operating," David instructed.

Singh spontaneously came up with an idea. He ordered his teams to do the job in half the time than what was required. Apart from these engineers, all the scientists and engineers at the office were called in, and were ordered to throw any attack they knew at the new system, which was now running a dummy database. This would help in testing the system in a much smaller time. He gave them exactly six hours to do so, after his team finished integration and linking the various modules. The final testing stage was to throw the actual dummy Ashtray that Shukla had used earlier at the system and check if the response was under the limits. All the people got to work.

The new attack on the system was averted again. But this time, the attack seemed to do nothing. It just sent a lot of ping messages, no changes were made to the databases. In fact, it didn't even touch the database, and was handled by the server itself, which threw it somewhere else. David was monitoring the attack. There was no message this time, and it seemed as if it was a futile attempt by some novice. On careful consideration, one could see that it was the quarantined state of the old system which was doing its job.

Was Ashtray leaked? Was Shukla tricked into doing something wrong? David had a feeling that something bigger was impending, as this attack was not sending any other signal.

FILTERS FOR HARMONY

April 12

It was 9.00 pm. While the filters had been deployed to the respective systems and the fission procedure initiated, it was not yet clear how they would work in real time environments. Shukla and Jai had not tested the code even once on a real system. They did not have the time to do that. It was risky to install the filters without testing them, but it was the only solution they had. Shukla now ordered Jai to test if the systems were actually compatible with the computers in Building 3. Jai did not have a choice there, if the systems were not compatible, he had to make them compatible. Shukla started getting into the depth of his initial plan, working out a strategy to port the filters out to the old NIC system.

Shukla was thinking of ways to get the filters out to each system present on the earth. He thought that the way the filters were being created here, a fission could be started to make the filters reach every computer. The old NIC system was, of course, the starting point of this. But he soon realised the restrictions to this. Jai had by now lessened the time requirement for the filter fission, but the time was small only for the systems here.

On the earth, according to Shukla's computer, it was to take exactly 79 days to replicate the filter on each computing device connected to the internet, provided the fission would not stop. He had estimated this based on the total number of processors that were sold by various companies in the past 8 years. This gave him a rough estimate of the number, and he added a buffer to it. But, there was no guarantee of it happening in the estimated time span. Nobody could have determined how the filter fission would spread. Since it was to be a virus-like program, the information systems could just filter it or scatter it the way the NIC database had done the first time. To add to this problem, the Governments of different countries would not risk putting out the specifications and details of their highly secure computers, hence Shukla would not be able to know if the filter actually had been placed. While securing the NIC, Shukla could use his knowledge of the systems there, but what was he going to do when he could not gather data from other systems?

The problems were numerous. He did not even know how many countries would agree to it, and if it was to be done diplomatically, there was no way that the world would ever come to a conclusion. The votes and vetoes would take up a considerable amount of time before anything could actually happen. Also, the enemy countries would not accept the proposal to work together. In such a case, the solution would be to commercialise the filters, and sell them with regulations. But the issue with this was that Shukla would not be able to control it, as companies would add unnecessary products to it to sell them, and in such cases, the primary goals of the filters might get lost. Plus, there was the problem of competition in such cases. The companies, as they would monetise the product, would fight for money. All these were forcing him to not think about porting the filters to the earth.

But the biggest problem Shukla faced was that he would have to reveal the filter, and ultimately how vulnerable the old NIC database was. Revealing the filter would mean giving open access to enemy countries to the NIC's computers. If reverse engineered properly, the NIC's system would be exposed. Infact, any system could be hacked if the filters were properly reverse engineered. Shukla was not ready to be rebuked and bear the caustic criticism that would arise out of this.

Jai was busy hitting the keys on his laptop, developing the test cases. These test cases were to be built considering the mighty nature of this project. Also, the test cases had to be designed considering that it was a live system that they were working on. So, Jai designed them in such a way that they could be deleted from the code that they were inserted into, if tested successfully. In all, he had 36 test cases. The test cases were built in the next two hours, before Shukla took his keeper and broadcasted a message to be displayed on the big screen.

"Testing about to begin. Hope for the best."

Within a span of 5 minutes, Nicole and Mr Hans were at Shukla's office, and there was a crowd gathering in the main hall, watching the big screen. Shukla once again went through the test cases to ensure that accidentally no test case would spoil the project. When he was assured, he gave a go-ahead to Jai. Mr Hans stood there spectating the events, while Nicole left to supervise other work and to check if any other aberrations were reported in the meanwhile.

Jai started with the first case. This was a simple case, which was about dealing with inputs. The test ran for a while, as Shukla used his own set of standards for the inputs. He had developed standard inputs that were to be fed. If the system gave the desired outputs, the system would pass. He had used these test cases effectively over the years. The first five cases passed without any problems, but the sixth one created a problem, though it was resolved very soon. No damage was done.

The real damage was discovered later, when the twenty-seventh test case was being executed. This was one of the internal coordination and communication checks. The problem, unnoticed till now, was worse than they had thought. The filters were designed to see that if Ashtray bypassed them, they would stop its further penetration into other computers. So, the problem here occurred when Jai realised that the filters were not able to curtail the internal damage that was done to the system. And this damage was not an alteration or modification, it was about the internal communication between various components of a computer. So, further internal transmission would not stop.

The message sending between various components too showed fission-like qualities. And although Shukla had verified the filter program himself, it did not occur to him that something so obvious could skip his eyes the first time. So, Jai had to make a patch to the original filters. All the people at the building were taken aback at the thought of installing the filters again, the same long procedure. But Jai had made it as a patch, so it was just to be transmitted to each computer there, which was not a problem. There was no fission involved, nor any physical work needed.

Testing took another two hours, and the updated filter program was ready to be sent to each system present in Building 3. Jai sent a text to Vineet and Nicole to come to his workplace, and told Shukla that the program was ready. Shukla wanted to check it himself and gave it just a glance, trusting that Jai would have tested it extensively. Shukla gave his final nod to Jai. Shukla had been putting messages for people to view on the big screen. It was as if he was posting updates on social media from time to time. The final one read-"Filters are about to be deployed now. Testing complete. Results in a while."

This message raised the anxiety of everyone present in building 3 on that day. For calculation of results of time needed to compute, more time would be needed. Shukla took a pen in his hand, and turned his keeper into a calculator screen. He then checked the difference between the actual time taken to run and the time that would ideally be needed. The time required for calculation and detection of an Ashtray attack was the most important part. If the time for detection went overboard, Ashtray might just penetrate the database. Shukla did his calculations and showed them to Jai to verify them. Jai approved them without much delay.

Shukla posted on his keeper- "Time taken for detection within bounds. Successful testing. Minor additions to the filters to be made."

There were some changes to be made to the filters, owing to

the test cases that did not pass easily. The twenty-seventh test case uncovered a major loophole in the system, and it was to be rectified, apart from some minor fixtures. The coding was to take some more time. Everyone just hoped that in the meantime, the filters would hold Ashtray somehow. If not kill it, just hold it. It took Jai and Shukla a while to design the solution to this minor problem.

The simple yet effective solution that Shukla had found was to isolate the attacked system from others, so that Ashtray would not advance further. How was this to be done? If the system recognised similar requests from multiple neighbours in quick succession or simultaneously, there was a high probability that the requests were generated by Ashtray. This strategy had a few drawbacks, for example, it could block requests in cases where they shouldn't be, at times. But it was a small drawback. Although multiple requests came to the system all the time, they were for fetching data, and not for updating it, while Ashtray fiddled with the data. This was the main principle behind the design.

Now the patch code for this solution was to be built. But Jai was no expert in the communication systems at Building 3. So he delegated the work to the maintenance department, which did the job in just 20 minutes. Jai was amazed at the swiftness of the people in the maintenance department. They speedily handed over the code to Jai. Jai was about to start patching up the previous code with this one.

Nicole and Vineet arrived in some time. Jai explained to both of them what exactly was to happen, and what the estimated time that would be taken was. The time taken was not a big factor this time, unlike when they had to embed filters into the Datrees along the barriers. Jai sought Nicole's permission to go ahead with it, and told Vineet to check the details.

"I will be right back. I need to check with authorities, although it looks promising." Nicole replied. "Yeah go ahead," said Shukla, as she left.

"Vineet, what are these authorities that she always keeps talking about? Earlier, this place looked like a farce to me, but I just decided to believe in it. So far I have believed in what we have done till now. But..." said Shukla.

"I have seen the working and everything. Although it is too good to be true, something tells me it is not right. This cannot be it," he continued.

"Sir, I understand. I have been in the maintenance department for a reason. I initially was supposed to work with you both, but I was appointed to work in some other department. I just had to verify that all this was correct. You were right in posting me there. All this while, I have looked at every possible nuance of this place, and sir, it certainly is the correct place. I can prove it to you if you want," replied Vineet.

"No that would not be required, I believe you. Right now, let's finish this problem and then look at the bigger one," said Shukla and started thinking again. Vineet and Jai started looking at the implementation details, as Vineet was the person who would initiate the action this time. Vineet was responsible for loading the program into the nerve centre's main computer, and then run it. Jai was going to monitor the whole operation, and had to tag each system, just the way Shukla had done the last time. Shukla was to be with Jai to assist in tagging, as this time the number of tags was going to be very large. But it was nothing to worry about. Jai had embedded the code for auto-tagging of a system after it was equipped with the filters and all the procedures were completed. So, their job was mere supervision, and in case a tag was missed, then they had to do it explicitly.

They started the work and the tagging began on its own. In a few moments, it was clear that the process was going on smoothly and it was time to relax. Although not completely, but they could take it easy now. Shukla was still thinking of porting the filters to the world. But he was still unsure of his strategy. And he could not discuss this with Jai as he was too busy at the moment.

"Listen, you both can handle this operation. I will think about the larger filter in the meantime. If anything is needed, I am here," said Shukla. Jai and Vineet had to agree to him. Nicole returned in a while, and gave a go-ahead to the team, but soon realized that the job had already started. Nicole was not angry this time; she was rather happy that they had started.

Shukla got busy calculating some figures on a piece of paper. Then he searched for the number of computers that were present in the world that day. This was going to need some time to analyse. Imagine any device in the world that could connect to the internet, be it computers, phones, laptops, tablets, other machines, etc. Every computer needed to have a filter. He was basically revising his earlier estimate of 79 days.

By now Shukla had decided that the job was to be done without informing anyone on earth. He had thought a lot about the consequences of announcing the threat. The problem was, how was he going to tell the Governments of other countries to allow the filters into their system? There was no chance that he could get everyone to agree on the concept of filters. This had been hovering over him for some time and he finally decided not to let anyone know about the filters. He had to find a way to secretly port it to all the computers. But the time estimate was too big. Nevertheless, he was working on his plan.

Vineet went straight to the maintenance department and briefed his team of four people about the patch operation when pinning was about to be completed. The maintenance department had some concerns with the patch program that was being run.

First, it was necessary to shut down the fission after all the nodes were equipped with the filter. Though this was a simple task, it would need a lot of time, as the fission process had to be stopped at the nodes reached most recently. That is, if eight nodes went through the process in the last stage, then the fission had to be halted at all the eight nodes. Vineet had his trusted team ready for this job. This was to be done so that all the nodes had the final patched code up and running in them.

Second, when the filtering process was on, it could happen that the node could go out of operation, as the node's scripts were being tweaked. And after this, it needed to be refreshed and connected to the nerve centre, where it would be double pinned on Jai's keeper, which was now being projected on the big screen too. These issues were to be resolved during the implementation itself. The teams had to make sure that the refreshing of the nodes happened in such a way that the backup nerve centre was connected to the nerve centre at all times, so that even if the data might not be available, the query could still be put into a wait state.

Although they had these concerns, they proceeded with the work. Vineet's team did very well to make sure that while the patch was being done, none of the systems caused any serious trouble. They were able to curtail anything that could make that system useless. The pinning of the systems was happening rapidly now. Having that extra time in which Jai could make the program for the pinning was a major factor that fastened the process.

After all the nodes were pinned, the backup nerve centre was to be accoutred with the filters, making the whole of building 3 secure.

Jai initiated the procedure and ordered Vineet to proceed with loading the program. The double pinning began in some time, with a small pin appearing on each node that was visible on the giant screens all over, with a characteristic 'ping' sound. The pins continued to spread all over, and Jai was happy to see that all was working smoothly. His time estimate was about 35-40 minutes until the whole place was secure.

All the nodes were to be backed-up by the backup nerve centre all this while. The engineers earlier had specially designed a backup nerve centre that could last that long, as the older one was not capable enough. This backup system was the one on which Vineet had been working on earlier. It was capable of standing for about two hours, before going down. But it was capable of only keeping the system working, no querying was possible on it. It would instead queue the requests. When Ashtray had attacked and the system was in hibernation, the maintenance department had not allowed Vineet to use this backup system. The reason stated was that this system was newly built, and it was surely unable to handle Ashtray. Vineet wanted to pick up the risk then, but could not.

All the nodes were pinned in exactly 36 minutes, and the backup nerve centre was immediately disconnected from them after completion of this task to prevent any damage to it. The maintenance team got into action now, as Jai reported the nodes where fission had to be stopped. He called out the number of each node to which the maintenance department had to act on. They stopped the fission reaction at all the nodes, 32767 exactly. Now, the backup nerve centre had to undergo a similar procedure and the task was performed effortlessly in the next 5 minutes. The maintenance team initiated an automatic testing and error check program which they had built for all the databases there, and declared everything to be perfect after "TESTED O.K." was displayed on the screens. All the databases were safe!

Shukla was looking at Jai's laptop, who was sitting beside him giving orders all this while. "Good job!" he exclaimed, and felt really happy. Jai and Vineet would now have felt blissful. All the operations there were done, and they could go home after that, they thought. Jai was excited as he would be getting a new job at the NIC, as Shukla had promised him. "These poor lads," Shukla said to himself, as he decided not to tell them the reality. They were looking ecstatic and Shukla did not want to spoil the moment. After some time, Jai even suggested Shukla that they could add filters to each device on earth, and he would undertake the whole operation when they got back to NIC. Shukla did not react to this.

Meanwhile, the alert buzzer began ringing, the big screen showing- "Backup system multiple alterations."

MAYDAY

April 12,13

The system at NIC had just experienced some abrupt movements, and so did the one at Building 3. Was it coincidental? Or had the ultimate destruction begun? Despite the filters and all the drama that had happened to put them in place, all the sleepless hours put in by Shukla, Jai and the others seemed to have done nothing substantial. It could be expected that Ashtray might attack the NIC system, but how did it attack the backup biological IS? It was equipped with the filters, and was being tested. So what went wrong? And if the backup system was attacked, it was highly probable that the original system would be attacked in some time. It was time for some speed.

The problem had happened because while the patch program was being inserted into the Datrees-Ashtray had already reached them. They were pinned only after Ashtray had reached them. This allowed Ashtray enough time to get into action. But since the filters were operative and only the patchwork was not done, the spreading of the attack was curtailed to a few nodes only. In all, forty-one fields were updated, which was a small number compared to the size of that database. But if the criticality of that data was to be thought of, it was a significant number.

The maintenance team now had to nullify the effect of this attack. They did not have any sophisticated tool to do it. They had to check each modified field, and copy the data from the original database to it, to nullify the effect. It seemed like a simple task, but it was critical. If a field had a time in the death time field that corresponded to the current time, it was needed right now. Thus, the main system would be busy satisfying the request, and the field would not be copied. In such a case, there would be multiple attempts to copy, which could lead to errors.

The team first checked the times from the main database, and selected a time that would be free for all the fields. The team could copy the fields at this instant. It was set to 8.27 pm, 31 seconds that day. The team gave instructions to the system to update the fields at that time. The job was done automatically by the system.

Up in their office, Jai and Shukla popped their keepers to view the whole modifications that were made to the backup system, trying to get a hold of the impact this time. Fortunately, it had not reached the core system. Nicole suggested building another backup system, as, although the backup system's data was restored, there was a chance that Ashtray might reach it. What Nicole suggested was to build a new backup system and isolate it from the outside world. It had to have contact with only the main system, and would be hibernated when it was idle. Whenever a threat to the main system would be detected, the main system would hibernate itself, and forward the requests to this backup system. This would reduce the chances of the backup system being attacked. This way, there would be three systems: the main system, the first backup system and this second backup system.

This seemed to be a very good plan, of course, if the implementation reduced contact with the outside world to a zero. And since there was only a one-point connection to the main system, the chances of this system being attacked were nil, unless the filters could not detect attacks at the main system. She discussed the plan with the maintenance team. Vineet delegated the work to the other maintenance staff. They were ordered to finish the construction of this system in the next 4 days. Shukla and Jai did not have to bother themselves with this work. Vineet was required to give this new system a final check after it was created. And he was sure that it would work just fine. So, this was the time for a bit of relaxation. All of them had not slept properly for a long time now, and decided to do just that.

After sleeping for only a few minutes in his office chair itself, Shukla took out the same piece of paper from his pocket on which he had been performing the calculations earlier. He was working on some sort of a plan, and looking at him, it was visible that he was getting nowhere. But he was constantly scribbling something on that paper. After about thirty minutes, he thought that he had enough to tell others. Shukla readied himself to explain his plans to all the people present in Building 3. He might need their support for the work he was planning. And he knew that no one would be willing to help him at first, considering it was not their job. He started preparing a speech to convince all the teams present there. But he soon discovered that the content he had to explain was not powerful enough for him to convince them.

Vineet was sleeping in his bedroom, when his keeper buzzed very loudly. He didn't hear it the first time, but the second time, he almost fell down off his bed due to the high volume. The keeper's volume was controlled by Nicole, who had raised it. He was summoned by Mr Hans to his office for some reason which Nicole did not know. He asked for permission for an extra half an hour to complete his slumber. He had not slept for the past two days, and his sleep before that too was not very comforting. He set the alarm for half an hour from now, and went back to sleep. He woke up at the scheduled time, and straight away went to Mr Hans' office. On reaching there, he found Mr Hans having a look at the report of the backup system attack that the maintenance department had handed over to him.

"Hi Vineet. Hope you slept well. Did you?"

"Sir, sleeping well is not permitted at this time. Although I did sleep enough."

"Yeah, I guess that is okay. Do you need tea or coffee or anything else?"

"Sir, a cup of tea would be fine." Mr Hans himself went to the machine and prepared a cup of tea and a cup of coffee. He took the coffee for himself. He offered the tea to Vineet, and sat back in his chair.

"Sir, how may I help you?" Vineet asked.

"Yes, you definitely can help me. I just read the report of the attack on the backup system. Do you think something might have happened to the original system as well?"

"Sir, from the data that we gathered, there was no effect on the original system. Only the backup system was affected."

"Okay, if you say so, I agree with you there." Mr Hans sipped his coffee. "Did you have any private meetings with Shukla?"

"Yes sir, we met once to discuss the work."

"Okay, any personal discussions?"

"No sir. But is there something I should know?"

"Yes. He is working on something on his own. If he asks for a meeting with you alone, please inform me first. It might help us all."

"But, is there anything I should be wary of?"

"No. I guess that would be it. You may get back to work."

Vineet finished the tea in his glass and went to the adjoining washroom that Shukla had earlier thought to be an exit. But Vineet did not notice the EXIT sign over there, he knew that it was a washroom. He then went to his bedroom to get changed, post which, he had to be at the maintenance department.

All this while he kept thinking about what Mr Hans meant by what he said. After thinking a lot, he could zero in on a few reasons. He had noticed that Shukla had acted weird on a few occasions since he was here, and he thought this could be the reason. Also, Shukla's scepticism towards the whole concept of Building 3 which was cleared by Vineet could be the reason for Mr Hans to think there was something wrong with Shukla. He decided not to think much about it, as the reasons Shukla had were trivial, and Shukla was now convinced that the place was real. But he agreed with Mr Hans when he said that Shukla was working on something on his own.

Shukla till now had an eclectic list of possible solutions, all too futile to prevent Ashtray on earth. He had spoken to Jai briefly about a solution, and Jai could easily explain how Ashtray would penetrate a system which included that solution. Shukla's only possible way now was to implement the filters designed for here over there-a time consuming, money eating procedure. Before that, he would have to explain all these concerns to the people at building 3.

Shukla decided to defer talking to people about it for some time. He first spoke to Jai about the solutions that he planned. He had a note in his hand which read:

1. Back filter

2. Substitution

3. Crash: kill the systems

4. Hibernate the virus

After a lot of researching and thinking, Shukla had decided that the final solution was one amongst these. So he started explaining each one of them to Jai.

"I talked to you about implementing the filters for the whole world, right. So now with the improved solutions, and some more optimisations, we can think of doing it, like setting standards in the world where all the people would have to update their systems," started Shukla.

"Yes sir, but you also mentioned the problems of Governments and secret agencies not cooperating, which could make it futile. Also, there is the time restriction, sir. Who knows how much time it would take for each person to get the implemented version from the internet even though we create a free ware," added Jai.

"That is what is bothering me. But it is something that needs to be looked into a lot more Jai, as it could be our best chance," Shukla explained.

"Let me first explain to you everything that I have thought which could give us a chance. The second technique that I have thought would be to substitute Ashtray. If we make Ashtray into a system which can act as a vaccine to itself, maybe we could have a chance, right? What I mean by that is if we modify the original program so that it becomes self-inhibitory, the job could be done. But again, you can see the problems clearly. We do not know how to inject this into the original program which is currently killing jaguars. I have absolutely no clue."

Jai nodded, waiting to hear the next solution.

"Which brings me to the next solution-to hibernate the virus for some time. You get what I mean by it?"

"To some extent. You want me to change the sequencing of the virus so that it is not able to attack the systems that it reaches for some time; after which it may continue on its path. That is, delay the action of Ashtray, right?"

"Absolutely, we need to make sure that there is enough time for the owner of the system to install the filters. Again, the problem here is that we cannot insert this change into the original Ashtray, I guess," continued Shukla.

"Yes sir. In both the cases, it is required that the original program be modified. But as you can see, the original program has already begun its journey into the outside world, and it won't be possible to curtail it, unless…" He paused for a second, and then continued- "Sir, you may continue. I will think on it later."

"The fourth solution is simple, we need to just put a program in the systems such that the system switches off as soon as Ashtray reaches it, and thus it would not progress further. Although it will stay in the system, it will not cause any further harm. But, switching off? Not a good solution at all."

Jai continued Shukla's explanation, "And there is an added risk if the system ever connects to the internet unless Ashtray is completely removed from that system. Removing Ashtray from an attacked system is a tough process sir. We have seen it already over here. Earth will be a lot more complex than what we have done here, I suppose."

"Oh yes, you are right. It will be a lot more complex. But still, we need to think of something."

"So I need you to think a lot about all these, and try each of them to secure the planet," said Shukla, as Jai nodded. "Of course, you will have to improvise a lot on these. These are just the primary level solutions that I could think of. Think of what you can do with these possible solutions. The answer lies somewhere near these."

"Yes sir, let me see what I can do with these solutions, and pick up the best one of them." Jai immediately got to work, switching from his keeper to his laptop. Shukla decided to go to Nicole, and report all that he had till now. He told her his plan to replicate the filters for earth as well. He tried to convince her that it was necessary, and he and Vineet were already working on it.

While there were problems with his methods, there was a far bigger problem. Shukla had realised that to make any of the solutions work, he would have to send out messages and codes to the starting point of the chain reaction. But how? He had thought of sending out messages in a way which he had used earlier, but there was a huge risk associated with it. The last time it was done, order on earth had been disrupted. That time, only 31 jaguars were killed. Who knew what could happen this time. Even though they had secured Building 3, why take the risk? Although there were filters in place for Ashtray now for the biological IS, it was not known to anyone what would happen if Ashtray reached the nerve centre somehow, as the filters were available only to prevent the virus from the biological system.

They did not stop the propagation of the virus. And there were other ISs too. The danger of Ashtray affecting the other ISs still remained. This would make sending messages like last time impossible, at least until the other ISs were secured with filters.

Nicole heard out Shukla's plans, and clearly told him that the management would not approve of the opening of the barriers again.

"Leave aside the databases of the earth. It would cause harm, of course, but not so much that humans would be wiped out," Nicole added to her discussion.

Shukla, on the other hand, was doggedly putting forth his statements to make sure that the human race would not face the brunt of a data wipe out. Both of them kept arguing, and they could find no solution to the problems. Towards the end of it, Nicole had given Shukla permission to first find a perfect solution of the four that he had chosen, and then she would make a pitch to the senior management. Shukla was elated at the victory.

But she had to remind him that his job with the Informatics of Earth was not done. He was yet to secure the other ISs. Only the biological IS was secured. All that was linked to it was at a much bigger risk now, as Ashtray was in the system, although dormant. Shukla and Jai did not have the time to secure the other ISs under the circumstances. Shukla had to convince her that the job was similar to the biological IS, and the maintenance team would be able to handle it. They would also secure the nerve centre, so that the barriers could be opened. Or someone else could, if they were too busy. He convinced her that his job now was to secure the earth from a data disaster.

Jai had started working on the solutions, the first one of which, the filters, was just about reducing the time requirements and the linkages. He had been able to reduce the complexity to a mere 30 milliseconds for the filter to install on a system, after which the system would have to be restarted. Although the time seemed too small for one system, it was still large, as all the systems would take 30 milliseconds each to have an active filter, after the filters reached their systems. Jai started thinking about the next solution.

Substitution required the original program to be modified, and to make those modifications, Jai would have to implement new strategies. He started working on his laptop, when his keeper showed a pop-up- "Hooray! Permission almost done," from Shukla. He could see how Shukla must have negotiated with Nicole and Mr Hans. He promptly replied to Shukla and told him to get back as soon as possible. He continued with his work on the second solution, then the fourth and finally, the third, the easiest of them all. But again, none of it was constructive enough to make it a complete, fool proof mechanism, and he was frustrated by now.

Shukla had to make a stop at Mr Hans' office to explain what he was about to do. He decided to do it himself this time, as he felt that Nicole herself was reluctant about the solution. So if she had to talk about it, she might take away the permission from him.

Meanwhile, Ashtray had started bouncing back and forth between the NIC office and the Building 3 core network, as the effects were felt on the old NIC database, via the smaller, harmless attack. Although this seemed to be a dummy attack, it was as if ashtray was learning something from the system, and would pitch a stronger and more impactful attack in the near future. Shukla was back at his place when all this started to happen, and while the maintenance team was able to shut down the backup system to prevent further attacks, he knew his colleagues at NIC would be facing trouble.

Shukla ordered reports to where the attack had reached from the NIC's system, and started thinking of ways to combat the attack through a channel to the NIC. All the information from the earth that he needed was available to him. He was now almost certain that he would be able to negotiate a deal to let him form a tunnel for communicating again.

After a few minutes, Vineet delivered the reports Shukla had requested. It was clearly visible that the attack had reached not just the NIC, but some systems that were connected to the NIC-the President's Office, the Prime Minister's Office, some Governmental sites, and the Unique Identification Database. Some foreign agencies were also in trouble, it seemed. Shukla only saw the reports of the systems linked to the NIC. He could only imagine what would be happening to the internet around the world. It was mayday.

DELIRIUM

April 13

It was the day of destruction, Shukla had realised. Building 3 seemed calm everywhere, except Jai and Shukla's office. Vineet had joined them, and was monitoring the report along with Shukla. Jai was continuously staring at his laptop, and the sound of his fingers hitting the keys was irritating Shukla now. But Shukla was in no mood to say anything to him. It was the early hours of the 13th of April now, and the placid atmosphere at the building was enough for Shukla's eyes to shut down. But his mind said otherwise. Shukla was desperate to do something for the earth. He was frustrated now.

This was the time when he needed Mohan the most. Mohan had always been there in times like these, and he always had stories to tell which would cheer Shukla up. Also, through these stories, Shukla had always found some or the other inspiration or a solution, somehow. And it was not that Mohan told stories which were new. They were the most common ones, but he made sure that he told the right story at the right time. Shukla tried to recall all of his stories that could help him find a solution or an inspiration.

"Vineet, can you tell me a story, the way Mohan used to tell always?" asked Shukla

"Even I am searching for something inspirational Shuklaji. I just wish Mohan was here. Should we call him?"

"No. Please don't. No more people are to be called here. Please."

"Okay sir, okay. I won't."

To refresh his mind, Shukla took some time off. His eyes did not allow him to stay awake anymore, and he slept in Jai's bedroom, which was near their office. After about two hours, he woke up, tensed and still not knowing what to do. He still felt dizzy, but he could not sleep. He went to the washroom to take a shower, and decided to return to the office after changing.

Jai and Vineet started with their own jobs-Jai working on the solutions, and Vineet predicting the next systems that would be under attack, or already were under attack. Vineet's keeper was constantly refreshing with updates on systems on the earth that were under attack.

Jai had been working on a way to shut down the systems that Ashtray attacked. This solution looked a bit more promising to him than the others. His plan was simple, if Ashtray was detected, the system would go off completely without any backup. All unsaved data would be lost. Jai had not had the time to think of any solutions of his own. And his mind was not in a state of thinking of something new anymore. He had decided to just implement each one of them, with improvisations to them.

After a gruelling coding session, Jai had each one of the solutions implemented partially, but not to his surprise, none of them was enough for preventing destruction. In fact, two of them could actually act like vaccines to Ashtray, and make it immune to such defences later on. He felt that his job was useless. But due to the mental fatigue he was experiencing, he did not even have the power to argue with Shukla about it. The exercise was taking a toll on him now, but he could not afford to rest, at least not before explaining to Shukla what he had implemented. After that, if there was some time, he could try to get some sleep. Vineet was watching him when he was implementing, he could clearly see that his eyes were blood red, and the ire showed on his face.

Shukla met Nicole on his way back to his and Jai's office. It seemed like she was rushing towards the office. Shukla asked her what the matter was. "You remember the boss telling you how you will never go back? Well, I am going to deliver the same message to your colleagues. I will make it quick. It is time they knew. You don't have to worry about it anymore," said Nicole.

"Oh no, please do not do it so early. My team would break if you told them so early. Please let's just wait till I find a solution to the problems out there. And I can see that it will happen sometime soon. Please allow me a little time. If needed, I myself will deliver the message to them, just that I won't do it now. Please, Nicole!" Shukla begged. But she was helpless this time, it was her boss who had strict orders for her, and she would be punished if they were not followed. "Can I talk to the boss once?" Shukla asked, realising from the looks on her face that it was not under her control.

"No, the boss is firm on it, he does not want anyone to have any false beliefs," replied Nicole.

"Well if that is the case, why didn't you explain it to them earlier? Why now, when we are thinking specifically about the human race, and not the whole ecosystem? We have finished our job of securing this place to a fair extent, and I think we deserve a chance to save the human-made systems. Aye?" replied Shukla, his tone rising in frustration. Nicole ignored him and went ahead anyways to explain the situation to Jai and Vineet.

Shukla called up Mr Hans straight away.

"Mr Hans, I came to know from Nicole that you have told her to deliver the message to my team as well. Sir, I am sure that it will worsen the current situation, and there is a lot of work left. Please understand my point of view."

"Shukla, what I have told her to do is a decision taken with the utmost care and consideration for everyone. I am sure that this is the best time to tell them. They will not take much time to get back to work; even you were back to work pretty soon when I told you about it. I must say, Shukla- you have a brave heart."

"All that is fine. But do I have to tell you again that this is a very critical juncture in the mission. We almost have the code for saving every system on the earth." He paused after he said this. He felt breathless for a moment. He thought, "Is this deliberately being done so that humans become extinct? Is it seriously the end?"

"Shukla, please do not worry about anything. It won't be a problem in the long term. Let Nicole do her job," replied Mr Hans.

But Shukla was thinking now. Was apocalypse going to happen so soon? And in this way? The answer to these questions was given by Mr Hans to him just before he disconnected the keeper.

"Shukla, I am saying this one last time. Nothing is going to happen. Don't be so sceptical." Although Shukla had reservations, he also knew that Mr Hans was a noble man above everything else. So he believed in him. And at the same time, he trusted Nicole as well. She was not someone who would be easily influenced by someone else's decision, even if it was Mr Hans. She must have thought it through before coming to their office for explaining it to Jai and Vineet.

She delivered the message in one go, loud enough and clear. Both Jai and Vineet remained stunned, the revelation was just too hard to digest. Pictures started running through their brains, and everything looked hazy to them. Shukla imagined what those boys were going through and himself felt guilty of keeping the information about not returning from them. It was going to take some time, perhaps long before the boys came to their senses and did their jobs.

Shukla himself was reminded of the time when Mr Hans had shaken him with this news. And for a while he felt low. But this time, he wondered what had actually happened with their database entries when they came here. If they were dead, their fields in the database would have to be modified, but since Shukla had arrived, he had not seen any deliberate alteration to the database (he got the reports of any update to the database on his keeper) apart from the time Ashtray attacked the IS. So, was this a signal that he was still alive? Or was he really dead, and no one cared to tell him that the fields were modified. Or was there a different procedure altogether? But he saw hope due to this thought.

Before he knew it, his mind was thinking about the escape plan which he had conceptualized of earlier. He had estimated that he would use Ashtray, the original one, to do the job for him. For this, he would need to locate the database entries against his name. By this time, he knew that the database entries were not stored with names, but using some unique IDs. He had no idea how these IDs were generated, but he thought that the computer which used to predict the lifetimes of people would be the one doing the job. Although it was a wild guess, Shukla had always been positive that he would eventually find his way out. It took him some time to come out of this impossible diversion.

Instead of talking to Vineet and Jai, he left them alone, thinking that time alone shall teach them. He took up the job from Vineet, and started monitoring the systems under attack. Looking at Vineet's keeper was painful, it showed the world falling apart, in a way. This might be the beginning of the dawn of the information age. Various thoughts were flashing through his mind. But he had the grit to try and improve upon the one solution present. He decided that instead of monitoring which systems were going down, it would be better if he thought about which systems were to be prevented from the damage. And he knew that there were a lot of them, the number was still huge. He decided to look up at Jai's implementations of the solutions, to suggest possible improvements, although time was running out.

Before that, Shukla looked at the database audits of the NIA database that were performed a day earlier, looking at the disruptions in the fields of databases. He had just received news that the NIA system had been shut down, and the Government was performing checks and restoration of lost data. This was another reason for him to be on earth. He knew exactly how to handle everyone while performing his duties. According to his estimates, a new system would be ready by now at the NIC in all probability, and the old NIC system would be demolished any moment now.

He was thinking of sending a message again, but owing to the complexity and the negotiations required to get permissions from the authorities, he aborted the plan. Also, he would not be able to do it illegally, as the maintenance department had ensured that such communications would not be possible in the future.

Jai and Vineet were still in their period of sorrow, and time did not allow them to even weep properly. The time called for work, and Jai realised it sooner than Vineet. He was back to work within 15 minutes since Nicole had told them. The plan was now being discussed. Shukla had the permission for making the tunnels to the old NIC system. In fact, Shukla had done the whole job of forming communication channels in the form of these tunnels to the NIC database. Only the program for the filters was not ready. And Shukla himself was not able to finalise which method would suit the project.

Meanwhile, Singh announced that the implementation of Raakh 1.1 was complete, and the old system would be crushed as soon as David gave the orders. It was 9 pm on the 13th of April. The job was done well before its deadline, and David was pleased at the team's effort. He called Mohan to his office, and the three of them got into discussions about switching off the old one.

Mohan had piously held to his support for Shukla, and told David that they should not do anything to the system unless a message was received. But Singh and David were of the opposite view. As the attack had resurfaced, it would be the best to turn it off at that instant.

"But, Shukla wants that system for implementing his antivirus, maybe. What will he do without our support," reiterated Mohan.

"Yeah, but what if Shukla has been turned?" said Singh. Again he stated the reasons which were still in his mind. But this time he could be believed; after the first communication from Shukla, there was no further communication. Why was there no communication if Shukla wanted the old system desperately? Above all, why was Shukla not in the office if he had to find solutions? Well, maybe Jai wanted to do it furtively and include only Shukla. But why would Shukla not inform the NIC? All these were reasons enough for Singh to strengthen his belief that Shukla was on the other side of this war.

Singh was finally able to put forth his views about the matter to David again assertively, and this time he put it in such a way that David could not shun him. This time, David could not thrash Singh. The reasons of Singh's disbelief were same as before, but the time was different now. Project Raakh was complete now. David had to choose a side, Mohan on one side, and Singh on the other.

David was in a dilemma over the whole issue, and could not pick up what he should do to stop the destruction. "There has to be a trade-off, right?" he asked both of them. He ordered Singh to discuss the possibilities with each one of his team members and come back to him, within an hour. He ordered Mohan to try communicating with Shukla, by trying to set up a channel to the location from where the dummy Ashtray had arrived.

Mohan had already tried all the methods he knew to find the address, to no success. But he decided to give it another shot. The path through which the message arrived earlier was too complex. The only way he could communicate was if he embedded the message in the Ashtray source code. If this reached the sender, that is, Shukla through an attack, his job was done. But this was cumbersome and tedious, so David did not allow him to do this. He told him to rather concentrate on finding the source, and then send the message. Never in his career had Mohan seen his team take so much time to find the location of a computer. They would usually find out every detail of a computer within minutes.

After exhausting the small probability of embedding the message in Ashtray, Mohan was unable to think. But he had to think of some alternative way to communicate with Shukla. After losing all hopes of finding a perfect method to send the message, he decided to float the message on an open channel, and hoped that it would reach Shukla somehow.

The message read-

"SIR, OLD NEEDED?"

It was as if he wrote a message on a piece of paper, made a paper boat, and hoped that it would reach the destination, once he put it in water. He had not worried about the direction of flow, the currents, and the possibility of the paper getting wet. In this case, the message could be lost due to time outs in the communication channels. It could also be stolen by anyone, and altered as well. But he did not care about anything, he just wanted to have some conversation with Shukla.

He also had to submit the report of the whole project Raakh, so that it could be mailed to all the governmental agencies whose systems were not directly under the NIC, for example the NIA. All the systems that were under the NIC were protected automatically. But others would have to implement a package that these people had developed that would work to stop Ashtray from penetrating systems. The package would also make sure that Ashtray's sender was uncorrupted due to Ashtray. It would also be sent to the latest sender automatically to destroy Ashtray over there as well. The NIC claimed that once this was installed, the offices could buy enough time for the creation of a new system, with full-fledged features similar to the new NIC database. NIC issued highly detailed guidelines for each office to create a new system, along with the antivirus package.

After his meeting with David, Singh headed straight to his team, and found half of them planning parties, while the others were in deep slumber. He woke each one of them personally, and brought each person into the central hall. He took a mike from the podium, and started talking in a desperate but confident voice.

"Fellow mates, congratulations on completing the job before time. Every one of you has performed extremely well, and we shall surely party in some time. It's just that, we need to make sure that the calamity is completely circumvented. I need your help, probably for the last time before we can celebrate. All of you must be knowing about the dilemma over Shukla. So the question is, should we shut down the system right now, or should we wait for a communication from Shukla. I need each one of you to explain your reasons, so please think about it before speaking. Please explain your reasons! Am I clear? Any doubts?"

Everyone nodded to this, and started thinking. In a few minutes, David decided to hear the verdict of each person. He also decided to take a vote. People started throwing up their thoughts, and most of them had already been thought over by David, Singh and Mohan. A few people told bizarre stuff that was risible, at first. Of these, someone mentioned that it was a bad time for Shukla and Vineet, and the NIC would have to conduct a 'Puja' in office that very day to bring them back. One person maintained that Shukla and all the missing people might have been picked up by the intelligence agencies, and the NIC's database was used as a propaganda to spread something similar to the virus, and collect all the data. It seemed ridiculous, as David personally knew the top bosses of all the intelligence agencies there. But what if Shukla was recruited by a foreign intelligence agency? It was worth giving a thought.

After listening to the verdicts of people, David found himself more confused. He was unable to get over the delirium. After some thinking, he decided that they should just wait for some more time, and then activate the procedures for destruction. Mohan and Singh, although partially in disagreement over the issue, had to accede to their boss. The time for beginning the destruction of the old system was set to four hours from now. The time limit had been set up after considering the time gap it normally took for their system to completely shut down in case of an attack. Although it was not a logically justified move, they just thought that it must be related and went ahead. They just had to wait now for the next four hours for a message to arrive from Shukla.

THE REAL ONE STRIKES

April 12, 13, 14

A young engineer working on his start-up website in Silicon Valley had just found out that his website had been under a major DDoS attack. He brought this to the notice of an expert in security, who tried his best to resolve the attack. But the attack happened again and again. After a few attempts, it became so severe that the system on which the server was hosted started crashing multiple times. And this engineer did not have enough money to have a backup server. He was disappointed now and had started losing hopes of his company ever making it big in the valley. He was already facing problems acquiring funding for his venture. The security expert could not even analyse the system properly, as every time he tried to, the system would collapse. But he made notes on the technical aspects of the attack.

As was a rule with these techies, they would report any serious attacks over forums and social networking sites. So the security guy went on, updated his Facebook and twitter statuses, and posted the nature of the attack in a blog. He also posted it on a few forums that were restricted only to his friends, and cautioned everyone. They both were helpless, unless someone really good at this could help them.

After a while, he had a few comments and updates that the attack was not only on his computer, but was spreading wildly. It had reached 251 peers, when he checked. This was only the number of people who posted about the attack on the internet. There must be a large number of people who would not post, he estimated. But this seemed severe enough for implementing new protocols and standards, he thought.

After about 4 hours, the whole internet was filled with stories of similar attacks, and no one could help. Only those companies who had multiple servers were likely to survive it for longer. This was very much evident. The tech giants sitting in Silicon Valley, the outsourcing industry in India, the research universities throughout the world were looking at this attack, wondering where this big loophole had been. This loophole was not restricted to a few computers; it was with the essentials of computing. This was clear to everyone.

A newspaper article published in Australia was titled: The Dawn of the New: Computer age faces its biggest challenge ever. The article clearly described the scope of this attack. It stated that the end of the current world of computing could come, unless something which was quick and globally distributable was not thought of at once. The Internet Engineering Task Force (IETF), the security agencies governing the internet and the tech companies ruling the internet met online on that day itself, to decide what to do about it.

They had concluded that the attack was spreading fast, so they had to shut down the most vulnerable systems for a while. But there lay the problem, the internet is so loose, that to find which ones are vulnerable would not just be tough, it would be like finding blunt needles in a bundle of billions of needles. To design a software for the purpose was too tough as they had no clue about the nature of this virus. The best engineers in the world were recruited and made to decide policies which could guide the implementation of such a system. It was unanimously decided to keep money out of it, not because there was no scope for monetisation, but because there was not enough time for it. It would take months for commercialising a product.

While this meeting was happening, systems reported crashing around the world. Many countries' government websites started facing flak from the common people, as their work was being delayed. There were momentary crashes in even the most secure websites. As a result, people started deferring online payments, not trusting the payment gateways anymore, online booking systems started to fail, and the losses grew at an expeditious rate. The app ecosystems that had people hooked on to them were going through their toughest tests. Many apps failed to connect to their servers, and all the ones who had a centralised system could have gone down any moment from now.

Till now, there were always talks that the current generation was a slave of computers and technology. It was the first time now that these slaves were unable to eat their bread as the masters were unable to take care of themselves, let alone feeding the slaves and paying them.

Mr Goyal, Jai's father was reading reports of this crisis in the world. His hands trembled as he wondered if his child was involved in this attack, by any chance. He had heard that Jai was assisting in matters of national importance. His son disappearing all of a sudden; NIC, NIA getting involved to search for him; his phone not reachable for days now; no report on him; it was easy for him to connect the dots. But he had to stay calm at this moment, it might be the other way round as well. Maybe he was the one who would act against this crisis and save the world, he would be a hero then. There was a lot that he could speculate. He convinced himself not to, but after intervals, the thoughts would come to his mind.

In the evening that day, Mr Goyal decided to call Shukla. He got his number from a telephone directory and called him straightaway, only to be disappointed. He then called the NIC headquarters. As soon as he said, "This is Mr Goyal, Jai's father," the phone was redirected to David by an associate. David explained to him the scenario just enough, not disclosing details that his son was the culprit, neither did he say anything about his whereabouts. He just assured him that he would be safe soon, and he was not involved in this crisis. But Mr Goyal was not convinced. He was silenced just for the time being.

A reply was posted to a thread started by the security expert earlier. The reply was from one Dr Aravind Sharma, and it was a detailed description of what could have happened. Basically, Aravind had posted whatever he could infer from the one talk he had with Shukla a few days earlier. He did not post details about Shukla, as he knew that Shukla's job was very secretive, and he could not disclose details publicly. But the description of the attack that he posted was intricate. It didn't take much time for the IETF to notice this. Soon, he was requested to be in a chat session with the conclave that had met earlier to discuss and implement the solutions to this problem.

Aravind was speaking with people from China, India, USA, Germany, Australia, Singapore, Russia and Brazil at once. The task force consisted of 36 people now, and they were looking at the possible solutions. Aravind was eager to call Shukla. He had tried earlier but Shukla's phone had been unreachable. Once or twice it even occurred to his mind that he should tell the people about that discussion he had with Shukla, but he first wanted to speak to Shukla. The meeting went on for the next 45 minutes, during which Aravind explained all the details, and also built some speculations about the virus. All the people were now able to see the scope of the virus fully. They decided to meet online the next day with recommendations from each person on how to implement new and better security protocols to deal with the problem.

After the meeting was done, Aravind called Shukla again, only to be disappointed once more. He tried to reach Shukla four times, and then searched the internet for the NIC headquarter's number. Although he did not have hopes to find anyone at this late hour, he just wanted to try once. His call to the NIC office was received by Mr AB Khan. He was surprised to see that at this late hour in the night, there were people at the NIC office. Busy people with all these threats lingering, he assumed.

Mr Khan was prompt to report the matter to David at once, who was in a meeting with Singh's team working on Raakh 1.1. He had completely isolated himself from the world for the past few days, as he was too busy at the office. Aravind showed him the complete picture of what was happening over the internet currently. They decided to meet in the night itself to discuss what the NIC had been doing, and how the task force should work in order to save the world. David requested Singh to be there for the meeting as well.

Aravind arrived at the NIC office for the meeting with David at 11.00 pm. Aravind wanted to pen down his own observations about the solution NIC had devised and put them forth to the task force and tell them how they could work.

"Hello sir, I am Aravind," he said to David.

"Yes Mr Aravind. Let's discuss whatever you had to," David replied.

Aravind started describing the recent attacks and then moved to his talks with Shukla. He then asked about the NIC's stand on the problem and their solutions. David was at first sceptical about telling him the complete story of Shukla and Jai's disappearance, and the solutions that the NIC had built. He decided to give him an insight into the solutions, but refrain from discussing the disappearance of people. "Aravind would be considerate, and would know that the NIC would not give the complete picture to him," he thought to himself.

So David asked Singh to explain the abstract architecture of the new system built, but refrain from mentioning Shukla's disappearance. Also, he was told not to discuss the old system that the NIC had kept active. Singh gave Aravind a tour of the new system under construction. It was the 12th of April, and Raakh 1.1 was not yet completed.

As Singh and Aravind were going through the various components of the system, a report appeared on the big screen that was flashing the news. "Big News: The days of internet are almost over," it was titled. David was completely engrossed with the news as soon as he read the headline, and stood frozen in front of the screen Aravind left after explaining everything he wanted to, and gathering information that he needed. He felt that he had a moral obligation now to discuss the matter with the world. He went to his office once the advertisement break began, and kept thinking about what to do.

David desperately wanted to discuss the matter with someone who would appease the situation, but the only name that came to his mind was Shukla. He finally called Amit, deciding to tell him that he was informing the higher governmental officials, specifically, the Prime Minister. Amit himself wanted to do the same, but had withheld it because David had requested him to be secretive.

David and Amit then scheduled an appointment to meet the Prime Minister to inform him so that he could handle the international complications involved.

But before that, Amit was informed by one of his associates that Jai's father had taken it to the media to find his son. He had published newspaper and television ads to urge people to find his son. In a video he uploaded on YouTube, he also described the complete story of his son's disappearance. He had let out all the secrets; he had spoken about his meeting with Shukla earlier, about how his son was going to be a 'hero' as described by Shukla among others.

Amit was stunned to know all this, and straight-away called Mr Goyal, Jai's father. Mr Goyal was busy going through the daily activities of his son. Although he knew that the NIA was investigating, their investigation was a farce to him. He had lost all hope from the government. He had even hired a private detective for the matter. But that could be handled, the big problem was the media coverage that the whole case could get.

The YouTube video was already getting attention. The internet giants were making sure that the video was not related to the current predicament that the internet was going through. The video had also started trending on Twitter and Facebook. Google's result for the query "viruses" gave this video as the first thing in the video search results for a while. It was time that David dealt with the situation. He had estimated that the Prime Minister would want to pitch the solution that was developed at the NIC to the world, and then call for a vote. David wanted to convince him against doing this, for obvious reasons. He kept thinking about this for a lot of time, before leaving for his home to ready himself for the meeting with the PM. While in his car, he called up Mohan and told him to end the situation with Jai's father. He told him to call the NIA investigators and suppress the matter as early as possible.

The meeting with the Prime Minister of India had been scheduled at 4.30 am on the 13th of April, considering the priority given by the Prime Minister to Amit. Amit and David reached the PM's office, and waited for a while. The Prime Minister's secretary had been a busy person, and he hated the fact that he had to wait so late in the night for scheduling meetings. He was talking on the phone for a long time, entering appointments in the calendar and making more calls. After keeping them waiting for a while, he showed David and Amit into the office, and continued talking on the phone.

They went into the Prime Minister's office, and were greeted warmly by him. Amit introduced David to him, after which they started discussing the matter.

"The news about the internet going down, we know what is happening. We can reduce the effects," said David.

"I had followed the news yesterday. Please explain the whole scenario to me and what needs to be done. And, since when has all this being to been going on, Amit?" asked the Prime Minister.

"Sir, David will answer all your questions," replied Amit, pointing to David.

"It has been complete chaos for the past ten days at the NIC office. The problem started on the 31st of March," he started to explain. He explained the complete scenario to him, the stature of the problem and its effects that were visible now. He was yet to explain Shukla, Vineet and Jai's disappearance.

"Is this the same Jai Goyal, whose reports I am getting from my PR team?" questioned the Prime Minister, as David explained the origin of the virus.

"Yes, sir. That takes the problem to a whole new level," replied David.

"But he has disappeared, right? That means he could…" he stopped, and his eyes opened wide.

"Yes, sir. You are thinking right. He could have been turned. But there is another view of the story that needs to be considered. It's not only Jai who has disappeared, but two others with him, both from the NIC."

"That is grave. Continue."

"Sir, I am not sure, but I think you must know Mr Rajinder Shukla. You might have interacted with him; he was advising the Prime Minister's office."

"Yes, I know him. I know him well."

"Even he has disappeared."

The Prime Minister was stunned on hearing this. But he wanted to hear the full thing first. So he gestured David to continue. David explained the disappearance of Jai, Vineet and Shukla, and then told him about the communication that they had with Shukla. He also mentioned that the NIC and NIA both believed that Shukla was with them in the matter. But the Prime Minister did not believe this. He would naturally have been concerned. It took Amit some time to explain to him that this was something that the NIC had to believe, it could save the future ultimately.

The meeting lasted more than two hours. It was early morning now. David planned to go to the NIC office, and Amit went home. On the way, David called Singh to check the status of work at the office, and was relieved to know that the new system was about to be ready in some time from now. Thus, he went home, and slept in peace for some time.

Before he reached office, he got a call from Mohan.

"Sir, the video is trending everywhere. All the common people are scared. What to do?" he asked.

"That was bound to happen. Poor thinking from this Mr Goyal. I don't know what to say to this," he uttered in displeasure.

"I am calling him to the office today, and then we should speak to him. Okay?"

"Yes that would be necessary I guess. Call him. I will speak to him," he said, and cut the phone.

He turned to his PC and saw the video, discovering what it was really about. Although the focus of the video was to urge the people to find Jai, NIC and NIA were badly criticised. And this irked him enough. Mr Goyal was going to face a lot of a heat when he would come to the office.

David sat down with Singh and Mohan to discuss how to deal with Mr Goyal. Amit was to arrive in some time. Singh was happy to see that David was actually very angry at someone. This was perhaps the first time he had seen him like that. And he felt that his anger was justified. Just that, if expressed, it could go the wrong way as well.

Amit received a call from the Prime Minister himself.

"Amit, I saw the video just now. I want this matter to be over as soon as possible. First settle this, then look at the internet problem."

"Sir, we are trying to do that. Give us some time."

"I don't know all that. Just talk to him, do anything needed, stop him from making such comments about the Government right now. I have a UN conference coming up next month, so this is not the best time for such controversies. I am going to address the world at that time, so please..."

"Yes sir, I realise that. I assure you that we will deal with this matter."

"Okay, good. Bye," and the phone went off.

Amit realised the gravity of this situation now. It was going to hamper India's image in the world, if not dealt with promptly. His car just drove into the parking lots of the NIC, and he headed straight to David's office. David, Mohan and Singh were waiting for him.

"Okay, I just got a call from the Prime Minister. He saw the video. I don't think I need to speak more on what to do now," Amit said.

The Silicon Valley was in a state of panic over the matter. Over the past two days, services of 79 small companies had gone down. Two banks had completely frozen their online transactions to avoid any impact, and many more were about to follow them. But there was one good thing that happened.

All the tech giants; Google, Microsoft, HP, Dell, Apple, Samsung, LG, Amazon among others were working together to mitigate the threat. The only reason these giants were able to survive till now was that they had enough replicas of their systems, so their full systems would not crash, even if one site crashed. There was no thought of competition about the matter among them. It was inherently necessary that the internet should not crash for all of them to keep their businesses intact.

The larger impact of the virus was now clear to the whole world.

IMPACT DEEPENS

When the world awoke to the sun of April 13th, people read similar news again. The NIC building had received calls from other governmental informatics systems, to notify them of the attack. The other countries were not yet aware that one solution was actually being implemented here. The only limitation was that it just gave enough time to build a new system with a better defence system.

The internet symposium was to be held later this week, but the issue at hand was too fearful to wait till then. Thus, it was held on this day itself, through the internet. All the agenda that was originally planned for the meeting was kept aside, and the issue at hand was discussed at great lengths.

"Hello everyone. I am Dr Aravind Sharma, and I know what is happening here. I spoke to a friend of mine…" As he said this, the audio went off, only the video was visible. In a span of a few seconds, the video was also off. On retrying connecting, the system gave errors and crashed again. It was evident, the server which was handling this web-chat had crashed. The engineers tried different ways to start the system, but nothing worked. At first, people were baffled to see this. But later they realised that it was the same attack. The obvious reason for this was Ashtray. The people attending took some time to decide on another platform, this time going for a strictly public network with a lot of backup servers available, thus avoiding similar problems.

Aravind was about to name Shukla and everything that he came to know about NIC's system. But the connection going away pointed towards another direction, he felt. He decided against giving out the details, and speak only about the problem. He also had to give the solution he learnt at NIC as a proposal. He started speaking again.

"People, I thought about a strategy for this, and have come up with a solution. But it is a tedious one, and is best only for the most critical data. This is not permanent, but could prevent some damage," he started. "I tried this theoretically, and feel that this could work against the DDoS. The first step here is to quarantine the current system using some parameters that I am putting up on the blackboard," he kept talking as the blackboard on the right half of the screens showed a bulleted list. The list contained all the elements that the NIC team had developed. As he went on, people were amazed at the level of detail with which he had dealt with the problem. The task force had gone to the initial level of solutions, but it would take them another 3-4 days to get to as detailed a solution as Aravind presented.

The symposium lasted 3 hours, after which there was an online press conference. It was decided unanimously that Aravind should lead the task force now, considering his solutions and the quickness with which he had delivered them. So he had to address the conference.

"The meeting was fruitful. We ensure you that the task force will deal with the matter in a short span of time. The fluctuations and whims of the internet would be gone in a very small time from now," he mentioned to the reporters.

"But Dr Sharma, can you tell us specifically till when we would be able to see a concrete solution? And whatever you are doing, will it require efforts from all of us, or will the problem be dealt with automatically?"

"We have tentatively set the date as April 20 to give everyone an idea of what we are doing. I won't be able to disclose any other details right now."

"Can we do anything right now to stop it?" asked another reporter, as Aravind accepted her request for a question.

"Certainly, start backing up your data."

A series of questions about the current situation came, and Aravind handled all of them deftly. The final question was the real troubling one:

"Any news about the culprit?"

Aravind momentarily thought about giving out the details that NIC and NIA were investigating, but then told them what he had been asked to tell:

"No. The case has been handed over to the Interpol, and you may ask questions regarding the case to them directly. I guess that should be it," he tried to wrap up the conference.

The press conference did not last long, and Aravind had his priorities clearly stated to his team now. He had the world's best engineers at his disposal now. His goal was to develop a framework so that the work done at NIC could be standardized for all the computers worldwide and published by April 20. He had set apart a group of 16 engineers to find out a temporary way to quarantine critically endangered systems. He then decided to head to the NIC headquarters, to see their quarantining ways. But he was apprehensive of whether they would share the details of their quarantining protocol.

Raakh 1.1 was not yet ready for the outer world.

Aravind made a three-member team who were ordered to make a document that would be sent worldwide, to all companies. This document was to have details of the problems that could arise for that particular class of companies. The various classes that were identified were:

- Financial
- Informative
- Entertainment
- Governmental
- Completely internet based (included all internet-only companies)
- Software development and deployment
- Manufacturing
- Product based
- Service oriented

All the websites were to be categorised into these categories, and a class-specific document was to be given to them. The team developed separate documents for each class, and then they added specific criteria to classify a business into these classes. These documents were released through a new website hosted on servers of many internet-based giants. Anyone could download the document from these servers.

After viewing the global outlook of the problem, Aravind now had to see the impact the systems were to have on the government websites, be it of any country. David made him see this picture when they met. The meeting happened at 9.30 am. The discussion went on and Aravind soon queried about the quarantining protocol. David tried to dodge the question by saying that it was a confidential matter as the government websites depended on it. If made public, there was a high possibility that the attacker could modify NIC's system to bypass the quarantine. Aravind was completely aware of this, but he wanted to get something out of David that could help him. But David did not give in.

Instead, David told him that the small program the NIC had built for other Indian Government offices such as NIA would be made generic by the NIC and made available to the world. Aravind was negative on this too, as it would take a lot of time for them to build a generic system, considering the smaller workforce at the NIC. So he asked if he could get the principles of the protection mechanisms used, and the task force would implement them. David instead suggested a better solution. He told Aravind to add additional components to the small program that the NIC built, which would lead to a reduction in time. Aravind readily agreed. Singh was again asked to give Aravind a description of the quarantine program.

Aravind was to learn all the principles, and then present these principles to his team of developers and engineers as if he had developed them himself. The NIC wanted to keep its involvement secret, and Aravind respected that.

As he had spoken on the call to the Prime Minister earlier, Amit himself went to clear the matter with Jai's father. Jai's father was distressed about his missing son, and no one was helping to find him, it seemed. While going, Amit had taken two sets of papers with him; one, the reports of the NIA's investigation on Jai till now, two, a highly concise investigation report that picked some details from the other one, but did not reveal the actual complete details. He met Mr Goyal in a hotel. But he did not find the place safe to have such a high level discussion there, so he took him to his car instead.

They started discussing in the car, as the driver drove towards the NIC headquarters.

"Do you realise what you have done? Of course not, I know!" Amit asked rhetorically. "I saw what you have done, and need to show you something," he said, handing over the concise reports to Mr Goyal.

"What is it?" Mr Goyal asked. Amit did not bother to answer the question, and looked at the papers as Mr Goyal started reading.

"But, if all this was happening, why was I never informed? Why always call it a matter of 'national importance'?" he asked. Amit was about to answer those questions but he instead showed him the call record he had with the PM the earlier day.

"The Prime Minister called me to get rid of it. Tell me now, after reading the report, do you still feel that we are not working? Please acknowledge some things about us. We are not allowed to give details to anyone about our working and the missions, you should be knowing. Posting such videos over the internet, worrying the public and creating a hype, is exactly what we do not want. But now that you have done it, please do not do anything further without our permission. I am taking you to the NIC headquarters to give you a demo of what your son has developed. These internet problems you see these days, are because of his work. We all want to save him from trouble, but… So please stop creating trouble for us."

Mr Goyal was speechless, and felt an ache in his throat as he tried to speak. He could not speak for a while, and felt seriously guilty. His suspicions about his son's involvement in something serious were coming true. They reached the NIC office, with no dialogue happening between them in the meantime. David greeted Mr Goyal in a very cold manner, and looked at him as if he was a criminal. They sat in David's cabin, as David offered both of them refreshments. Tea arrived for them in some time, but Mr Goyal was in no mood for anything now.

Both David and Amit were in a mood to berate Mr Goyal, but the problem had already occurred, and it was time for recovery. So they just placidly told him the complete problem, and made him realise what he had done. After discussing for some time, David and Amit ordered him to follow their plan.

They had already thought of a strategy for dealing with the problem, but Mr Goyal was a mere pawn in this plan. While the world could see the video which Mr Goyal uploaded, it could also see the videos that others would make. Plagiarism was their solution to this problem. When Mr Goyal came to meet Amit in the morning that day, 16 videos similar to Mr Goyal's video had already been uploaded on the web. Apart from videos, tweets, statuses and blogs were written of a similar kind. Not just uploaded, they were also being promoted worldwide.

All the videos were based on a general theme- someone's close relative or friend had gone missing, and people urged the world to find their loved ones. David and Amit were experts in dealing with such situations, and they knew how the media reacted to such situations. While someone's someone going missing was always reported to the police, this was not a problem as the NIA handled it. Amit had a team of engineers develop a series of dummy videos and social media content stating the police record numbers. The aliases used for developing these videos were from different parts of the world, so the Prime Minister's concern would be taken care of, although not addressed completely. This was because if concerns were to be raised, they would happen globally and would not be restricted to India. While it was true that some concerns would be raised about Mr Goyal's video, it was certain that the attention that this video was getting would be diverted to an extent. Basically, people would now start ignoring such stuff unless it appeared on their personal spaces such as their Facebook wall or email or if someone tagged them. A video saying someone was missing was less likely to be watched by everyone now and Mr Goyal's video would be 'just another missing person report'.

After discussing the problem with Mr Goyal, they both told him his role- 'to not give any details about the project his son was working on; to never think of relating his son to the current scenario and to not make any statements unless someone asked him questions.' They were not going to figure out the ways to do all this for him, but had one man follow up every activity of his till the crisis would be over. He was told that he would be followed everywhere, so there was no secrecy involved there. Mr Goyal left only after David was absolutely sure that he completely understood. Amit then called up the Prime Minister's assistant to tell him that the job was done. Then he left to carry on with his office work. His office work had been side-lined for sometime now, as he had been making frequent visits to the NIC office.

Mr Goyal abided by what he had been asked to do, and there was no hype created by him after this. But his concern for his son remained, naturally. At the same time, he was sure that since people of such high authority were involved, there was a high chance that he would see him soon.

The various members of the task force kept working on Aravind's instructions. Since they could not take the risk of their server going down, all the communication happened over public networks, and secrecy could seriously be affected. But that was a much smaller problem at the moment. They kept working, looking at the deadline and keeping in mind the threat if the deadline was not met.

In all, till April 12, a total of 1041 websites were reported completely inaccessible, and many more were partially inaccessible. Physical security at data farms located all over the world was doubled, some data farms were already turned off by their owners to avoid complete breakdown. Their thinking was simple-it was better to bear some losses than to have a debacle.

Shukla monitored all this activity from up there, and felt utterly useless. He also wondered about the effect that the death of those Jaguars was going to have on the other animals and plants. That is, the effects that would be caused due to the biological IS's automatic adjustments to adjust to the changes.

As was expected by people at building 3 earlier, the 31 fields that were modified would affect many other fields too, as the whole food chain would have to be balanced. And the results of these changes were visible soon, when everyone's keepers started giving alerts. There were a total of 4,246,762 fields that were modified. It included the flora and fauna from the start of the food chains that led to members higher up in the food chain. It took the computers at Building 3 about seventy hours to calculate all these effects and make the changes. Imagine the effects if a few more fields were allowed to change because of Ashtray.

CRASH THE ASH

April 13, 14

The message for which NIC was waiting arrived, as people felt increasingly anxious. It was just the onset of the third hour since David had declared the four hour waiting period, when it did. David and Singh rushed to the old system as it started beeping out an alert, and it was maybe the first time at NIC that everyone was happy to see the system being attacked. The screening of the test report was happening at the central screen in the auditorium now, and almost everyone had gathered there.

The system was certainly under attack. But it was something different this time. David checked the database to see the inconsistencies that were caused. In a few fields, the modified fields read-"Shukla. Please note." And this was not just for one field, it was as if Shukla was trying to be certain that the changes were duly noted. And, there was no question of this being a dummy attack. The reason being that the changes made were in the most privileged entries, only accessible to the administrators at NIC. David trusted Shukla considering his impeccable record at the NIC. And he decided to just follow the instructions that were displayed.

Singh and Mohan started scrutinising every entry that was modified, all of them had the same message as above, except one. Here, the procedure to be followed was explained fully.

"Do not turn off the system at any cost. Remove it from quarantine, and wait until the screen pops up 'RESTART'. When it does, switch to the NIC new system. No need to build new systems anywhere after this."

That was all. There was no explanation made to it, neither were any solutions from these people expected. But all the people decided to trust Shukla, and went ahead. The system was taken off from quarantine first. It was made openly accessible to the world. Then, all eyes turned to the screen. First, there was a message stating that a field was modified, then another, and then a bunch of similar messages came by. The terminal showed rapid activity now, and at times, it paused for a while. Everyone watched anxiously. They were anticipating a RESTART message sooner or later. But no one moved from their chairs. All those who were sleeping were completely awake now, with eyes wide open.

It took a wait of about 35 minutes before the screen turned green, blinking in capital, bold letters- 'RESTART'. Singh looked towards David, who nodded one time, and Singh sprang into action.

The switch of the system was locked inside a cage, the key to which was the retina print of 5 people at NIC. Singh was one of them. He opened the cage, and tripped off the switch gently, as his heart pounded loudly. It felt as if it would fall out of his mouth in some time. The system started buzzing loudly. The backup power was on, to which David attended carefully, and switched it off in a similar procedure. The buzzing now turned into a calm, serene beep, which was coming from an alerting machine. All the focus now shifted to the new system, which was about to go through its toughest test yet. It was not even 12 hours into its service before it was going to experience the toughest attack, but it was made for survival.

The atmosphere at the NIC office was now tranquil. Not even a faint noise apart from the beep alert could be heard. All the people held on to their seats in the auditorium. Singh and David reached the auditorium, to find everyone holding onto their seats. David reached his seat, deciding not to say anything at that moment. Singh, on the other hand, took to the stage. In a fragile voice he spoke-"I guess this is it. Wait for some time, I will let you know about the team which I still want here, others may leave the office." Nothing, nothing could deter Singh from his job. He started picking up people in his mind, thinking what would be a good enough number to pick, only to find that he did not know how many people would be required in the office. He instead asked both the core teams to stay, and others were dismissed. David did not utter a word while all this was happening. Mohan had his eyes stuck to the screen, viewing the status reports of the new system.

If one looked at the auditorium, it looked as if a big movie release was about to happen, and that auditorium was the stage for the launch. People were anxious to see what would happen. Although only the core teams had to stay, all the people were in the auditorium. No one had left. It was going to take a while to get it done. But for the first time, Singh himself was feeling positive about Shukla. He was convinced that Shukla was on their side, and the solution that Shukla had planned must have been a really good one.

He was standing at the right side of the stage. In fact, after some time, while looking at the screen, he almost fell off the stage. But his eyes stayed on the screen. He decided to sit in a chair, and watched the scene from the front row. All the people were just waiting. The core team was in the front row, thinking that prompt action might be needed at anytime. The system was still restarting. It was taking much longer than usual to restart.

They waited, waited and waited. The system restarted finally, and Singh went to the terminal log straight away. He was about to see what magic Shukla had created now. Everyone looked at the number of requests that the system was sending to other systems nearby, and how the systems were responding to it. Just by looking at it, anyone could say that the number was huge. The terminal had stopped updating only once, when the system's alert message was delivered.

Singh had proceeded to cancel this alert, but as he was walking to the laptop, the message disappeared. Shukla had taken care of everything. He knew the system at NIC so well that even the alerts that would usually have appeared did not manage to do so. Shukla's program took care of all things.

The alert message was about the high number of requests that were being sent. The system at NIC was designed in such a manner that administrator permission was needed in case a large number of requests were being sent. Shukla had put additional features into his program so that the people at NIC would not have to do anything. The basic idea behind this was to avoid any in coherency and delay.

After 4 hours, David finally told each one of them to be at ease, to trust Shukla and get some rest. He told them to come to office after having a good sleep, and then they would think ahead. In the meantime, the offices would install their patch programs and begin working on their own new systems. But the concern here was, after what Shukla had done just now, what would be the status of all the systems. Will it be 'safe' or 'quarantined' or 'still vulnerable'? No one could tell unless some message arrived from the other end. But people had ignored the fact that the message was embedded in the database alterations that Shukla had made earlier. When they searched again, it appeared in bold.

Yes, the systems were safe.

There was another message attached to it-"Copy the file named secure (no extensions visible) to the product package being built. Autorun capabilities already added to it."

Hooray! The antivirus was to go to every system now as a part of this product about to be handed over to Aravind for global transmission.

All the drama that began on the 30th of March had come to an end, although it did not seem to be a hysterical, climactic end. All the people had to figure out ways to get back to their normal lives now. Everyone had had the greatest adventure of their lives. Mohan also was told to go home, and Singh insisted that he would stay there for checking the new system's performance. Mohan and David left for home.

Singh waited in the office, with only two other people. He was too relieved to sleep at that moment. He waited for a while, about an hour, before he went to sleep. The others who were with him went home. He did not realise that he had slept for about six hours, before he could hear loud music from the auditorium speakers. As he opened his eyes, he found his colleagues dancing and partying. He ran up to the music controller and changed the song to a bhangra, and performed a scintillating solo dance. Everyone was happy that the worst was over. It was time to get back to normal lives now.

EARLIER...

Shukla ran through Jai's codes of all the solutions for about half an hour before both Jai and Vineet joined him. Rather than letting emotions get the better of them, they started working on the solutions. Shukla told Vineet to work on the last solution as he saw some potential there. Jai kept working on the other methods as well, being biased towards turning the systems off, the third solution. So he kept on thinking over ways to do it, and at the same time, partly thinking of the first two as well.

Meanwhile, Shukla modified his plan to make the communications work. From the dummy attack Shukla had made earlier, he had an experience with the old NIC system. This was to be put to use. Shukla copied the code of the dummy virus into a new one, and integrated some elements of Ashtray that he got from Jai's computer. These elements were those required for handling the AI part, and most of the ones that had been left out for the dummy attack. He then started with something of his own.

He chose one Datree as the anchor which was to be used for the communication. Then, he implemented a tunnel from this Datree to the NIC's computer, which bypassed the barriers. He could easily bypass the barriers this time as Vineet had access to all the control lists of the barriers, which he could easily modify for the area around that Datree. Then this anchor Datree was cut off from the system inside, only one link was active for use from external agencies, that is, the system was available from the outside, but linkages to other Datrees were disabled. The tunnel was to be opened for only a span of 25 seconds, which was to be used for the transmission and retransmission of the code, as there was no guarantee of receiving acknowledgements.

The sending of an initial message was to be followed by the transmission of the whole program. But the span of 25 seconds was not enough to retransmit the program thrice. Thrice, because retransmission would increase chances of reaching the destination. The program could only be sent twice in the timespan. But Shukla's mind was still not at ease. The program for the filter was not yet ready, and he did not know if it would ever be ready.

"Sir, let me share a story with you. Remember the time when you used to be our mentor. We were a batch of 30 people. The instructions that you had given us were humongous in number and we found them hard to memorise. We had decided to share the work. We had made four teams, who would answer different sets of questions. We had prepared our own sets of doubts as well. If you asked a question to someone, and he did not know the answer, we would make sure that the person who knew the answer would give it to him, through gestures we had prepared. So, it made answering yes/no questions very easy. In fact, every kid must have developed such techniques in school or college. We all had the habit of sharing the work and performing the task. Teamwork, sir."

Shukla remembered this anecdote from a conversation he had with Mohan some years ago. It had done the job for him, at least he had something to think of now. For the next thirty minutes, he kept thinking alone. People asked him twice or thrice what he was thinking, but he ignored them each time. He finally had a concrete idea in his mind.

Shukla said to Jai- "If the methods of prevention are not effective independently, can we think of combining everything? We just have to link all the methods in proper order, and our job is done."

"Sir, can that work?" Vineet and Jai were dubious about the method.

"Yeah it will. We do the following steps." Shukla started explaining in his extremely procedural manner. He showed him a piece of paper on which he had written the instructions.

1. As soon as the antivirus reaches a node, we get the logs of that system to check if it has been under attack, if it is, we check the logs for changes to the system since the time it was attacked, that is, the time when DDoS started. All these changes have to be nullified, keeping only those that can be verified by the administrator. The administrator is asked to verify them, and the others are discarded.

If the system is not under attack:

2. The altered program first tries to install filters into the system

3. The substitution will begin then. Since a filter is installed, the vaccine will be effective. That is, Ashtray would act as a vaccine to itself.

4. If a filter is not yet installed, and Ashtray reaches there, we hibernate Ashtray. The process for hibernation must be clear to you. You must have seen by now, the program for hibernation would be the first to be installed.

5. After all this is done, we restart the system. If none of these steps has happened and the system is under attack while we install, we use the third solution, that is, we kill the system.

If the system is under attack:

1. After the discarding of the changes from logs is done, the virus is hibernated.

2. Then, we install the filters, and make sure that the system responds to the filters. If it does not respond properly, we shut down the system (this should not be required).

3. We now check the computer that would follow the current computer in the process of fission of Ashtray, and mark them. We then substitute the original Ashtray that has attacked.

4. The system is now restarted.

5. The changes to the system are notified to the administrator, followed by normal cycles.

The transmission to NIC is almost similar to the previous time, although I am implementing a direct tunnel this time.

"Masterpiece sir! Masterpiece," uttered Vineet.

"Jai has already found a way to implement these solutions. So Jai, I hope you can code it quickly, so that this job can be done soon," he spoke, looking at Jai.

Jai had developed a method through which the filters could be accommodated in each computer connected to the internet, however heterogeneous its configuration may be. He had decided to design the filters such that they would operate cross-platform and across all device categories. He was going to do this by targeting the web browsers. Since the number of browsers was a known figure, he had to code the filters such that they would be compatible across all the browsers; a small task for the skill set that Jai possessed.

"Apart from this, I want some features for easy and seamless transmission to the NIC system. Also, I will implement some features to optimise the program to be used at NIC. It will eliminate unnecessary security features NIC would use. So, once you are done, please let me know. I will add the latter part," Shukla told Jai. Jai and Vineet worked on integrating the four solutions now.

After the filters were installed at the NIC, they were to be transmitted to the other systems automatically. His original estimate of 79 days was brought down to five days only, considering the involvement of Aravind. Since the antivirus was automatically going to be there in the product package that the NIC was building, once Aravind got a hold of it, the transmission across the globe was going to happen seamlessly and quickly. Basically, all the places where the

NIC's product would reach, would act as the first point from where the fission reaction would begin. And, there was no need to build new systems either.

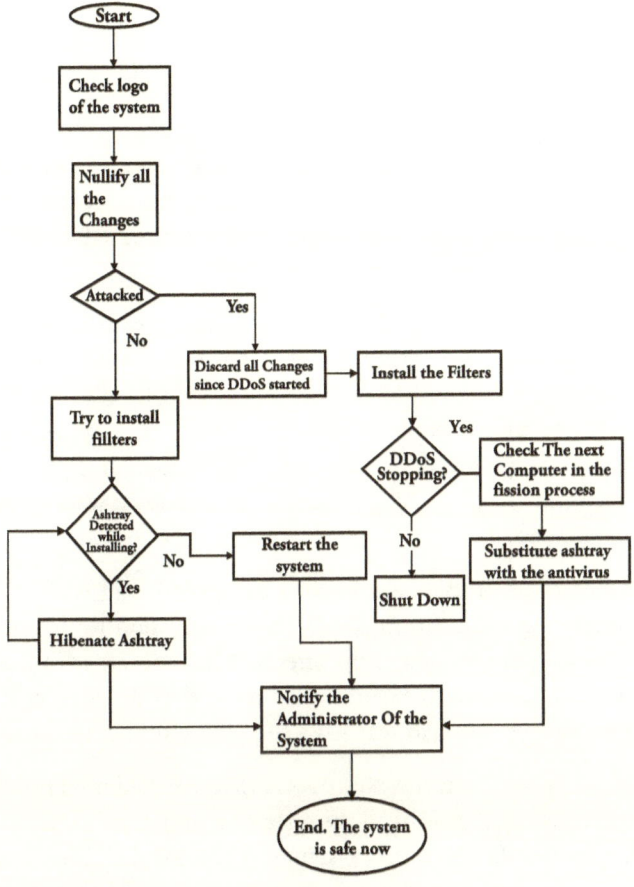

Final Solution

All the points that were stated were integrated into the system and a final program was built for the task. Shukla intentionally put some additional instructions in the antivirus, and it was set to go. The spreading of this was to happen again through fission itself. This was the reply to Ashtray, and Shukla was sure that any system would be able to survive attacks of the level of Ashtray, using the filters and the enhancements.

Shukla called Vineet and gave him a piece of paper which had a message saying

"Let's do it, Let's secure the world."

Shukla wrote it on a piece of paper as he wanted it to be symbolic, and the piece of paper would always be with him as a memento.

Vineet did not utter a word, he continued adding lines of code into the program that Jai had built. Jai was going to be very angry with Shukla once all this was over. He already was, but the job had the highest priority right now. Shukla had promised Jai a job at the NIC although he knew that they would never go back.

When the coding was done, Vineet got into action, feeding in some values and establishing the closed tunnel Shukla had built. Shukla took a final word from Nicole. He actually did not bother to take her opinion this time. He just told her that they were about to begin. And she agreed. She also told Mr Hans about it, who then came to Shukla's office. All of them were anxiously waiting to see what would happen.

Shukla ordered for the tunnel to be opened, and within those 25 seconds, the work was finished. The transmission was complete. Now they just had to look at the effects of the antivirus. To prevent re-propagation, the old system needed to be shut down after it was sure that the antivirus had reached a sufficient number of systems.

Shukla's keeper was the workstation that they had used this time. It started showing details of all the systems that it reached. It showed whether the installation onto a system was successful or not. Also, the reports of the old NIC database's performance were being recorded and displayed. Everyone's eyes were on Shukla's keeper. They had planned 39 systems that would be reached in the first round. The addresses of these 39 systems had been deliberately added. Apart from these addresses, the product was to reach many more systems in the further stages. From there, Ashtray's capability to reach all the nodes was to be put to use.

All the tasks were swiftly performed, and the 'virus containing the antivirus' was doing its job. All the three were viewing reports collected on Shukla's keeper. After 34 minutes, Shukla was convinced that a sufficient number of systems were penetrated by this virus, and the NIC system could now be restarted.

All the jobs were now done, all three of them could finally breathe in peace. All three of them had worked tirelessly till now. They were excused to be tired now. But the combined effect of guilt and relief took it all away. Jai started weeping at the thought of not being able to go back home. Vineet looked completely dejected as the whole world had literally ended for him. Shukla by this time had told himself that it was not possible and was not thinking of going back. All three of them would have to serve this place, and of course, Mother Earth: a noble job.

Neither were the people at the NIC too happy. Their hero, Shukla was missing. But they knew that he was with them always. His father-like shield was with them always, and people were about to revere him as God. Were they right? Perhaps they were.

EPILOGUE

Vineet, Shukla and Jai were still not able to digest all that had happened in these few days. While the world had slept in peace, they had no time to even express sorrow over the sad news they had heard. Vineet now found the time to weep, still hoping there was a way back. Shukla tried consoling him, but the effort was in complete vain. Shukla himself was devastated, and decided to talk to Mr Hans to try one more time. He reached his office without prior notice.

"Sir, is there any way of…" asked Shukla.

"Do not even think about it. I cannot help you there, Shukla ji," Mr Hans pre-empted Shukla.

They talked, Shukla trying his best to negotiate a way out.

"If it was just me, I would have given you the permission, but Shukla please know that there are rules. We are mere pawns. The king controls the game," Mr Hans replied. Shukla felt hopeless on hearing this. He finally gave up all hopes, and returned to his team.

Jai thought that he was the only person responsible for all the trouble, and expressed it to both Vineet and Shukla.

"Jai, if you would not have done this, someone else might have created havoc. I see you as a smart kid, perhaps the smartest I have ever known. You have helped save the world from a possible end, so please... You are the unsung hero this generation would always want to find about. And I think Vineet will agree with me on this. Besides, what has happened has happened. It's up to us now to be together and save this place from trouble, every time. We belong here now, aye?" Shukla replied, giving Jai the confidence that he rightly deserved.

Vineet too was influenced by the words he had just heard, and happily looked around, this was his new office. Oh, what a promotion it had been, he would always cherish this one. From an associate at NIC to a maintenance manager at Building 3. His keeper beeped as a smile came to his face.

"Shuklaji, movie tonight? Krishnakant Rao just texted me about the new sound design he has implemented," asked Vineet.

"Oh yes, absolutely going. Let us celebrate!"

Jai was very sad about the happenings. The same thought had occupied his mind-"If I hadn't created Ashtray, nothing of this sort would have happened. If only I could rewind time and erase all the hard disks before testing Ashtray." Shukla knew that his sorrow would take some time to heal.

Aravind took NIC's package from them and had his team follow the plan for installation everywhere, which they did. He had to wait for two days before he could see stability reports, and the number of web site crash reports coming down. On the 6th day since his team started installing the software, the reports of being attacked by a DDoS attack had fallen below a threshold level. It was victory for him and his team, and of course, the world.

The day after Shukla's filters had been installed at the NIC office, everyone talked about when Shukla would return along with his heroes, or whether he ever would. David had formed a three-member team, headed by Mohan, to find Shukla. He did not care even if it cost a fortune. He had given them access to all the resources he could. Mohan and his team worked for three days, scouring each place they thought Shukla could be, before some news reached them.

Shukla was reported dead in a car accident on April 7, his car was just found in a forest that did not attract many people. Vineet was reported dead only when his body was washed up the shore in Mumbai, reports claimed that he died due to lack of food and water. Jai was still not confirmed dead, but a body which matched Jai's physique was found in a valley near the Indo-Chinese border.

Would Mohan have believed it? He would not, but he seemed to have no choice. Would the death of all three of them simultaneously not have raised suspicion in the minds of Singh, the questioner? It certainly would have. But what could he do about it? It was God's will, he thought and left the matter aside.

All through his career, Amit had seen spies and agents making some of the finest stories, but none of them were revealed. "Another story that needs to be told but would go unsung," thought Amit.

The world would know nothing about Jai, Vineet and Shukla, which was good. Informatics of the heavens was safe as no one knew about it. Because it was safe now, the world was safe.

www.ingramcontent.com/pod-product-compliance
Lightning Source LLC
Chambersburg PA
CBHW030408020726
47493CB00003B/980